Highlander Defied

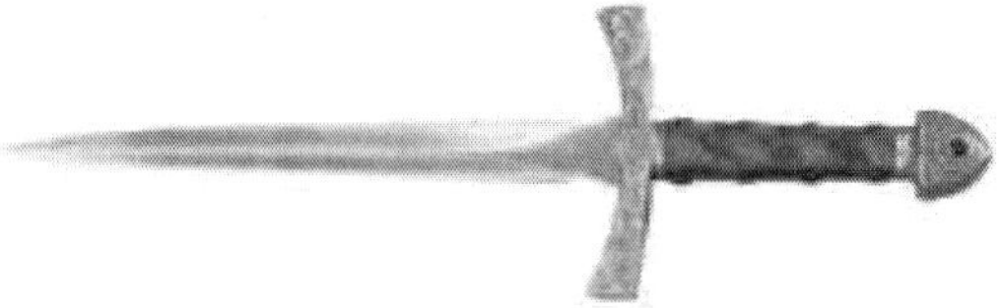

Courageous Highland Hearts
Book One

Jayne Castel

All characters and situations in this publication are fictitious, and any resemblance to living persons is purely coincidental.

Highlander Defied, by Jayne Castel

Copyright © 2022 by Jayne Castel. All rights reserved. No part of this publication may be reproduced, stored in a retrieval system, or transmitted in any form or by any means—electronic, mechanical, recording, or otherwise—without the prior written permission of the author.

Published by Winter Mist Press

Edited by Tim Burton
Cover design by Winter Mist Press
Cover photography courtesy of www.shutterstock.com
Dagger vector image courtesy of www.pixabay.com

Visit Jayne's website: www.jaynecastel.com

What happens when an arrogant clan-chief, who faces down his enemies without flinching, is terrified of loving his wife? A marriage of convenience turns into a battle of wills in Medieval Scotland.

Beth Munro needs a husband. On the cusp of spinsterhood, she's had a run of ill fortune—one that has earned her the moniker 'The Cursed Bride'. But when a proposal arrives from the Mackay clan-chief, Beth believes her luck has finally changed.

Niel Mackay needs a wife. He doesn't care about the rumors that follow his bride-to-be. After nearly a decade in prison, he's focused on two things: gaining vengeance against his enemies and ensuring his bloodline survives.

Love isn't part of the arrangement.

But even carefully laid plans can be doomed to failure. Beth struggles in a marriage with a man who shares his body but not his soul. Meanwhile, Niel fights against his growing feelings for his passionate wife.

Not all battles draw blood ... yet who will emerge the victor?

HIGHLANDER DEFIED is Book One of the Courageous Highland Hearts series. This steamy and emotional follow-up to Jayne Castel's bestselling Stolen Highland Hearts series follows the lives of four battle-hardened Highland warriors and the courageous sisters who capture their hearts.

Historical Romances by Jayne Castel

DARK AGES BRITAIN

The Kingdom of the East Angles series
Night Shadows (prequel novella)
Dark Under the Cover of Night (Book One)
Nightfall till Daybreak (Book Two)
The Deepening Night (Book Three)
The Kingdom of the East Angles: The Complete Series

The Kingdom of Mercia series
The Breaking Dawn (Book One)
Darkest before Dawn (Book Two)
Dawn of Wolves (Book Three)
The Kingdom of Mercia: The Complete Series

The Kingdom of Northumbria series
The Whispering Wind (Book One)
Wind Song (Book Two)
Lord of the North Wind (Book Three)
The Kingdom of Northumbria: The Complete Series

DARK AGES SCOTLAND

The Warrior Brothers of Skye series
Blood Feud (Book One)
Barbarian Slave (Book Two)
Battle Eagle (Book Three)
The Warrior Brothers of Skye: The Complete Series

The Pict Wars series
Warrior's Heart (Book One)
Warrior's Secret (Book Two)
Warrior's Wrath (Book Three)

The Pict Wars: The Complete Series

Novellas
Winter's Promise

MEDIEVAL SCOTLAND

The Brides of Skye series
The Beast's Bride (Book One)
The Outlaw's Bride (Book Two)
The Rogue's Bride (Book Three)
The Brides of Skye: The Complete Series

The Sisters of Kilbride series
Unforgotten (Book One)
Awoken (Book Two)
Fallen (Book Three)
Claimed (Epilogue novella)
The Sisters of Kilbride: The Complete Series

The Immortal Highland Centurions series
Maximus (Book One)
Cassian (Book Two)
Draco (Book Three)
The Laird's Return (Epilogue festive novella)
The Immortal Highland Centurions: The Complete Series

Stolen Highland Hearts series
Highlander Deceived (Book One)
Highlander Entangled (Book Two)
Highlander Forbidden (Book Three)
Highlander Pledged (Book Four)

Guardians of Alba series
Nessa's Seduction (Book One)
Fyfa's Sacrifice (Book Two)
Breanna's Surrender (Book Three)

Courageous Highland Hearts series
Highlander Defied (Book One)

Epic Fantasy Romances by Jayne Castel

Light and Darkness series
Ruled by Shadows (Book One)
The Lost Swallow (Book Two)
Path of the Dark (Book Three)
Light and Darkness: The Complete Series

***

For Grandad.

***

*"To fear love is to fear life,
and those who fear life
are already three parts dead."*
—Bertrand Russell

1

FORTUNE SHINES UPON YE

Bass Rock, Firth of Forth
Scotland

February, 1437

HIS MIND WAS blank this eve, his soul leaden. Numbness cloaked him, an emptiness that drilled deep into his bones.

The constant sound of dripping water had a lulling effect. The steady, rhythmic drip on stone echoed in the silence of Niel Mackay's cell. The drops seemed to splash with the beat of his heart and even fall in time with the slow rasp of his breathing.

Niel leaned against the pitted rock wall—made of the same dull stone as the island upon which this prison sat—and rested his chin on the sill, his fingers clasped around the thick iron bars. He'd been moved to new accommodation a few weeks—or it could have been months—earlier. And unlike his former lodgings, this cell had a window low enough for him to peer through.

Granted, the window was tiny and he had to stand on his sleeping pallet in order to see outside, yet it was enough.

It looked west, toward the mainland, and right now the setting sun painted the sky with fiery hues. The cold and grey had seemed endless, and day after day of mist meant that this was the first time in a while Niel had been able to see beyond his gaol.

This isle was a cold, bleak rock, even at the height of summer. Over the years, he'd grown used to the raucous, throaty cries of the gannets that populated this rock and the eye-watering stench of their droppings that wafted into his cell when the wind blew in a certain direction. He also didn't flinch at the heavy tread of guards passing by his cell, the rattle of iron keys, and the occasional grunts, cries, and shouts from the other prisoners.

However, a frisson of fear still tightened in his gut when the door opened and two, or more, guards entered.

That signaled a beating was coming.

He caught the scuff of booted feet then, warning that someone was approaching his cell. Was it time for supper? Time lost any meaning when one's world shrank to four damp walls.

Niel didn't move. Instead, he remained at the window, gaze trained west, watching the fiery sunset: a splash of color and light in his otherwise drab existence.

The scrape of a key in the lock didn't make him shift position either.

Supper wasn't anything to get excited about. More often than not, it was moldy bread and sulfurous pottage. Nonetheless, hunger was a constant companion, gnawing like a rat at Niel's belly. His body and mind had started to feel increasingly disconnected of late, yet the survival instinct was stronger—and so he forced down the awful food the guards brought him.

They hadn't yet broken him—but these days, it had started to dawn upon him that one day they would.

The creak of unoiled hinges intruded then, and Niel waited for the rattle and thud of his supper being set down on the stone floor.

After a lengthy pause, he heard it. However, the door didn't close.

Niel tensed, his bowels turning to water. Whoever had brought his supper wasn't leaving.

Satan's cods. Those bastards hadn't come for him again? His bruises had only just faded from the last kicking.

He stubbornly refused to tear his gaze away from the sunset though. The beauty of the flames of red and gold that danced across the sky was too precious to ignore. If they wanted to use their fists on him, they'd have to drag him away from the window.

"Mackay," a gruff voice intruded then. "Fortune shines upon ye this eve."

The comment surprised him. Niel drew back from the window and turned. However, his gaze alighted upon just one guard. Dark-haired and stocky in build, he was younger than most of the men who worked at Bass Rock Castle: this island fortress prison. Unlike some of the guards, who smirked and growled insults at him whenever they entered his cell to bring food and water, or empty his privy, this one had a solemn face and usually said little.

Niel stared back at him, not answering. He wondered if the guard had fallen prey to the malaise that usually infected the guards here after a while: boredom. It eventually turned them mean and vicious. Niel waited for the young guard to continue—no doubt he'd come to toy with him.

Entering the cell, the guard stepped over the bowl of grey-colored vegetable stew, and the stale bread, and drew the dirk at his waist.

Niel's belly twisted. His warrior instincts, which had once been honed, were blunted these days. He was unarmed, his body weak from years of incarceration. If the guard wished to slit his throat or gut him, he'd be easy prey.

But the guard didn't approach him. Instead, he moved to the wall next to Niel and started digging into the mortar around one of the bricks.

Niel watched him, the cramp in his guts draining away.

What was this fool doing?

The mortar around the brick was dry and crumbly, and it took the man only a short while to loosen the stone. The dirk's thin, sharp blade was the perfect tool. He then dug his fingers in and heaved, pulling the rough brick free. In fact, it came away with surprising ease.

Rising to his feet, the guard cast Niel a grim smile. "As I said, ye are a fortunate one, Mackay. Ye have a friend here, it seems."

Niel stared back at him, still not comprehending what the man was getting at. He swallowed, his lips parting. He spoke rarely these days—words had to be dredged from him. "A friend?" he croaked.

The guard's grey-blue eyes gleamed. "Aye." His gaze met Niel's. "Are ye ready to leave this place?"

Niel twitched.

Aye, this whoreson was playing with him. It wouldn't be the first time—and once they'd been at Bass Rock a year or two, some of the guards went to great lengths to entertain themselves.

As if reading his thoughts, the guard's mouth twisted. "Ye think this is a ruse ... but it isn't." He weighed the brick in his hand. "This is how it's going to work, Mackay. Unbeknownst to us, ye have been using a wooden spoon to dig out the mortar around this brick here." He paused then, studying Niel's face as if ensuring he was taking all of this in. "I brought ye supper this eve, but ye were lying in wait for me ... and smashed me hard over the back of the head with yer new weapon, knocking me out cold. Ye then stole my dirk and made yer escape." His gaze never wavered from Niel's as he continued. "After that, ye made yer way down to West Landing, where ye stole a rowboat and fled across the firth to the mainland."

The guard stepped forward then and held out the brick. "Go on ... try not to cave my skull in though. I'd like to wake up afterward."

Niel stared at him. He was struggling to accept the man's words. It felt as if his head were filled with porridge. Had all these years of incarceration dulled his once sharp wits?

Surely the guard wasn't offering him his freedom?

Wordlessly, he took the brick, his fingers fastening around the rough stone.

"I don't understand," he finally managed. "Why would ye help me?"

The younger man's mouth quirked, although his gaze was shuttered. "There's no time for explanations." He glanced over his shoulder then. "We'll have company shortly ... ye'd better not delay this." With that, the guard turned his back on him. "Come on." His voice tightened, betraying his nervousness at what would come next. "Get on with it."

Niel licked his parched lips, his gaze dropping to the brick once more. It felt heavy in his palm. A weapon at last.

However, this situation felt as if he were night walking. Freedom didn't come so easily. This had to be a trick of some kind.

"*Do it*, Mackay." The guard's tone was flint-edged now.

Niel tightened his grip on the brick and raised it high, hesitating. "How do ye know I won't kill ye?" he asked.

The guard huffed a humorless laugh. "I don't ... it's an act of trust."

The fresh sea air hit Niel's face when he pushed upon the heavy wooden door and took the narrow, winding steps down the cliff-face.

I'm free!

His legs felt wobbly. Years of being locked up had taken their toll. He hated feeling so unsteady, as if his heavy feet would trip him up and send him careening head-first down these perilous steps.

The last of the light was fading from the sky now, as was the bloody sunset. Even so, Niel blinked like a sleepy owl thrust out into the noon sun. After the dimness of his cell, the light stung his eyes.

The winter air cut through the thin material of his tattered lèine and braies. His teeth started to chatter, and he clenched his jaw tight in an effort to control the reaction to the cold.

Hades, he was so frail these days.

He had to be careful in the half-light not to miss a step, especially on shaky legs. The wind buffeted the rocky isle, pushing at him like rough hands as he inched his way down, leaving the crenelated bulk of the prison and guard barracks behind. The stairs wrapped around the edge of the Bastian, a large tower with high windows peering out like blind eyes.

Despite the cold, sweat beaded on Niel's top lip. What if someone was watching him from there? What if guards appeared at any moment? He couldn't run, couldn't hide. The thought of being dragged back to his cell made his heart buck wildly against his ribs.

Calming himself, Niel tightened his grip upon the dirk he'd taken from the guard. Aye, he was cornered, yet he was no longer unarmed.

Teeth gritted, he continued down the stairs toward the West Landing, where dark water lapped against a narrow jetty. Curse him, his legs swayed under him like those of a newborn colt. They could barely hold him up. If guards came after him now, he'd be done for.

Moored to the landing was a small wooden rowboat. And despite the gloaming, which now wrapped around Bass Rock in a grey blanket, he spied a cloaked figure awaiting him.

Niel's already violently beating heart started to echo in his ears.

His fingers clenched hard around the bone hilt of his dirk. The guard hadn't warned him that someone would be waiting for him at the boat.

Cautiously, he approached, each muscle coiled.

He was free now, and he wouldn't have anyone rip it from him. The gelid winter air stung his cheeks, and the scent of brine in his lungs sharpened his dulled senses. A spark—a shadow of the man he'd once been—returned, and he clung to it.

As he neared the jetty, the cloaked figure pushed back its hood.

Niel's breathing caught, surprise flooding over him when he saw a woman's face looking back at him.

"Who are ye?" he rasped, halting before her.

The woman, who looked to be around five and twenty winters, with curly dark hair and solemn blue eyes, stared back at him a moment before her mouth lifted at the corners. "We are kin, Niel ... I'm Amelia ... yer cousin."

Cousin? Niel stared hard at her face before a memory returned. Aye, he recalled her now. They'd met but once. She'd been a waif of a girl at one of the Mackay clan gatherings. He'd never known his aunt. His father had rarely mentioned her, and the woman had died young. "What are ye doing here?" It felt odd to talk, his voice was rusty, hoarse with disuse.

Her features tightened. "I'm wed to Sir Robert Lauder ... the governor of Bass Rock Castle." Amelia cast a glance up toward the Bastian, her expression suddenly nervous. One look at her face, and Niel knew that her marriage wasn't a happy one. There was no mistaking the fear that shadowed the woman's face.

"Why would ye help me?" he asked, frowning. Aye, there had been a time when his mind was as sharp as a whetted blade, yet his head felt woolly this eve. He was having trouble grasping the situation.

Her gaze shifted back to Niel once more. "Ye are the rightful clan-chief of the Mackays ... and ye have been locked up here for too long."

Niel stared back at her, a chill washing over him. "So my father is dead then?"

A nerve flickered in her cheek. "Did the guards not tell ye?"

He shook his head.

"Angus Mackay died four years ago," she replied, her voice brittle now. "And I would tell ye everything I know concerning it, but there isn't time."

Niel drew in a slow breath. His mind churned at this news; the knowledge that his father was gone was a punch to the gut. Yet he knew she was right—they didn't have time for this.

"This is a terrible risk ye take, lass," he said, his throat tightening. "Yer husband could come across us at any moment."

She shook her head. "Robert is ensconced with a messenger from the mainland this eve. King James has been murdered ... and since it was by his decree that ye were sent here, the king can no longer have ye arrested and returned to Bass Rock."

Niel sucked in a deep breath. Angus Mackay dead and King James murdered—what had been happening in the world beyond this island prison?

"Go now." Amelia stepped close to him, her gaze shining in the gloaming. "Take the boat directly across the firth ... a horse is waiting for ye in the woods just back from the shore. Take it, and ride swiftly for the Highlands."

Niel nodded, even if his mind scrabbled to keep up.

"The guard," he began, searching her face. "How did ye—"

"Ye didn't hurt Graeme too badly, did ye?" Amelia's face had gone rigid.

In an instant the veil lifted, and Niel understood. Of course—they were lovers. Why else would one of the guards set him free?

He shook his head. "Worry not about him," he assured her. "Although he'll have a lump the size of an egg on the back of his head when he wakes." He reached out then and took her hand. It was slender and ice-cold, although her palms were damp, betraying her nervousness. "I only hope this act doesn't lay the blame at yer feet."

She shook her head. "It shouldn't ... my husband thinks I'm abed with a headache, and Graeme has made it look as if ye used a spoon to pry a brick free of the wall over time ... before assaulting him. That's why we moved ye to a different cell ... one where he'd already loosened one of the bricks in readiness for this day." Her throat bobbed then. "Hurry, Niel. We can't remain here like this much longer. Someone will see us."

Niel nodded. He didn't need further urging to be gone from this place. Releasing her hand, he crossed to where the rowboat bobbed against the landing. He then climbed in, discovering that she'd left him a cloak and a small leather pack.

Warmth seeped through him, despite the biting wind and the chill spray of seawater. Amelia's kindness, after so many years of suffering, was a balm to his arid soul. He wished she would come with him—yet it was clear she wouldn't leave her lover.

"Why don't ye and Graeme come with me?" he asked then, glancing up into her shadowed face. "It would be safer for ye both."

Amelia stared down at him. "We can't leave," she replied, her voice cracking.

Whyever not?

Niel's lips parted, as he readied himself to question her further. However, there was something in her tone—a blend of brittleness and panic—that checked him.

"There's no time for this," Amelia choked out, taking a step back from the mooring. "Go ... now!"

Shrugging on the cloak, Niel untied the boat from its mooring and pushed himself away with an oar.

He then glanced back up at the slender cloaked figure. "Thank ye, Amelia ... yer act will never be forgotten." The wind whipped away his words, and for a moment, he thought she hadn't heard him.

However, the governor's wife nodded and raised a hand. "Go well, Niel Mackay." And with that, she gathered her cloak close and slipped away, the darkness swallowing her.

Settling himself down upon the slat of wood in the center of the rowboat, Niel picked up the second oar. It was perilous this close to the rocks, for the waves swelled and foamed against the sharp edges, and he struggled to turn the craft around and strike out, toward the shore. The muscles in his shoulders and arms—weak after years of disuse—screamed for mercy as he rowed, yet Niel clenched his teeth and forced himself on.

His gaze remained fixed upon Bass Rock: an austere, craggy pinnacle thrusting out of the sea that was now outlined against an indigo sky. There had been times over the years when he'd thought he'd never leave that rock, never see freedom again. He'd believed he'd die there.

But fate—in the form of a loyal Mackay kinswoman, a cousin he'd forgotten he even had, and her brave lover—had set him free.

And with each stroke of the oars, the numbness that had shrouded Niel for so long fell away.

For the first period of his incarceration, thoughts of the reckoning he'd take on his father and the treacherous Gunns—the clan who'd caused the king to turn on the Mackays at Inverness all those years ago—had fueled him. Initially, it had kept despair at bay, until time and misery wore him down. After that, he'd sunk deep into a strange torpor, where nothing mattered anymore.

But as he allowed himself to reflect on all he'd suffered, his instincts flared to life once more. Heat kindled in his belly, and his blood caught afire.

Anger burned like a stoked furnace in his gut.

Niel had been robbed of the chance to face his father again. He'd wanted the Mackay to pay for sacrificing his only son to save his own neck. He'd dreamed of confronting the old bastard one day.

But as the moments passed, he reminded himself that George Gunn and his spawn likely still lived.

A harsh smile split Niel's face, and he bared his teeth to the outline of Bass Rock, which drew smaller with each pull of the oars.

Aye, he'd still be able to take his revenge against those who had wronged him—and he would savor every last bit of it.

2

GHOSTS OF THE PAST

Tongue
Strathnaver, Scotland

Three weeks later ...

IT WAS A great pity one couldn't take retribution against the dead.

If he could, Niel Mackay would have beaten his father to a bloody pulp. But as it was, Angus-Dow Mackay, the former clan-chief of the Mackays, was buried six feet under. His father was nothing more than food for the worms now; Niel couldn't do him any further damage.

Even so, Niel's hands clenched into fists at his sides as he glared down upon the headstone. He stood in the windswept kirkyard, his eyes dry and burning. Next to his father's grave sat his mother's. The etching upon her headstone indicated that she had perished in 1428—a year after his incarceration.

"How did my mother die?" he asked softly, glancing at the man who stood nearby. John Mackay of Aberach had drawn up a respectful distance from the graves.

His cousin's lean face was somber as he met Niel's eye. "Estelle took ill a few months after the council at Inverness ... a wasting sickness." John paused then, his features tightening. "She was never the same after ye were taken."

Niel shifted his focus back to his mother's grave, letting silence fall between him and his cousin once more. Perhaps in contemplation, he'd feel something.

After all, he hadn't had an acrimonious relationship with his mother.

But there wasn't any place in his heart for grief, not now.

He recalled Estelle Mackay's shrill, pleading wails then, ten years earlier, as he'd been dragged away in chains. His mother had been a self-contained woman—he'd never witnessed her lose control before.

But she had that day.

In an instant, Niel was back there—standing before King James in the great hall of Inverness Castle. The king had just threatened his father with the axe before asking why he shouldn't take his head. Niel would never forget his father's response.

I offer ye my son, Niel. Take him prisoner. Hold him as proof of my word that I will never again disobey ye.

And James had—but not before Niel had gotten his hands around the clan-chief's throat and attempted to throttle him.

He would never forget his mother's screams. They'd haunted him for a while afterward.

She sickened and died because of it.

Niel drew in a deep breath as a hard lump rose in his throat.

His mother hadn't been a bad woman, but neither her husband nor her son had paid her much attention over the years.

Niel shut his eyes for a moment, blocking out the sight of her headstone.

Aye, Estelle Mackay likely deserved much better than the lot she'd been given—but then, so did most folk.

Exhaling sharply, Niel opened his eyes once more. He moved his full attention back to Angus Mackay's headstone, and as he did so, a serpent coiled in his belly.

Rage. It had burned within him constantly since he'd rowed away from Bass Rock.

"Treacherous, shit-eating bastard," he muttered under his breath. "I should spit upon yer grave."

Next to him, he heard John shift uncomfortably. No doubt, his cousin thought him overly harsh, unfeeling.

But they both knew what the clan-chief had done to his only son.

Time stretched out in the kirkyard, and neither Niel nor John spoke. An icy breeze gusted in off the Kyle of Tongue, the wide body of water that stretched north to the coast and to the south dwindled into Kinloch River.

Stepping back from the graves, Niel reached up and massaged a stiff muscle in his shoulder. Tension reverberated off him these days, the need for action writhing in his gut. He inhaled the sharp mountain air laced with the scent of wood smoke. He then swept his gaze over his surroundings, taking it all in.

The two men stood a few yards away from a squat stone kirk with a slate pitched roof on the outskirts of the village of Tongue. Niel had only been back here a day, and it was still so new—it was as if he were looking upon this landscape for the first time.

Behind him rose a lofty bush-clad promontory, and upon its crest perched a stone fortress: Castle Varrich, seat of the Mackay clan. Beyond the castle rose the sculpted outline of two great mountains: Ben Loyal and Ben Hope.

Niel took in the majesty of the mountains. He'd missed his home terribly in those first days of incarceration—but after a while, he'd forced himself not to think about everything that had been ripped from him.

It was dangerous to long for something he might never see again.

"I'd forgotten just how beautiful it is here," he said finally, his voice gentler now that he'd shifted his attention from the graves.

"Aye," John murmured. "I shall be sad to leave it ... and return to Achness."

Niel looked his cousin's way. "There's no need for ye to go yet, John ... I've only just arrived."

His cousin nodded, although his expression was now serious. "As ye wish ... but I repeat what I told ye last night: I was merely a custodian of Castle Varrich in yer absence. Now that ye have returned to the clan, I willingly surrender all lands to ye."

Niel inclined his head in thanks. "And I thank ye for that, cousin." He paused then, anger curdling his belly once more. "At least *ye* are loyal to me."

"Many of yer clansmen are too," John replied, his tone firming. "Connor Mackay of Farr, Hugh Mackay of Loch Stach, Robin Mackay of Melness … and many others of the clan see ye as the rightful clan-chief. News of yer return will spread like wildfire through the Highlands."

Niel huffed a laugh, although there was little humor in it. "Aye … that'll surprise them."

His gaze settled upon the younger man, taking him in. He hadn't recognized his cousin when he'd come out to meet him. He remembered John as a tall, lanky youth with dark curly hair, an eager face—and guileless blue eyes.

The man before him bore little resemblance to that lad.

Time, age, and battles had changed John Mackay irrevocably. Niel recalled that, before his incarceration, John had already been the laird of Achness. The role was thrust on him early, for he'd lost both his parents young.

John was still tall and lean, yet his arms and legs were heavily muscled and his shoulders had broadened. His face was no longer so eager or earnest. And the patch he wore over his left eye, and the wooden hand that emerged from his right sleeve, told the story of a warrior who would carry a reminder of the battles he'd won for the rest of his days.

His single blue eye—the hue of a winter's sky—watched Niel steadily.

"I know ye don't wish to hear it," John said after a moment, "but yer father was sorry for what he did."

Niel's jaw clenched. John was right—he didn't want anyone making excuses for Angus Mackay.

"The old fazart might have been sorry," he growled, "but it changes nothing. He never lodged an appeal to free me, did he?"

John's mouth pursed, acknowledging that this was true. "No, it was the Mackays of Farr that championed ye. Morgan Mackay even went to Scone on yer behalf."

Something unknotted deep within Niel's chest at this news.

He'd grown up with Connor and Morgan Mackay. Morgan, the laird's younger brother, had always been a bit of a hot-head compared to steadfast Connor. But then he recalled the last time he'd seen the brothers in the dungeon of Inverness Castle—and he remembered the determination in Morgan's eye as he'd made him a promise.

We won't give up on ye, Niel. I give ye my word.

But his own father had. The moment he'd handed Niel over to the king in his place, he'd lost his only son.

Niel turned then and made his way out of the kirkyard. It was late morning, and the noon meal awaited. The cooks were preparing a banquet to welcome him back, but Niel had needed to visit his parents' graves before sitting down to eat.

They took the path away from the village and over a stone bridge. Cottars, tilling earth for the coming spring plantings in a field behind the kirk, glanced up at their approach.

"Laird!" One of the men shouted, joy rippling across his face. "The best of mornings to ye!"

"We are happy to have ye home, Mackay!" A woman called out a moment later. "Where ye belong."

Niel's step faltered, an unexpected warmth replacing the chill his father had left in his gut. These were his people—and from their expressions, they welcomed his return.

"Morning," he called back, waving to the cottars.

He and John kept walking. The castle loomed overhead now, although it was a steep climb up a winding road to reach it.

"They love ye," John observed. "As they did yer father."

At the mention of Angus Mackay, Niel's mouth thinned. "He brought dishonor upon our clan," he replied, his tone biting. "By rights, they should loathe the bastard."

As I do.

"Do ye wish to know how Angus died?" John asked then.

Niel cut his cousin a sharp look. Part of him didn't wish to ever speak of his father again, and yet another part was curious. "Tell me then," he grunted. He might as well get this done with too. Once he knew, he could leave his father's ghost behind him.

"He wasn't well enough to fight in the Battle of Drumnacoub," John began. "And so he watched from afar as the two sides met." His cousin's gaze remained fixed upon the path ahead as he spoke, his expression distant as if he'd returned to that battle, four years earlier, that had taken his eye and hand.

"The clash was a cruel one," John continued. "But I was determined not to let yer father's traitorous cousins win out. Our victory was hard-won, even if I fell upon the field. In the end, there were few alive on either side. Afterward Angus, who was unable to walk well, ordered men to carry him down to the battlefield upon a litter. He was searching for the corpses of his faithless cousins … and for me … but in the end, a skulking Sutherland man, hiding in a nearby bush, killed him with an arrow."

Niel listened to this tale dispassionately.

It was an irony indeed that the once formidable Angus-Dow Mackay had been reduced to watching the battle that would decide his fate as clan-chief, only to be struck down afterward by an assassin. His own cousins had attempted to take his lands, and they'd been backed by warriors from the Clan Sutherland. Niel could only imagine how betrayed his father would have felt.

Niel's jaw tightened. He hoped the disloyalty of his own kin had cut Angus deep. He hoped his father had wept in rage and despair.

Shoving aside such thoughts, which only made his belly ache with the need for vengeance against a dead man, Niel glanced at his cousin once more. They'd begun the steep climb toward the castle now.

"He was indeed fortunate that ye led his army, John," he replied. "Although Drumnacoub cost ye dearly."

John's mouth twisted before he shook his head. "I lived."

The words held a heavy, resigned edge to them. Aye, John had lived—but no man wished to end up maimed after a battle. Better to have fallen.

"It wasn't the only time during yer absence that Mackay fought Mackay," John continued, shifting the topic away from himself. "A few months after ye were imprisoned, two Mackay chieftains turned on yer father during a clan gathering hosted by the Mackays of Farr." His cousin's face turned grim. "But we bested them too, and William Mackay of Dun Ugadale and Robert Mackay of Balnakeil were beheaded in Castle Varrich's bailey ... their heads mounted on pikes outside the gates."

This grim tale cast a shadow over Niel's already dark mood.

He'd once thought of William and Robert as friends. He'd hunted with them, fought with them, and downed horns of ale with them on many occasions.

"Why did they do it?" he asked after a pause.

"Yer father's behavior at Inverness weakened him in their eyes," John replied. "They didn't think him fit to rule the Mackays."

Niel's mouth thinned. In that, he was in agreement. Even so, it didn't excuse their behavior.

The two men stopped talking for a spell as the way steepened—it was a long walk up. John navigated the path easily, while Niel's breathing quickly became labored. Despite his missing eye and hand, his cousin was still a man in his prime. Niel felt weak and wasted in comparison. They were the same height, yet he was still painfully thin, and these days, every one of his five and thirty winters weighed heavily upon him. Even the three-week journey north on horseback hadn't done much to strengthen his body.

Niel's brow furrowed. That would change. If he was to become a clan-chief to be feared, and was to have the reckoning he craved, he needed to be strong and fighting fit. He resolved to begin training with John daily and to make sure he ate meat regularly in order to regain the muscle he'd lost.

Halfway up the hill, Niel was forced to stop. Breathing hard, he placed his hands on his hips and shifted his attention out across the glittering kyle. It was a bright day for this time of year, and he could almost taste the coming of spring in the air.

"I'm not interested in fighting my clansmen, John," he said, gasping out the words as his sorely underused lungs heaved like forge bellows. "Instead, I wish to focus on those who have done me *real* wrong."

John halted and turned to face him, his gaze wary. His cousin knew that this declaration was coming. "The Gunns," he said, his tone flat.

Niel nodded. "If it wasn't for them, the king would never have dished out such harsh punishment against our clan."

John pulled a face. "There's something about the Gunns ye should know, Niel."

"Aye … what's that?"

"George Gunn died a few years back. However, it isn't Alexander who rules the clan now, but his younger brother Tavish."

Niel stilled. Disappointment flooded through him then. Ever since escaping from Bass Rock, thoughts of what he'd do to George Gunn and his eldest son, Alexander, had driven him forward. Now, he would need to focus his ire upon a man he'd never even faced in battle: Tavish Gunn.

"And what happened to the Gunn first-born?" he asked.

A sigh gusted out of John, and he raked a hand through his mop of curly dark hair. "Aye, well *there's* a tale, Niel … although I think ye need to be seated with an ale in yer hand to hear it."

Niel's gaze narrowed. He was tempted to demand his cousin just tell him now, yet something in John's voice warned him this wouldn't be a brief account. After their discussion in the kirkyard, an ache had formed either side of Niel's eyes.

Talking of the past was wearing upon him. Instead, he needed to think of the future: of the reckoning he would have upon his enemies, and of what he would need to do in order to ensure his bloodline endured.

He wouldn't leave himself weakened and open to challenge, as his father had, by bearing just one son.

"I'll have my vengeance upon those Gunn dogs," he growled after a pause. "But first, I must get my own house in order." He met John's eye then and favored him with a tight smile. "And I'll need yer help, cousin ... for I must find myself a wife."

3
THE CURSED BRIDE

Strathnaver, Scotland

A month later ...

"I SEE IT!"

Neave's excited voice made Beth's chin kick up, her pulse quickening. She glanced over at where her sister rode upon a sturdy pony beside her. "Really ... where?"

Her sister's hazel-green eyes gleamed as she grinned back. "Look due north!"

Doing as bid, Beth's gaze scanned the northern horizon. They were riding over open hills now, having left the shadow of the mighty Ben Loyal and the loch by the same name behind them. The highway was rutted and winding, and the journey had been slow—especially as they had brought a large wagon, laden with dowry gifts, with them. It was a four-day journey from Foulis Castle in the southern Highlands, and Beth had never yet traveled so far north.

Excitement danced in her belly, as did nerves. Her palms, gripping the reins, were damp. This remote corner of the Highlands, the seat of the Mackay territory, would soon be her home.

Squinting, Beth focused upon the bulk of a fortress, outlined against a windswept sky. Castle Varrich sat high upon an outcrop, a swathe of green underneath it, looking over the breathtaking landscape it commanded. The late afternoon sun bathed its dun-colored walls, turning them gold.

A smile curved Beth's lips, and a little of her apprehension eased.

She'd thought the setting of Foulis Castle lovely, and although the gentle woodland and meadows surrounding it were, her home paled in comparison to the dramatic sweep of the wide cradle they now rode into and the great mountains that framed it.

Her belly flip-flopped.

I will be mistress of all of this.

It was still almost too much to take in.

At six and twenty winters, she'd started to believe that she was doomed to become a spinster, especially after three betrothals had all ended with the death of the men she'd hoped to wed.

A shadow fell over Beth then, and her smile faded—as did a little of her excitement.

The Cursed Bride.

That was the name folk had given her after the third of her husbands-to-be, Ian MacLeod, had gotten himself skewered by a boar.

No one ever dared say it to her face, yet she'd heard the whispers, seen the veiled glances, and the smirks at gatherings. Folk were superstitious about such things. Indeed, they thought her ill-luck for any man.

Beth drew in a sharp breath and glanced away from the hill-top fortress, back to Neave. She then twisted in the saddle, her gaze alighting upon her two other sisters, Jean and Eilidh, who rode directly behind them.

And of course, if she was cursed, so would her younger sisters likely be.

Of late, none of them had received visits from suitors—and Beth couldn't help but think her reputation had tainted them all.

Jean met Beth's eye, favoring her with a quick smile. However, her grey-green eyes were solemn, as always. "Are ye ready to meet him?" she asked.

"Aye," Beth replied with more bravery than she felt. Thinking about her 'cursed' past had made misgiving knot under her ribcage. What if this marriage too never came to pass? What if they arrived at Castle Varrich only to discover that her future husband had choked on a piece of meat?

"I wonder though, if Niel Mackay is ready to meet *ye*." Neave piped up once more. Beth cut her sister another look to see she was grinning. Neave's eyes gleamed with impish good humor. "Surely, he won't expect such a force of nature."

Beth snorted. It wasn't a ladylike sound at all, and no doubt their stepmother, who was riding ahead with their father, would have been horrified if she'd heard her. However, Laila Munro wasn't within earshot, so she was spared the pained look.

"After a decade in prison, I doubt Niel Mackay will be cowed by the likes of me," she replied archly.

"But aren't ye a little worried about what sort of man he is?" Jean asked, a note of concern in her voice. "Incarceration may have turned him cruel."

Beth pursed her lips, turning back to Jean. Of all her sisters, Jean was always the voice of doom. Always the worrier, the one who fretted over what the future might bring.

Actually, Beth was more intrigued than concerned about the character of the man who'd sent her a proposal of marriage. She'd heard that, previous to his imprisonment, Niel Mackay had been an arrogant, headstrong warrior.

Next to Jean, their youngest sister, Eilidh, sighed before rolling her eyes. "Ye were there when Beth read out Niel Mackay's letter," she pointed out. "He appeared articulate and reasonable."

Jean sighed. "Aye, but anyone can appear so in a missive." Her attention remained upon Beth. "If I were ye, I'd be wary."

"Mother Mary, listen to ye," Neave scoffed. "An old woman at two and twenty. What choice does our Beth have? She'll never have an offer of marriage as fine as this one."

Beth turned back to face the direction of travel, her gaze shifting to her father's broad back. He and Laila rode so close that their thighs almost brushed. Her stepmother had just laughed at something George Munro had said, the light, musical sound of her mirth carrying through the afternoon air.

Neave had echoed her own thoughts perfectly.

Aye, she was a clan-chief's daughter. However, her history had caused all offers of marriage to cease.

Niel Mackay was nearly ten years her elder, a man wishing to make a fresh start since his escape from Bass Rock. He was an unexpectedly good match.

Her father had been delighted when the missive had come from Castle Varrich three weeks earlier and had sent off a reply the following morning. And, like Eilidh, Beth had been impressed by the respectful tone of Niel Mackay's correspondence.

This marriage would form a powerful union between the Mackays and the Munros—and it was up to George Munro's eldest daughter to ensure that this alliance flourished.

Beth's jaw firmed. Jean fretted unnecessarily.

She stood upon the threshold of a new life, an adventure—and she couldn't wait to embark on it.

Niel awaited his future bride in the bailey. He'd been helping the farrier shoe his stallion when word had reached him that the Munro party approached.

Glancing down at the dirt and sweat-stained lèine and braies he wore, Niel's mouth thinned. It wasn't the right attire to meet Elizabeth Munro in, yet there was no time to bathe and change clothing.

She would just have to put up with him as he was.

"They're nearing the gates now," John advised him. His cousin approached, his long stride eating up the distance between them. He winked then. "Prepared to meet yer bride?"

"Aye," Niel replied, keeping his face expressionless.

It had been John who'd suggested this match. He'd been blunt about it too—informing him that Elizabeth Munro was on the cusp of spinsterhood yet was attractive enough. He'd also told Niel of the name that folk whispered behind her back: *The Cursed Bride*. Apparently, all three of the men she'd been betrothed to had met untimely ends.

Such a tale would have put many men off, but not Niel. He wanted a well-born wife, and Elizabeth Munro was a clan-chief's daughter. After the things he'd endured over the past decade, Highland gossip didn't bother him.

Nonetheless, misgiving wreathed up within him as he waited, like smoke from a kindling fire.

"Ye have actually *seen* the woman?" Niel asked his cousin. It occurred to him that he might have heard of her attractiveness second-hand. Elizabeth Munro might be in reality horse-faced.

John nodded. "Aye, years ago now, at a summer gathering." Meeting Niel's eye, his mouth lifted at the corners. "Fear not, I remember her as a comely lass. A bright and lively one too."

Niel pulled a face. He was satisfied to hear that his bride-to-be wasn't a hag, but he couldn't have cared less if she was 'bright and lively'. He wanted a wife, not a confidant. He was in his mid-thirties and wedding far later than he should have been. It was enough that it wouldn't be an ordeal to bed her. He hoped too that she was fecund and would bear him plenty of sons. He cared little about anything else.

The thud of horses' hooves drew his attention away from musings on Elizabeth Munro. He turned from his cousin and looked to the gate, where the first of the newcomers clattered into the bailey.

A middle-aged man with thick greying brown hair and a neatly trimmed beard led the way, a pretty blonde woman swathed in fur following close behind.

Niel observed them keenly. This would be George Munro, Tenth Baron of Foulis, and his second wife, Laila. Niel remembered George Munro from many years earlier. He'd been at that fateful council at Inverness with his first wife.

Four lasses upon sturdy garrons entered the bailey then, passing through the gate in pairs. A knot of armed warriors followed them in, and a large wooden wagon brought up the rear.

Niel's gaze swept over the four young women astride the Highland ponies.

Which one is she?

He knew that Elizabeth Munro was the eldest of four sisters—in fact, she had written to him in person a fortnight earlier, requesting that she might bring her three younger siblings to live with her at Castle Varrich.

Niel had replied that she indeed could. It hadn't been a difficult decision, for this castle lacked females. Since his mother's death, there had been no Lady Mackay in residence, and there was much work to be done to make it a proper home once more.

Upon his return, Niel had noted how quiet the castle was these days. The mood was somber, and few of the servants smiled. He intended Castle Varrich to prosper, and that meant doing away with the old and welcoming the new.

Even so, he wished John had imparted a little more detail about what his bride-to-be looked like, for 'comely' described them all to varying degrees. Each of the four lasses before them had her own distinct appeal, and each held herself differently.

Niel's attention rested upon the first two: one had a thick dark walnut-brown mane, milky skin, and a pugnacious jaw, while her companion had elfin features, a mischievous twinkle in her eye, and braided hair that was more chestnut in hue. Behind them, one of the lasses, with curly mousey-brown locks scraped back into a bun, wore a worried expression, while next to her perched a lass of gamine beauty. Everything about this one was delicate, from the swanlike neck to her fine oaken-colored hair.

Those last two had a younger appearance than the first pair, and so Niel's attention shifted back to where the darker-haired sister was now dismounting her garron.

If he had to make an educated guess, he'd say that *this* was Elizabeth Munro.

She had a maturity to her, a poise that spoke of being the eldest sibling.

Relief uncoiled within him as he noted that his cousin hadn't lied. She *was* pleasing to the eye. The heavy fur-trimmed cloak she wore swished back to reveal a small yet curvaceous figure clad in a jade-green kirtle. She had broad hips, which boded well for childbearing.

The woman turned then, her attention sweeping the bailey and the crowd that was rapidly amassing there.

She's looking for me.

Niel fought a rueful smile, wondering if she'd spy him. Dressed as he was—he doubted it.

He tensed in surprise when a frank hazel-eyed gaze met his—and held.

A heartbeat passed, and then Elizabeth Munro's full lips curved into a smile.

4
THE DEED

"MACKAY, MAY I introduce ye to my first-born daughter, Beth."

George Munro's voice boomed across the bailey. The clan-chief swung down from his courser and moved to where the woman who had so boldly met Niel's eye still stood, staring at him.

Niel's mouth lifted at the corners. However, he couldn't help feel a little disdain for Munro and the pride with which he introduced his daughter. Aye, this was a good match for her—although a man who'd sired four daughters and not one son should appear a little more humble, a little embarrassed even.

What good were daughters to a clan-chief? Who would continue George Munro's line? Niel glanced then at the Munro's wife. The woman was still fairly young—perhaps she could achieve what his first wife hadn't been able to, and bear him an heir.

Niel shifted forward then, approaching George Munro and his daughter.

The lass still watched him, with an appraising look that surprised him. Aye, he'd noted the stubborn set to her jaw as she'd ridden into the bailey. His bride-to-be certainly wasn't a meek mouse.

Niel wasn't sure how he felt about that. He'd once appreciated a feisty woman—Jaimee Mackay, Connor Mackay of Farr's younger sister, had caught his eye—but he wasn't in the market for such a wife. He wanted a biddable yet capable spouse who'd take care of his household without a word of complaint.

Niel halted before her and dipped his chin. "Greetings, Elizabeth," he said, still holding her gaze.

Her full lips parted, and she nodded to him. "Please ... call me Beth," she replied.

Niel stilled. Hades—her voice, husky and low, sent an unexpected jolt of lust straight through his groin.

His body's reaction was so sharp that he didn't know how to react. A moment passed, and mastering himself, Niel then shifted his attention to George Munro. The two men clasped arms.

"It has been too long, Niel," Munro greeted him warmly. "I'm glad to see ye back where ye belong."

Niel smiled once more. "And I'm glad to be home." He stepped back then, gesturing to the keep behind him. While the Munro clan-chief resided at Varrich, Niel intended to inform him about his desire to move against the Gunns. Elizabeth Munro's father would make a powerful ally. "Come, George ... let my men see to yer mounts while ye join me for an ale before supper."

Beth followed the men into the keep, her arm looped around Neave's, her gaze fixed upon the back of her husband-to-be.

"He's handsome," Neave whispered to her. Beth tore her attention from the Mackay to see her sister wore a knowing smile, her green eyes, flecked with brown, glinting.

"Aye," Beth replied with a smile of her own. There was no doubt about it, Niel Mackay drew a woman's eye. He was tall and lean—although painfully so. His lèine and braies hung on him—hardly surprising since he'd recently escaped from prison. A mane of wild dark hair, yet unmarked with grey, fell to broad shoulders, and he had the most penetrating blue eyes she'd ever seen. His face had an angular beauty, emphasized by slightly sharp features and a short beard trimmed close to his jaw.

But it wasn't his good looks that intrigued her, as much as the aura of strength and confidence that exuded from him. Despite the rough and dirtied clothing he wore, she'd spotted him easily in the crowd. The man's lordly bearing had given him away. And the impact of their gazes meeting had made her breathing catch.

"And he knew who ye were before Da introduced ye," Neave continued. "I saw the way ye looked at each other."

Beth emitted a strangled sound. "God's teeth, Neave ... ye do go on."

If she were honest, despite that he'd captured her attention, Beth was a little disappointed by the briefness of Niel's greeting. He'd clasped her father's arm yet hadn't even taken her hand. Now, instead of escorting her into the keep, the Mackay walked with her father—the pair of them chatting over old times.

Even so, her attention lingered upon the clan-chief's back. Sweat had soaked through his lèine, making the thin material stick to his spine and shoulders. Despite his leanness, this man exuded virility.

Aye, their introductions had been over too quickly, but she had plenty of time to remedy that.

Just be grateful he isn't as superstitious as other Highland lairds, she told herself as she mounted the last of the steps before the oaken doors of the keep.

Indeed, she was fortunate that Niel Mackay didn't appear bothered by the rumors that followed her. This man had given her a future when she'd been staring spinsterhood in the eye—and for that, she'd always be grateful.

They entered a lofty entrance hall before the laird of Castle Varrich led them into the great hall itself.

Next to her, Neave caught her breath. "Lord, it's impressive."

Beth cast her gaze around the vast interior, noting the high ceiling, where heavy, smoke-blackened beams stretched like the ribcage of a great beast, and the two enormous hearths either end, where wolfhounds lounged, gnawing at shin bones. A bed of rushes covered the floor, and an array of weapons—shields, axes, and swords—hung from the stone walls. A large white banner stretched behind the dais.

As she approached the clan-chief's table upon the dais, Beth studied the banner, taking in the silken fabric and the blue embroidered rampant lion, along with a hand clutching a goblet and one of the Mackay mottos: *Bi tren*—be valiant.

This was the *Bratach Bhan*, the famous banner that the warriors of Angus Mackay had carried into the Battle of Drumnacoub four years earlier.

After that victory, it was fitting that the banner had pride of place here.

She then spied the crest carved into the back of the clan-chief's large wooden chair halfway down the table. The crest, one she'd seen upon the wax seals of the missives Mackay had sent her, bore a hand gripping an upright dagger along with the clan's second motto: *Manu Forti*—with a strong hand.

The skin on the back of Beth's arms prickled. The Mackays were a powerful and proud Highland clan. She could hardly believe she would soon be its chief's lady.

Settling herself into her seat next to Niel, Beth sneaked another glance at the man who would soon be her husband.

He reclined in his carven chair, still conversing with her father as servants circled with jugs of ale and ewers of wine. Despite Niel's apparently relaxed stance, she could sense the coiled tension within him.

His senses were sharp, his reflexes at the ready.

Beth's breathing quickened. Aye, she liked the edge this man had.

Nonetheless, Niel's attention remained upon her father. They were discussing the details of King James's assassination. It had been a doubly treacherous act, for one of James's relatives, his uncle Walter Stewart, had led it.

"They tortured Stewart for three days before they took his head," her father said with a scowl. "The fool ... did he really think he'd get away with it?"

"Ambition has blinded many a man," Niel replied with a shake of his head. "Not everyone has yer sharp wits, Munro ... or yer loyalty."

Beth smiled at these words. Indeed, her father was both shrewd and trustworthy. Over the years, he'd navigated the perilous relationships between the Highland clans with relative ease. He wasn't a man to let greed or ambition sway his loyalties.

It pleased her that Niel Mackay had noted this. Her husband-to-be appeared to be an astute judge of character.

The conversation between the two men continued, and Beth's attention shifted farther down the table to where her three sisters had also taken their places. A long-limbed warrior bearing an eye patch sat down next to Neave.

Beth recognized the man: she'd seen him many years earlier at a gathering. John Mackay of Aberach had been young then, thinner but with the same wild, curly dark hair. He'd filled out in the years in-between, and his curls had been tamed a little, although his hair still fell messily across his forehead. Beth had heard that despite his victory at Drumnacoub, he'd been disfigured in that battle—and she noted that he kept his right arm hidden under the table, raising his tankard of ale with his left.

"When will ye wed my bonny daughter then, Mackay?" George Munro's abrupt change of topic, and his booming voice, which echoed down the table, caused Beth to glance back at the two men seated beside her. Suppressing a wince, she took a sip of wine from the pewter goblet she'd just picked up. Hades, they'd only just arrived. She understood her father's eagerness; she just wished he didn't have to bellow it across the hall.

Niel Mackay's dark brows raised. "Soon enough," he replied, his mouth curving. "I have invited my chieftains to attend the wedding ... and once they arrive, the deed shall be done."

Beth pursed her lips. *The deed.*

That was hardly a romantic turn of phrase to describe their impending nuptials.

However, her father wasn't bothered. The Munro clan-chief beamed back at the younger man. "Aye, that's good to hear."

Niel Mackay did glance her way then, and their gazes fused. "I'm sure ye wish for time to prepare, Elizabeth?"

"Aye," she replied, cursing the heat that rose to her cheeks. She wasn't a blushing maid—not like the youngest of her sisters, Eilidh, who turned a charming shade of pink when she was embarrassed—yet the directness of the clan-chief's cobalt gaze threw her. "Although I already have a gown for the occasion."

"It was her mother's," George Munro added. "Beth is the image of Colleen at the same age."

Beth glanced over at her father—and in his warm hazel eyes that her sisters said were identical to hers, she saw a trace of sadness. He'd treated her mother like a queen—and although he loved his second wife, Laila, too, his four daughters were a constant reminder of the woman he'd lost.

To her father's left, Laila favored her husband with a soft smile before placing a hand on his arm. Beth's throat thickened at the sweet gesture. Laila was a good woman. It was common for a second wife to be jealous of the one that had preceded her—but that wasn't Laila's way. The bond between the couple appeared to grow stronger with each passing month.

In truth, Beth wished for a marriage like theirs. She wanted a man to look at her the way her father gazed at Laila. She'd liked all three of the men she'd been betrothed to—the last one, Ian MacLeod, perhaps the most. He'd been a good-humored, big-hearted man, who spoke frankly. She'd wept in earnest when she'd learned of his death three years earlier but had hoped that she'd be fortunate to find a man like him again.

Stealing another glance at Niel Mackay's profile as he raised his goblet of wine to his lips, Beth wondered what lay ahead for them both. She wasn't under any illusions as to why he'd chosen her. She understood that an alliance between the Mackays and the Munros would be highly advantageous to both clans.

And yet she couldn't help but compare her meeting with Niel in the bailey to the first time she and Ian had been introduced. Ian had winked at her before taking her hand and kissing it. He'd then teased her, and Beth had laughed. Ian had made her laugh frequently.

Would Niel Mackay eventually put her at ease as Ian MacLeod had?

Lifting her own goblet to her lips, Beth took another sip of wine. It was foolish to compare the two men, she decided, for they were as different as the moon was to the sun. Despite that she wasn't quite sure what to make of him, there was no denying that Mackay had a quick mind, and it warmed her that he understood her father's worth. They'd spoken little, but she liked him already. There was no reason at all they couldn't have a happy marriage.

This was a fresh start, and she would embrace it.

Warmth bathed the solar. Seated near the glowing hearth, Niel let out a deep sigh. After years of weevil-infested bread and watery grey pottage, he didn't take having a bellyful of rich food and drink for granted. Nor did he ignore that he was sitting in comfort and warmth.

He savored the sensations. Aye, there were some things he vowed never to overlook again.

Putting his feet up onto a settle, Niel's gaze fixed upon the flickering hearth. It had been a pleasant evening, and he'd had a productive conversation with George Munro. The man's loyalty to the Mackays seemed steadfast.

Good. If he was going to strike back against the Gunns—and by God, he would—he needed plenty more men like the Munro at his side.

Niel yawned then. It wasn't late, yet weariness stole over him. The Munro party, exhausted from their four-day journey north, had all retired after supper, and Niel had been relieved. Being in company tired him out—far more than it had used to. Strangely, he'd hated the isolation of imprisonment, yet now that he was a free man, he often sought out solitude.

John had teased him about it more than once over the past days. "Ye can't hide away in yer solar, man ... the Mackays need to see their clan-chief's face."

And his cousin was right. However, it drained him having to make conversation all evening.

Niel stretched back in his chair, his eyelids lowering. Perhaps he too would get an early night.

A soft knock at the door intruded then.

Eyes opening, Niel pursed his lips. Hadn't he told the servants he didn't wish to be interrupted for the rest of the evening? Perhaps it was John. Niel's jaw tightened. Although he enjoyed his cousin's company, he just wanted to be left alone for a while.

"Come in," he barked.

The door whispered open, revealing a small dark-haired woman.

Surprise tightened Niel's chest as his gaze rested upon his bride-to-be. She was still dressed in the becoming jade-green kirtle she'd arrived in earlier. However, since it was early spring, and the night air held a nip to it, she wore a woolen shawl around her shoulders. Elizabeth Munro was smiling, albeit hesitantly, although the tilt to her chin gave the woman a bossy air.

"Elizabeth." Removing his feet from the settle, Niel rose to his feet. "What are ye doing here?"

5
FRANK WORDS

IT WASN'T THE warmest of greetings Beth had ever received.

Remaining in the doorway, she suddenly questioned her impulse to visit Niel Mackay. Back in the chamber she shared with Neave, her sister had viewed her with wide eyes when she'd announced her intention.

"Should ye be spending time with him ... alone?" Neave asked as she brushed out her long chestnut-brown hair.

"We'll be wed soon enough, Neave," Beth had replied with an eye roll. "It's not like ye to caution me about such things."

Neave shrugged. "Suit yerself ... I suppose it doesn't matter if tongues wag."

Beth sniffed. "Let them."

In truth, she'd imagined that the clan-chief's cousin John would have been with him.

But he wasn't.

She'd opened the door to find Niel Mackay unaccompanied in his solar. The chamber was a large space. A magnificent stag's head looked down over the hearth, and deerskins covered the flagstone floor. A finely woven tapestry, depicting a battle scene, covered one wall, and the door to what would be the clan-chief's bed-chamber led off to her right.

Beth's belly swooped at the sight of her husband-to-be. He'd risen to his feet in a fluid gesture that spoke of a restive energy she'd already noted within him. Even when he was in repose, the man was never truly at ease.

And he was still a stranger—an individual she'd hardly spoken more than a handful of words to. She wished to remedy that.

Beth cleared her throat; under the clan-chief's penetrating stare, she suddenly felt awkward, exposed. "Good eve ... and apologies for the intrusion ... but I thought we might talk for a short while before retiring."

Niel Mackay's dark brows drew together, his eyes—a mesmerizing dark-blue—narrowing. "I'm weary," he replied. "Can we not talk tomorrow?"

Beth swallowed, her discomfort increasing at his dismissal, yet she forced herself to continue holding his eye. "Ye and my father are going hunting at first light," she pointed out, careful to keep her voice soft. Laila had advised her men preferred women who spoke thus. "The opportunity for us to converse won't come until later."

Silence fell between the pair of them. It was warm inside the solar, and she barely noticed the cold draft at her back from the open door. Self-consciousness made sweat bead upon her upper lip.

Perhaps this move had been hasty, after all. Clearly, he didn't want company. "If ye are tired, I will not bother ye," she said after an awkward pause. "Goodnight, Mackay."

She took a step back then and turned toward the door. However, his voice forestalled her.

"Wait, Elizabeth ... stay." Beth glanced his way once more to see that Niel was still frowning. Yet he gestured to the chair that faced the one he'd been seated upon in front of the hearth. "I apologize for my brusqueness ... please come in for a short while."

Her pulse fluttering in her throat, Beth moved into the solar, closing the door behind her, and walked to the chair, settling herself down upon it. "Please, do call me Beth," she requested. "No one calls me by my full name these days."

"As ye wish." The clan-chief moved across to a sideboard and gestured to a ewer there. "Wine?"

"Aye." Beth wet her lips. "Thank ye." Maybe a sip or two would ease the nerves that made her belly pitch as if she were at sea. She was usually unflappable, yet this man disrupted her equilibrium.

Niel poured them both small cups of wine before carrying them back to the hearth. He handed her one. As he did so, their fingers brushed. It was the first time they'd touched, and Beth noted the warmth of his skin against hers and the way her hand tingled in the aftermath.

However, the sensation was fleeting, and Niel drew back, his gaze veiled, and sank down into his chair, cradling his goblet of wine.

Seated opposite each other, listening to the crackling of the fire, the pair of them fell silent once more.

Beth shifted in her chair. *Well, this is uncomfortable.*

Silence didn't come easy to Beth, for having grown up with three sisters and a vivacious mother, she was used to filling gaps in conversation. But Niel didn't appear ruffled by it. Perhaps years of incarceration made one comfortable with quiet.

Eventually, Niel spoke. "It was forward of ye to pay me a visit at this hour, Beth ... does yer father know of this?"

Beth shook her head before she lifted her chin. "He trusts me."

Niel arched a brow. "I'm sure he enjoys having a willful daughter."

"He sees me as capable rather than willful," she replied, angling her chin a notch higher. "A good thing too ... as the eldest daughter, I had to manage things at Foulis Castle for a few years after my mother died."

Indeed, George Munro liked that she was plain of speech, like her mother. He didn't encourage meekness in his womenfolk and had sometimes chastised his youngest, Eilidh, for being biddable. "Ye are too softhearted by half, lass," he'd once told Eilidh after she'd let one of the servants bully her. "The world has teeth ... and if ye wish to survive, ye must grow sharper ones."

But observing the Mackay, Beth realized he likely held a different opinion about women.

She took a fortifying sip of wine, welcoming the heat of it pooling in her belly.

"Ye *do* appear capable," Niel admitted after a pause. "A woman who will run this castle without assistance." His gaze then traveled down her body—it was a look of pure male appreciation, and Beth's breathing caught. "And ye appear strong and healthy ... a boon indeed, if ye are to bear me bairns. I must have an heir, Beth ... or my bloodline will die with me."

Their gazes met once more and held.

Beth favored him with a tight smile. "I will do my best to provide ye with strapping sons then," she replied, unable to keep the teasing edge from her voice.

He nodded, his expression unchanging. "Fear not, the ceremony won't be delayed. As soon as my guests arrive, I will see it done."

Beth's smile faded. Once again, he made their wedding sound as if he were planning to have a boil on his arse lanced.

Fighting her irritation, she decided to change the subject. "Bass Rock must have been an ordeal for ye," she said, before taking another gulp of wine. "How did ye weather it?"

Niel Mackay observed her over the rim of his cup, a glint in his eye. "I had no choice."

"Aye, but it would have broken a weaker man."

Niel shrugged. "Time loses all meaning in gaol. After a while, ye just ... sink into yerself. Ye become numb. It's either that or go mad."

Beth frowned, caught off-guard by his sudden candidness. "And now?" she asked softly. "Do ye still feel numb?"

"No." Niel then leaned forward then, and Beth sucked in a breath, entranced by the intensity in his eyes. "As I rowed away from that rock I made myself a promise ... I told myself I'd have my reckoning." He paused then, his mouth twisting. "Those Gunns swayed the king's opinion ... and they all escaped punishment while I rotted in gaol."

Beth stilled. For the first time since entering the solar, it seemed as if Niel Mackay had truly come alive. Unfortunately though, the fire she saw in his eyes troubled her.

It made her realize just what a sheltered life she'd led.

This man had spent ten years in exile, locked up in a cold cell, fed gruel, and most likely beaten regularly. Most folk knew of Bass Rock, of the cruelty of the governor and the guards. Only Scotland's worst criminals were sent there, and only a handful of them saw daylight again.

Mackay had done what few had managed: he'd escaped. But Bass Rock appeared to have left its mark. It had made him vengeful.

Taking one more swallow of wine, she resolved not to let his words worry her. Her husband-to-be clearly needed a wife—and not for the reasons he'd so bluntly outlined earlier. A woman's patience and understanding would soothe him, smooth his sharp edges. And in time, a loving relationship would blossom between them.

Heedless to the direction of her thoughts, Niel drained the last of his wine and set his cup down on the low table between them.

"I think we have conversed sufficiently for the moment," he said, his tone veiled in the aftermath of his frank words. "I shall bid ye goodnight now, Beth."

6

NOTHING WILL BE AS IT WAS

"I MUST FIND a way to gain his trust."

Beth's murmured comment made Jean cut her a sharp look. The two sisters were inside the large kitchen of Castle Varrich, hands coated with flour as they helped bake venison pies for the coming wedding banquet.

Around them, the cooks, kitchen hands, and scullery maids kept favoring the two Munro sisters with puzzled and worried looks.

Clearly, the former Lady Mackay had never dirtied her hands in the kitchens. Beth's presence here made the servants uncomfortable.

But Beth had a love of baking. She was never happier than when kneading bread dough, mixing batter for her father's favorite cake, or rolling out suet pastry for a pie. Likewise, Jean enjoyed cooking—and so, after a few days at Castle Varrich, the sisters had decided to make themselves useful in the kitchens.

"Careful, Beth," Jean muttered. Her sister's frank grey-green eyes were wide as Beth met her gaze. "Ye hardly know the man."

The kitchens were noisy, what with one of the cooks berating a kitchen hand for dropping a basket of eggs, and the rhythmic thud of knives on oaken boards as other servants prepared vegetables for the coming supper. Nonetheless, the sisters' conversation was a private one, and Jean had been careful to keep her voice low.

Beth snorted. "Aye, and there lies the problem. Mackay's in dire need of a woman's influence." She paused then. "It'll help turn his mind from vengeance."

"So the rumors are true then?" Jean leaned close. As she did so, she raised a hand to brush a wiry curl that had escaped her braid off her cheek. The gesture left a streak of flour behind. "Niel Mackay plans to take revenge upon the Gunns ... for what happened in Inverness?"

Beth nodded, her jaw tightening. Jean was right—the castle was abuzz with whispers about what the Mackay planned to do to the clan he held responsible for his incarceration. Her father had told her of what had happened at the council held in Inverness a decade earlier—of how George Gunn managed to persuade King James that the slaughter at the Battle of Harpsdale had been the fault of the Mackays.

Niel Mackay had nursed that wrong like a bruise for many years and was eager to settle old scores—her conversation with him on the eve of her arrival left Beth in no doubt of that.

"Once we are wed, I intend to draw his attention to other matters," Beth announced then. She finished rolling out a sheet of pastry and carefully lifted it, placing the sheet over the filled pie dish on the table. She then started to crimp the edges with her fingers. "Castle Varrich lacks heart ... together we Munro sisters can breathe life and warmth into these walls."

Indeed, since her arrival, she'd marked the dour atmosphere here. It was as if the inhabitants of this castle still grieved the loss of their former laird and lady.

Jean nodded, her expression grave. "So Mackay will allow me, Neave, and Eilidh to stay on after the wedding?"

"Aye, he confirmed it yesterday."

The conversation the day before had been brief. Niel had just come back into the keep after sword practice. Clad in a sweat-soaked lèine and braies, his dark hair tied back at his nape, he'd been about to take the stairs up to his quarters when Beth had intercepted him. She'd enquired about his day and then had asked him to confirm that her sisters could indeed stay on at Castle Varrich.

She wanted to ensure he hadn't forgotten the promise he'd made her in that missive—and he hadn't.

It seemed Niel Mackay was a man of his word.

Beth's attention rested on her sister's face then, noting the furrows upon her brow. "What is it?" she asked, brushing flour off her hands.

Jean sighed.

"Don't ye like it here at Castle Varrich?"

"Aye ... it's just different, that's all."

"Would ye rather return to Foulis with Da and Laila then?"

Jean shook her head. The four of them had spoken about the future at length after Beth had received Niel Mackay's proposal. George Munro and Laila were starting a new life together. Just two days before leaving the Munro holding, her stepmother had learned that she carried the clan-chief's bairn. Would she soon give him the sons his first wife had never been able to—heirs who would carry his name and inherit his title?

George Munro would never admit as such, but his adult daughters had little place at Foulis Castle. By rights, all of them should have been wed by now. But with the eldest sister unwed, the remaining three had waited. There was nothing forbidding them from finding husbands of their own, but Beth's sisters hadn't wanted to humiliate her.

And the sisters were close—so close that Beth couldn't bear the thought of living far from them. There was no reason why Neave, Jean, and Eilidh couldn't find husbands here, and if they did, she'd get to see them more regularly than if they'd remained in Munro territory.

"No, it's just that change makes me nervous," Jean replied with an embarrassed grimace. "Ever since we arrived here, it feels like shifting sand beneath my feet." Her expression turned wistful then. "Nothing will be as it was ... and I sometimes feel sad about that."

A lump rose in Beth's throat at this admission, and she drew her sister into a floury hug. Pulling back, she then cleared her throat. "Don't be a goose, Jeanie. Nothing that really matters will change. Ye shall see."

Niel Mackay stood on the steps to the keep, watching as a company of horses rode into the bailey. Of all the guests he'd invited to his wedding, these were the ones he was looking forward to seeing the most.

It wasn't just a wedding he'd summoned them all to either—for he intended to make the most of having all his chieftains amassed to talk of the future.

Of revenge.

It was a windy, overcast afternoon, and despite that spring bulbs were poking up either side of the wide path winding up to the castle, and newborn lambs ran after their mothers on the hillsides surrounding the Kyle of Tongue, winter's bitter chill still lingered in the air. It bit through the quilted gambeson that Niel had donned and stung his face.

However, he wasn't paying attention to the cold at present, but to the newcomers: faces he hadn't seen in a decade.

Connor Mackay was easy to spot—a big man with a mane of golden hair as yet untouched by grey. He drew up his courser, his pine-green gaze sweeping across the bailey.

Niel knew whom he was looking for, and so wasn't surprised when the chieftain's attention halted upon him.

A heartbeat later, a smile split the man's face—and Niel found himself grinning back. He descended the last of the stairs and strode across the paved space to where Connor had swung down from his horse.

The two men embraced, and when Connor drew back, his gaze gleamed.

"Curse ye, Connor," Niel greeted him, still smiling. "Ye haven't aged a day."

"And ye are as lean as a hound," Connor replied, slapping him on the back. "Ye need to fatten yerself up, man."

Niel snorted, his attention going to where Connor's brother had stepped up. Morgan Mackay was grinning. "It's good to see ye again, Niel."

"Aye, likewise." Niel clasped arms with Morgan before the man yanked him into a bear-hug.

This time, it was Niel's eyes that were glistening when he drew back.

By blood and bone, he wasn't even sure where that surge of emotion had come from. However, besides John, these two men were the closest he had to brothers. Morgan Mackay had done his best to see Niel freed when his own father had turned his back on him.

"I heard what ye did for me, Morgan," Niel said, cursing the sudden roughness in his voice. "And I appreciate it."

Morgan's grin faded, his expression sobering. "Aye, well ... it did little in the end."

"At least ye didn't give up on me."

Niel's attention flicked between the two brothers. Neither of them had. "Well, fortune has finally shone upon me," he said, clearing his throat. "And since the man who sent me to Bass Rock is now dead ... I'm a free man."

He stepped back then, his gaze moving to the rest of the company. Keira, Connor's wife, had just dismounted from her courser and was waiting. A lass of around ten winters and two younger lads stood behind Keira. Her midnight-blue eyes regarded him, strands of brown hair from her braid whipping around her face. "Welcome home, Niel," she said, her mouth curving into a wide smile.

Niel returned her smile, before inclining his head. "Thank ye, Keira ... and who do we have here?"

"May I introduce, Rose, Rory, and Quinn," Connor said, pride lacing his voice.

"It's a relief to see ye alive and well, Niel." Another woman stepped up next to Keira. Small with raven-black hair and eyes the color of the sea, Maggie was as bonny as Niel recalled.

Maggie's uncle had once tried to pair Maggie and Niel off, and he'd flirted with the idea of taking her as his wife. But that was before that fateful day in the great hall of Inverness, when King James, and his own father, had torn his future from him.

At Inverness, during a supper he'd attended, he'd noted the way Maggie and Morgan's gazes met across the hall. It hadn't come as a great surprise when John had told him that Morgan and Maggie had wed in haste just days later, under the shadow of scandal. His cousin had added that their marriage had endured and appeared to be a happy one.

A lass, perhaps a couple of years younger than Rose—a girl with night-black hair and forest-green eyes—stepped up next to Maggie. "Tara." Maggie inclined her head to her daughter. "I'd like ye to meet Niel Mackay, our clan-chief."

The lass's cheeks grew pink before she dipped her head. "My laird."

Niel found himself grinning back. His pleasure at seeing the Mackays of Farr again shouldn't have surprised him, yet it did.

He noted then Jaimee Mackay's absence, and a little of his buoyant mood ebbed. John had eventually told him the tale of what had befallen the lass. Even now, Niel found it hard to believe that Alexander Gunn, the clan-chief's first-born, had cast aside his birthright to wed her. He couldn't reconcile John's story with the ruthless warrior who'd been George Gunn's right hand for so many years.

But apparently, it was true. Alexander Gunn had been Farr Castle's blacksmith for years now and had severed all ties with his kin.

Of course, Jaimee and Alexander wouldn't have attended this wedding. Connor and Morgan might have eventually welcomed Gunn into their midst, but Niel never would.

If he ever set eyes on the whoreson, he'd likely cut his throat.

Such thoughts soured Niel's joy at seeing the Mackays of Farr again. With difficulty, he shoved his resentment aside.

Connor and Morgan were still beaming at him, their green eyes shining. Not for the first time since his return home, Niel was reminded, yet again, that his people were relieved he'd survived Bass Rock.

It was humbling to know they wanted him as their clan-chief.

"We were glad to hear ye wasted no time finding yerself a bride," Morgan teased him.

The comment was innocently spoken, yet Niel's belly tensed all the same—it made him think of Beth Munro, and of the fact he couldn't seem to go two paces without crossing paths with her these days.

Wherever he turned, *there* she was.

Fortunately, in the three days she'd been resident at Castle Varrich, Beth hadn't tried to visit him again in his solar. Yet that didn't stop her from questioning him incessantly whenever she saw him.

And the laughter and chatter of Beth and her sisters at mealtimes often stretched his nerves to breaking point. His time at Bass Rock had made him less tolerant of noise, it seemed. After they were wed, he might start taking his meals in his solar—alone.

"Time is no longer my friend," Niel replied, slapping Morgan on the back and steering him toward the keep. "I've got sons to sire before old age comes for me."

Connor snorted. "Ye aren't in yer grave yet, man."

"No," Niel agreed, "but ten years are a lot to lose." He glanced over at Connor, their gazes fusing. "And imprisonment has a way of making a man's priorities clear."

Connor cocked his head. "Aye?"

"Once I've taken a wife, I'll focus on punishing those who helped put me on Bass Rock." Niel saw that Connor's expression sobered at these words, yet he didn't care. All of them needed to ready themselves for war, for bloodshed.

Slinging his free arm over Connor's shoulders, Niel cast him a smile. "But we'll talk about such things soon enough ... first let's break open a barrel of mead. It seems I have much to catch up on!"

7

A LIFETIME

BETH SPEARED A piece of mutton with her eating knife and took a bite, chewing slowly. And as she did so, her gaze traveled down the table upon the dais.

The castle had gotten increasingly busy over the past days, and this eve, there wasn't one space unoccupied. The last of the wedding guests had arrived. Everything was in place for the ceremony, which would take place the following day at noon.

Beth's belly fluttered at the thought, and she swallowed the mouthful of mutton with difficulty before reaching for her wine to wash it down.

The din of conversation was so loud in the great hall that she couldn't make out the words of those around her. She wasn't sitting with Niel this eve. Instead, he was downing horns of mead with the laird of Farr and his brother, the three of them ribbing each other while their wives and children were all engaged in animated discussion.

There were other Mackay chieftains at the table too. Of course, John Mackay was present, but so was Robin Mackay, laird of Melness, as well as Hugh Mackay of Loch Stach. Hugh—a portly older man with high-colored cheeks—had brought his beautiful blonde daughter, Janneth, with him. The lass smiled shyly as she engaged one of the chieftain's wives in conversation.

Robin Mackay sat opposite Beth. He was a man of around Niel's age, although of a shorter and sturdier build, with shaggy light-brown hair. Observing him, Beth thought the chieftain would have been attractive if he actually smiled occasionally. As it was though, Robin Mackay's face appeared carved into severe lines, his hazel eyes veiled. The tense set of his broad shoulders hinted that he wished to be elsewhere. Next to him, Hugh Mackay kept trying to draw the laird of Melness into conversation. However, he was having little success.

Taking another sip of wine, Beth glanced right, at where her stepmother sat. To her consternation, Laila was watching her.

It sometimes felt odd to think of this woman as her stepmother—for Laila was only two years her elder. Her stepmother had been a widow when she'd met George Munro, and her first marriage had not produced any children. But Laila was now with bairn. Her belly hadn't yet started to swell, yet the healer at Foulis had confirmed that she was indeed expecting.

Beth tensed under the intensity of her stepmother's gaze.

"Are ye nervous about tomorrow?" Laila asked, raising her voice to be heard over the din surrounding them.

"A little," Beth admitted.

"It's a fine match, indeed," Laila went on, favoring Beth with a gentle smile. "Despite his years of imprisonment, Niel Mackay is still a man in his prime." Her stepmother then took a dainty bite of mutton.

Beth nodded, her gaze shifting back down the table to where Niel was holding his drinking horn out for a passing servant to fill.

If the man kept drinking like that, he'd be in a sorry state by morning.

Her attention lingered upon him, noting how attractive her husband-to-be was this evening. He'd changed before supper into a charcoal-colored lèine, open at the neck, which revealed crisp dark hair upon his chest. His long peat-brown hair, which often had a wild, tangled appearance, had been brushed out over his shoulders.

And tonight, his cobalt eyes gleamed with good humor as he listened to his companions talk.

Beth's chest constricted then, as envy lanced through her. Why did Niel's visitors get to sit next to him, to talk with him, while she could not? How could she get him to pay *her* such close attention? Aye, their conversations at mealtimes could be a bit stilted, but she found Niel fascinating company nonetheless. She liked his dry sense of humor, although often when his gaze met hers, Beth's thoughts scattered.

She was usually quick-witted and liked to banter with men—yet Niel flustered her. He was a man who'd lived through much, and she sometimes worried that he found her uninteresting—after all, she couldn't begin to understand what he'd endured over the years.

Turning her gaze back to the woman beside her, Beth gnawed at her bottom lip. "Laila … may I ask ye something?"

Still smiling, Laila inclined her head. "Of course."

"When ye met Da … did ye have to do anything to win him over?"

Her stepmother held her gaze, her smile fading. "Not really," she admitted after a pause. "He sought me out … courted me." She gave a soft laugh. "Ye know what yer father is like."

Beth's mouth curved. Aye, she did. Despite that he'd been a warrior to be feared in his younger days, George Munro appreciated female company and respected the opinions of women. Even this eve, he made sure that his wife was seated beside him. And as the supper wore on, he didn't neglect Laila in favor of conversing with the men at the table.

Not like Niel.

Beth's smile faded. Noting her shift in mood, Laila reached out, placing a slender hand over hers upon the table. "What is it, lass?"

Beth favored Laila with a brittle smile. "I'm more nervous than I realized," she admitted. "I know I appear confident … but I have no idea what awaits me. What if I am ill-suited to be a wife?"

Laila's hand squeezed hers. "Take each day as it comes," she advised, her soft voice barely audible over the sudden burst of laughter at the far end of the table. "And remember that ye and Niel Mackay have a lifetime to get to know each other."

Beth was still mulling over her stepmother's words later that eve as she readied herself for bed.

A lifetime to get to know each other.

Laila's assurance had calmed her, eased a little of her worry.

Maybe she was fretting unnecessarily. Once the wedding was over and the guests departed, she and Niel would be able to settle into married life. Perhaps he too was a trifle nervous. After all, the man was in his third decade and hadn't yet wed.

Taking a seat by the fire, Beth closed her eyes as Greta, the maid who had accompanied her from Foulis Castle, and who waited upon all four sisters, brushed out her hair. Across the room, Neave was already tucked up in bed. Jean and Eilidh shared the chamber next door, although Greta had already helped them ready themselves for bed.

"There ye go, Beth," Greta said, stepping back and setting down the brush. "All done. Do ye want me to have a bath drawn for ye tomorrow morning, first thing?"

"Thank ye," Beth replied, turning to the lass. "That's a bonny idea. And can ye fetch some scented oils to add to it?"

The maid flashed her a smile before nodding.

"We want Beth to smell her best on her wedding day," Neave piped up with a wink.

"Aye, of roses and lavender," Greta answered. "Ye shall smell like a flower garden."

"Well, let's hope Niel Mackay appreciates the scent," Beth replied. Her tone was light, even if her nerves still jangled. The subject of conversation made her thoughts race forward to what would occur after the ceremony. Once they'd exchanged vows, once the revelry and feasting were done—they would have to consummate their marriage.

Tingling began then, dancing across Beth's skin, and she felt oddly breathless.

What would intimacy between husband and wife be like?

Of course, that was a question she'd never have asked Laila. She had no wish to learn about that aspect of her father's relationship with his second wife. Unfortunately, she had no one else to ask. Years earlier, her mother had briefly explained what happened in the marriage bed, and how a man's seed caused a bairn to grow in a woman's belly. But apart from those details, Beth knew little else.

Her mother was now dead, and her other sisters were all unwed, as was her maid.

Aye, she'd seen animals mate but had often wondered how it would be one day when she lay with her husband for the first time. Would it hurt? Would it forge a special bond between them?

Her pulse accelerated then, as she imagined what Niel would look like naked.

Beth bid Greta good night and padded across to the bed. Meanwhile, her maid set about rolling out her own bed—a sheepskin and blankets—before the hearth.

Shrugging off her robe, Beth climbed nude into bed. The bed ropes creaked as she shifted position and pulled the covers up under her chin. Despite the crackling hearth, the air inside the stone-walled chamber was chill; it was hard to believe that it was indeed spring.

"This is our last night sleeping in the same bed," Neave whispered a few moments later. "It will seem strange not having ye snoring beside me."

Beth snorted. "I don't snore."

"All the same ... I will miss our chats."

Beth swallowed, her throat constricting. "Aye ... so will I."

A pause followed before Neave murmured, "Ye are anxious about tomorrow, aren't ye?"

Beth pursed her lips and considered denying it. However, she and Neave were so close she knew such a denial would be useless—her sister would merely hound her until she got the truth. "A few days at Castle Varrich has made everything seem so ... real," she whispered after a pause. "I know I've been betrothed three times before ... but I've never managed to get this close to my wedding day."

"Ye aren't worried something will prevent yer marriage, are ye?"

"No ... I'm fretting more over what will happen *afterward*." There, she'd admitted it.

Neave was silent a few moments before answering, "At least Niel Mackay isn't a stranger. Ye have had a few days to get used to each other."

Beth pulled a face. "I thought we'd have spent more time together since my arrival ... but most of the time, it feels as if the man is avoiding me."

"He won't be able to for much longer."

Beth cast her sister a jaundiced look. "Aye ... thank ye for the reminder."

"Here's to yer last night as an unwedded man." Morgan Mackay's voice slurred slightly as he held his goblet aloft.

"Aye," John Mackay favored Niel with a mischievous grin. "Here's to the end of yer freedom."

Niel glowered at his cousin before muttering an oath under his breath. He'd consumed far too much ale, mead, and wine this eve—yet he wasn't nearly drunk enough. John's teasing needled him.

Morgan snorted. "That wasn't what I meant." His gaze met Niel's then and held. "Here's to years of happiness and plenty of strong, healthy bairns."

"Getting married was the best thing I ever did," Connor, laird of Farr, spoke then, with a beatific smile. He too had consumed a goodly amount of drink over the evening, but it had just put him in a mellow mood. "The right woman changes everything."

Niel's mouth thinned. *The right woman?* That was an irony coming from a man who'd wed his wife believing she was someone else. Things had come right in the end, yet Niel would never forget the eve they'd all learned that Connor Mackay's wife wasn't Rhianna Ross, as they'd believed, but Keira Gunn. An imposter.

Niel also remembered the rage that had exploded within him on that Samhuinn eve. He'd even drawn his dirk and lunged for the woman—and lord knew what he'd have done if Connor hadn't stepped between them. In the months following, Niel had come to realize that Keira wasn't a Gunn spy, but his suspicion of her had lingered until the parliament at Inverness.

After that, he'd had far more serious things to worry about.

These days, he accepted Keira as now part of the Mackay clan. But he'd *never* grant Alexander Gunn the same favor.

Nevertheless, even years ago, he'd noted how well-matched Connor and Keira were. A decade on, Niel would have been blind not to see the enduring bond between them.

But that wasn't what Niel Mackay was after.

This castle needed a mistress, someone to keep the servants in check, to ensure the floors were swept, food stores maintained, and the gardens tended—while he assumed his responsibilities as clan-chief. His quest for vengeance aside, Niel had a clan to govern. In the two months since his return, Niel and John had gone over detailed maps of the Mackay territory and discussed plans for various tracts of land. They'd also spoken with local farmers regarding the crops to be planted out in the coming spring across Niel's vast estate.

However, there was so much more that needed to be done.

Love be damned. He didn't want or need what Connor and Morgan had found.

Leaning back in his chair, Niel cradled his goblet of wine. It was still half-full, yet his belly suddenly felt sour.

Perhaps it was time to stop drinking now. If he didn't, he'd likely be puking his guts out all night.

A group of them—Niel, Morgan, Connor, John, Robin, and Hugh—sat in the clan-chief's solar before the dying embers of the fire. All of them were Mackays: the men who ruled the various corners of Niel's lands.

Hugh was asleep in his chair, whiskered chin planted on his broad chest as he snored gently. Next to him, Robin Mackay of Melness wore a shuttered expression as he cradled a goblet of wine. He'd said little all evening, and Niel noted the change in the man from when he'd known him before. The Robin he remembered from his old life had been shy yet affable.

When John had filled Niel in on the events that had transpired during his incarceration, he'd learned that Robin had endured a bitter betrayal a year earlier. His brother had run off with his wife—and not before the pair of them had tried to murder Robin first. It had been a bad business, and judging from the tense set of the man's jaw, and his shadowed gaze, it haunted him still.

Cynicism stabbed at Niel then. Aye, Robin Mackay was proof that not everyone had good fortune in love.

"Niel?" Connor's voice intruded then. "Did ye hear me?"

Jerking out of his musing, Niel glanced over at his friend. "Sorry ... I was leagues away," he replied, a trifle embarrassed. "What did ye say?" Ever since leaving Bass Rock, Niel found himself easily distracted. Sometimes John would be telling him something about his tenants or the crops they would be planting in the spring, and Niel would drift off into his own thoughts. He wasn't sure if it was a legacy of spending too many years with only his own thoughts for company, but it was an irksome habit nonetheless.

A groove formed between Connor's dark-blond brows. Unlike their companions—most of them now on the verge of falling asleep in their chairs, if they hadn't done so already—he appeared to have sobered up slightly. "I asked ye if yer choice in bride pleases ye?"

Niel flashed him a roguish grin. "Aye … as long as the woman minds her tongue and does her duty, I can get on with what really matters … making this clan strong once more."

8

YER DAY HAS COME

BETH VIEWED HER reflection in the looking-glass with a critical eye.

She'd never been a vain woman—for she'd always been too practical and industrious for such trivialities—yet this morning, she found herself wishing she were prettier.

Aye, she was pleasant enough to look upon, but her strong jaw and stubborn chin lent a severity to her face. The rest of her features were nothing extraordinary either. She didn't have Neave's elfin loveliness or Eilidh's delicate beauty.

It certainly wasn't a face to launch ships and bring down empires for.

Her body too—was compact and sturdy, like Jean's. Neave and Eilidh, although also small in stature, had much more willowy, elegant frames.

Beth frowned at the reflection, and the expression made the firm set of her jaw give her an almost bullish appearance.

By blood and bone, it did her no good to dwell upon her flaws. What foolish thoughts she was entertaining this morning. Before coming to Castle Varrich, she'd never indulged in such self-criticism.

Now wasn't the time to start.

"That kirtle looks lovely on ye, Beth," Laila said then, interrupting her brooding. "The moss-green brings out the color of yer eyes."

Beth fought the urge to deepen her frown, instead smoothing her brow. Unlike Neave, whose eyes were hazel flecked with shards of brilliant green, her own gaze was just a plain, unremarkable hazel.

Glancing at her stepmother, she forced a smile. Laila was being kind and encouraging, and she appreciated it, even if she felt a little fragile this morning.

She'd risen from her bed early and had soaked for a long while in a hot tub of scented water, while Greta washed and oiled her hair.

Afterward, the maid had dressed her with care. Indeed, the kirtle was one of her mother's. It was made of fine velvet, with long bell-like sleeves.

"I love the spring flowers in yer hair," Eilidh added, stepping up next to the mirror. Her sister wore a wide smile. "I knew snowdrops and bluebells would look bonny."

Beth smiled back at the youngest of her sisters, a little of her awkwardness easing. "That was so sweet of ye," she murmured, "to pick these for me." Indeed, Eilidh had headed out at first light, while Beth was still bathing, and had picked the delicate bonnets at the bottom of the promontory.

Greta had done an expert job of weaving them into her long hair. She'd pulled back the dark waves from around Beth's face and left the rest unbound, tumbling down her back. Her hair was one of her best features.

Smoothing her velvet skirts with her palms, Beth turned from the looking glass, her gaze sweeping over her three sisters, Laila, and their maid. They'd been locked up in this chamber all morning preparing, and she could see from the excitement gleaming in their eyes that midday was fast approaching.

"I'm glad ye are all staying on here with me," she said, her voice turning husky. Tears stung the back of her eyelids, yet she hurriedly blinked them back. She didn't want to arrive at the chapel with a blotchy face and red eyes. "I'd be lonely here without ye."

Her sisters, and Greta too, all smiled at her then, while Eilidh brushed away a glistening tear.

"And we are glad to remain here too," she replied. "I'll miss Da... and ye too, Laila, when ye go ... but it's right that we all make a fresh start."

"Aye," Jean agreed, the briskness of her tone belying the emotion that swirled just beneath. Her eyes glistened. "Fret not, ye aren't going to rid yerself of us."

"Coming to live at Castle Varrich is an adventure," Neave added, stepping close and taking Beth's hand. "Ye are the first of us four to wed ... but who knows what the future holds for me, Jean, and Eilidh."

"No doubt, ye shall all wed brave Mackay warriors too," Greta spoke up before giving a wistful sigh. "The castle is full of them at present." She then favored Neave with a grin. "Perhaps *ye* shall meet yer future husband at this wedding, Neave."

Neave laughed, the musical sound echoing through the chamber. Beth watched the merriment in her sister's eyes with a little envy. Neave had such a light-hearted approach to life—it was as if the cares of the world didn't touch her. She was interested in everyone and everything, and utterly fearless.

Neave was like a beautiful butterfly, fluttering from plant to plant, vibrant and free. The man who wished to wed her would have to net her first. And something told Beth that her sister wouldn't be easily caught.

A knock on the door intruded then.

"Come in," Laila sang out, and an instant later, the door opened and George Munro's familiar, broad-shouldered form stepped into the chamber. His hazel eyes widened when his attention settled upon his first-born daughter.

"Ye look lovely, lass," he murmured. "Finally, yer day has come."

Beth's throat thickened at the emotion she glimpsed in her father's eyes. He'd been worried for her after she'd lost all three of the men she'd previously been betrothed to. It must have been a relief to know that she'd finally found a husband—that he wouldn't have to concern himself with her future any longer.

"Aye," Laila piped up. "Yer husband-to-be will think ye a vision."

Lord, I hope so. In truth, Beth had no idea whether Niel would think her bonny, or not. The man was an enigma.

"I imagine Niel Mackay is as nervous as ye are," Eilidh murmured. Her sister was merely trying to make her feel better, yet the thought of Niel being apprehensive about his wedding, after everything the man had been through, was ridiculous.

Straightening her shoulders, Beth drew in a deep breath. The strain was getting to her. She was feeling a little light-headed this morning and needed to remember to breathe.

"Right then," she said with a briskness she didn't actually feel. Moving forward, she smiled at her father and linked her arm through his. "Let's not keep him waiting."

Niel shifted impatiently at the top of the steps to the chapel, just before the stone arch that framed a weathered oaken doorway. A wind raced across the bailey, and despite that it was relatively sheltered here—squeezed in between the curtain wall and the keep—the breeze still cut through the lèine, leather vest, and clan sash he wore.

The chapel, small with a pitched roof made of slate, had been built by his grandfather. Constructed from the same sandstone as the rest of the castle, the building's rough walls appeared to glow in the noon sun.

The chaplain, Father Lucas, stood next to Niel, his sagging face expressionless. In his gnarled hands, he held a length of Mackay plaid: a cross-hatching of sea blue, emerald, and forest green. Father Lucas would bind their hands with it while they spoke their vows.

Trying to curb his restlessness and not fidget, Niel's gaze swept the considerable crowd gathered at the foot of the steps. He was pleased to see that all his chieftains were in attendance for the wedding. After all the problems within the clan over the last few years, Niel wanted to ensure that he didn't inherit his father's legacy. He didn't want to ever give them reason to lose faith in his leadership.

Even the lairds of Balnakeil and Dun Ugadale had come. The two chieftains had arrived late during supper the night before. History with those two families had been strained in the past years, especially after their lairds had tried to topple Niel's father from power. However, Breac and Iver Mackay—both distant cousins of the former chieftains—ruled their brochs now, and there were no longer any whispers of discontent.

Niel's attention shifted then to where his cousin John stood near the foot of the steps. He cut a rakish figure with his black eye patch and matching attire of black leather and velvet. He looked like a pirate dressed so, and when he met Niel's eye, John gave a wink.

Since he'd returned to Castle Varrich and started spending time with his cousin again, it had become clear that John didn't have any plans to wed. Unlike Robin Mackay, he didn't appear bitter about marriage. Instead, he merely had the air of a man who wished to remain unfettered.

Niel fought a frown. That was well enough for a man like John. But *he* was a clan-chief. Taking a wife was necessary at his age. He'd once been content to flirt and enjoy women—but that was when he'd been young, and cocky enough to believe he had all the time in the world.

Shifting his weight from foot to foot, Niel did scowl then. Christ's blood, was he actually anxious about the coming ceremony? Aye, incarceration had changed him, but even before that he'd liked being a lone wolf. He realized then that he was loath to give up his newfound freedom. Irrationally, it felt as if he were about to go back in shackles.

Don't be an idiot, he chided himself. *Taking a wife isn't the same thing as being locked up in gaol. Ye just need to let Beth know what ye expect from her.*

Excited murmurs cut through the breezy air, and Niel's focus turned to where Beth appeared, walking at her father's side. They cut a path through the crowd, with her sisters and stepmother bringing up the rear.

And as his bride kissed her father on the cheek and left him at the foot of the steps, Niel studied her.

He'd noted from the first that Beth Munro was a comely woman, yet today she truly held his eye. The moss-green velvet kirtle she wore hugged her lush curves, its neckline dipping low to reveal a full cleavage. The gown's color emphasized the milkiness of her skin. A heavy gold chain girded her hips, showing off their womanly swell and the dip of her waist. She moved like a queen, straight-backed, with her head held high.

And when she climbed the stairs toward him, he saw that she had snowdrops and bluebells wreathed into her hair.

Despite himself, Niel's breathing slowed.

Soon, this woman would be his.

Unbalanced, he tore his gaze from Beth and tried to ignore the anticipation that prickled his skin—and the heat that pooled in his belly as he imagined what she'd look like naked, what she'd taste like, and feel like, when he was buried deep inside her.

Niel swallowed. Beth Munro talked too much and wasn't the biddable maid he'd hoped she'd be. Even so, there was no denying the visceral effect she'd just had on him.

Damping down his response, and telling himself it was a good thing he was attracted to the woman he was about to wed, Niel then stepped back to make space for her upon the wide step.

Father Lucas cleared his throat, glancing the clan-chief's way. "Shall we begin?" the chaplain asked, his gravelly voice carrying across the now silent bailey. All eyes were riveted upon Niel Mackay and his Munro bride, waiting for the ceremony to begin.

A heartbeat later, Niel nodded.

"I give ye my Spirit, 'til our Life shall be Done," Beth said softly, her gaze remaining steady upon Niel. He'd already said his vows and waited silently while the chaplain took Beth through hers. She'd just spoken the last sentence.

Beth found it difficult not to stare at him. He cut an especially striking figure today, clad in a black lèine and leather vest and trews, the blue and green Mackay clan sash across his chest.

And despite that she'd felt sick with nerves before the ceremony, excitement tightened her belly at the thought that in a few instants, this man would be hers.

"Ye are now husband and wife," the chaplain intoned. He then unbound the ribbon of plaid that tied their hands together. Beth didn't extract her grip from Niel's; she didn't want to let go of the warmth and strength of his hand. "May yer union be blessed." The older man paused, focusing upon the clan-chief. "Ye may kiss yer bride now, Mackay."

Beth's breathing hitched.

She'd lain awake over the past nights imagining this moment. What would her first kiss from Niel be like? Would it be rough or soft? Possessive or detached?

Still grasping her hand in his, Niel stepped forward, towering over her.

His free hand came up, and he gently took hold of her chin, lifting it so that her face rose to him. His eyes, as dark-blue as the sky after sunset, seared her, and Beth's pulse started to race.

He leaned in then, his lips brushing across hers once before his mouth claimed hers for a kiss. There was nothing hesitant about it. Niel's embrace was firm, demanding. Cheering erupted then, echoing off the surrounding walls.

Niel drew back, his gaze finding hers once more. His expression was serious, although there was no mistaking the heat smoldering in his eyes. Beth gazed up at him.

She could feel her cheeks ablaze and wished she could find it in herself to be as composed as he was.

She was sure everyone present could see how flushed her face was.

Niel's mouth quirked then, in a half-smile that made Beth's belly somersault. Heat washed over her. "Greetings, Lady Mackay," he murmured, his voice nearly drowned out by the noise the crowd beneath the chapel were making.

Lady Mackay.

Beth drew in a gulp of air, for she was starting to feel dizzy and realized that she'd forgotten to breathe.

I'm the 'Cursed Bride' no more.

The way Niel was looking at her at that moment made the raucous cheering die away, made her forget her burning cheeks and the insecurities that had plagued her ever since her arrival at Castle Varrich. Perhaps she'd misjudged him. What if he wasn't aloof, but merely wary, and had been waiting till their wedding day to bond properly with her?

If that was the case, it would be easier to establish a connection with him than she'd thought.

Giddying relief swept through Beth, as did desire— the sensation was so strong that it made her knees tremble.

Theirs might end up a love match, after all.

9

AN ADVANTAGEOUS ARRANGEMENT

THE NOISE INSIDE the great hall was deafening. The rumble of voices, punctuated by laughter and singing, almost drowned out the strains of the lyre and flute. A knot of musicians stood in a gallery on the far side of the space, playing valiantly.

Beth had started to sweat in her heavy velvet kirtle. Despite that she sat upon the dais away from most of the guests, who were seated at long trestle tables, she felt the press of bodies around her.

Seated at her side, Niel served them both a selection of food, including one of the venison pies, onto a platter they would share. After the ceremony had concluded, they hadn't had time to speak, for an excited crowd of well-wishers had swirled around the newly wedded couple, swallowing them up. The crowd had swept them off the steps of the chapel, across the bailey, and into the great hall. Ale, mead, and wine had then flowed, while Beth's father made a number of rousing toasts.

But now that the array of rich dishes had been served, the tables groaning under the weight of them, she and her husband could finally talk.

Husband. It felt odd to think of him that way, and Beth's belly fluttered when she thought of what would happen later, once the feasting and dancing were done and they retired alone to the clan-chief's bed-chamber. Of course, she'd often imagined what it would be like to lie with a man—having had three betrothals in the past—

but now the bedding was imminent, the blend of fear and anticipation that danced within her was oddly exhilarating.

Beth observed the clan-chief's proud profile for a moment before he picked up his goblet as if to take a sip. However, instead of doing so, he merely sat there, his gaze unfocused. It was as if her husband were staring at something only he could see.

"Niel?" she queried softly, intruding upon his reverie. "Is all well?"

Blinking, Niel turned to her, his gaze sharp once more. "Aye." He then motioned to the pie before them. "I hear ye had a hand in making these?"

"Aye," Beth replied, even as her cheeks warmed. She suddenly felt shy around him. "Pies are my specialty. My mother was a good cook ... and she taught me all she knew."

His mouth curved. "I'm pleased to see ye aren't above dirtying yer hands in the kitchens ... Lord knows, the cooks could do with some tuition these days."

Beth smiled. It hadn't escaped her, upon her arrival at Varrich, just how bland the meals had been. "Aye, my bannocks this morning were as heavy as river stones," she admitted. "I shall definitely be sharing my own recipe with the cooks ... that way, none of us risk breaking a tooth."

Niel huffed a laugh. "I'm confident ye will run my household with ease."

Beth continued to smile, even if the tingling excitement that had settled over her after the ceremony dimmed a little. Did he have to make their arrangement sound so utilitarian? It sounded as if what he really wished for was a chatelaine rather than a wife.

Only, a chatelaine can't provide him with the heir he wants.

As if sensing her shift in mood, Niel took a sip of wine and changed the subject. "Were ye close to yer mother?"

"Aye."

"How old were ye when ye lost her?"

"Not young. It was around five years ago." Beth picked up her goblet. It pleased her that Niel was asking her about herself. "She'd been ill for a while" —her voice lowered as the memory shadowed her mood— "with a growth in her belly that no physician could heal. Ma died after my second betrothal."

Her gaze dropped to the dark wine in her goblet. How she wished Colleen Munro could have been here today to see her wed. It had been an ordeal watching her mother sicken and die, helpless to prevent it. She hadn't slept easily for a long while afterward.

"Even so." Beth raised her chin to meet his eye once more. "Ma lived long enough to see us all grown. She always insisted we learn many skills ... not just those befitting a lady."

He arched an eyebrow. "So ye can wield a longbow then?"

Beth held his gaze, unsure whether he was teasing or mocking her. Even so, heat pooled in her lower belly at the awareness that now rippled between them, and she rose to his challenge. "As it happens, I *can* use a bow and arrow. My aim is true ... and I have bested many of my father's warriors at summer gatherings."

Niel Mackay grinned then, the expression so sudden that Beth sucked in a breath.

Mother Mary, the man had a smile that could melt a frozen loch. And the expression appeared genuine too, for his eyes gleamed as they continued to hold hers.

Beth hadn't meant to brag—for indeed, she did have some skill with a longbow. Her father had even taken her hunting on occasion. However, Niel had provoked her— and she enjoyed answering him.

"Well, this is something I must see for myself," he replied, taking a sip of wine.

"Aye ... perhaps ye and I can have a contest."

Both eyebrows raised then, although he didn't answer.

Beth drank from her goblet. It was a pity he hadn't accepted the challenge. She'd have liked to wipe that smug look off his face.

"Ye don't know what to make of me," she noted after a brief pause. "Do ye?"

Niel snorted. "How so?" He cut off a piece of pie and took a bite, his eyes widening as he chewed. "This is delicious."

Beth acknowledged the compliment with a nod before continuing, "Well, ye have no sisters … and I'd wager yer mother was nothing like me."

Niel took another bite of pie before washing it down with some more wine. "No, she wasn't."

"Tell me about her then."

Niel looked away and leaned against the carven armrest of his chair, swirling the wine in his goblet. Silence stretched out. The pause was so long that Beth was beginning to think he either hadn't heard or, or had chosen to ignore her. However, he finally replied, "Estelle Mackay was a woman who knew her place."

Heat prickled across Beth's chest. Was that a subtle warning she heard in his voice?

Moments passed, and then Beth cleared her throat. "Is that all ye have to say about her? What was she like? What were her passions, her fears?"

Beth was pushing him, yet she couldn't help herself.

And as she'd expected, the question seemed to unbalance Niel. Still not looking Beth's way, his dark brows drew together as if he was struggling to think of his mother at all. "She was quiet … severe," he said eventually. "But Ma ran this keep with great precision."

Well, that was a lackluster answer if ever she'd heard one. Beth wondered then if he'd ever paid his mother much attention. Had he known her at all?

"Yer parents … were they fond of each other?" she asked, unable to stop herself from interrogating him further.

Niel's mouth pursed. Aye, it was clear he wasn't enjoying the direction this conversation was taking. "In their own fashion," he replied, his tone off-hand now. "Not that it matters." He paused then, his gaze glinting as he turned to meet her eye once more. "But enough about my family. Earlier, ye mentioned yer second betrothal. I heard about yer run of ill-luck."

Beth stiffened. Tearing her gaze from his, she reached out and took a slice of roast goose from the platter they shared. She then helped herself to a walnut-studded bread bun. "Aye, everyone in the Highlands will have."

"Three betrothals ... and three men who met untimely deaths before their wedding day."

He was goading her. Beth had been about to take a bite of roast goose, yet she lowered her hand and met his eye, her gaze narrowing. "*The Cursed Bride* ... I'm sure ye heard the whispers," she replied, her voice cooling. "I'm surprised ye were brave enough to take me on."

The corners of Niel's mouth lifted, although his gaze remained shuttered. "I'm a clan-chief, and ye are the daughter of one my staunchest allies," he replied smoothly. "We both needed this marriage. It will be an arrangement advantageous to us both. I require a stalwart wife, for I shall be busy over the coming years, making my enemies pay and repairing the damage my father wreaked upon this clan."

Beth frowned. Aye, their marriage was indeed one of convenience—yet had he needed to be so brutally honest about it on their wedding day?

Niel held her gaze fast, while she stared back at him, her pulse quickening and her palms turning damp. Suddenly, the air around them felt charged, as if it were a late-summer afternoon and storm clouds hung overhead.

Over the past days, she'd told herself that, with a little work, she'd be able to win Niel Mackay over. After the ceremony, which had concluded in that lovely kiss, she'd thought her husband would be easier to woo than she'd previously believed.

But now she knew her task wasn't going to be an easy one at all.

Niel wasn't interested in being won over. He wasn't like her former suitors. There was a hardness to him, iron that went straight to the core. He possessed a sharp intelligence, and she had the sense that he always intended to be one step ahead of her.

Just beyond her reach.

Niel finished off the venison pie. It really was delicious—he hadn't been paying his wife a false compliment. The filling was rich, and the pastry was short and crumbly. He intended to help himself to another one.

Since his escape from Bass Rock, he'd managed to put on some weight. These days, he'd lost the skeletal appearance he'd first had upon his return to Castle Varrich. However, as Connor Mackay had noted, he was still too lean. For the campaign he wished to plan for the summer, he needed to bulk up.

A warrior needed to have strong muscles in order to wield a claidheamh-mòr—a heavy Scottish broadsword. When he faced the Gunns again, he wanted to be formidable.

Aye, he appreciated his wife's cookery skills—but not her boldness. The woman was entirely too free with her opinions.

A few of her observations and questions had vexed him. And yet at the same time, he was drawn to her. She met every challenge like an opponent in battle. He found it difficult to tear his attention from her proud face.

He observed her now, marking the faint flush highlighting her cheekbones. Her frank hazel eyes gleamed with what looked like thinly-veiled ire. She hadn't liked his last words, as he'd known she wouldn't. He'd made the comment on purpose.

She was a feisty one. What if his wife would be equally fiery in bed as out of it?

Niel's groin started to ache at the thought.

He held out his goblet for a passing serving lass to fill, his gaze never leaving Beth's.

His response to this woman surprised him. She made him react.

If they'd been alone, he'd have shown her other uses for her pert tongue. His erection swelled, pressing uncomfortably against his tight trews now, as the image of Beth on her knees before him, her mouth wrapped around his shaft as she eagerly sucked him, formed in his mind.

Niel shifted in his seat and took a deep draft of wine, in an effort to quell his arousal and the lustful thoughts that now plagued him.

In the past, such thoughts wouldn't have bothered him—for he'd made no secret of his urges for women—yet they did now. A wife was for getting with bairn and running his keep, not for going down on her knees before him. Perhaps he should take Angus Mackay's lead. His father had openly visited whores in Tongue over the years and had once told Niel that a wife wasn't to be used to satisfy a man's 'baser urges'.

But here Niel was, painfully aroused by the woman he'd just wed.

He was keenly aware of Beth, seated so close he could pull her onto his lap easily if he wished to. His senses felt heightened. Her scent, the warmth of her body, and the sight of her small, lush body encased in velvet made animal lust stir in his body.

Niel's jaw tightened as he tore his gaze from his wife and helped himself to some bread. Of late, he'd made a point of flouting every piece of advice his father had ever given him. It was his petty revenge against a dead man—and yet Angus Mackay's words on ensuring that a wife knew her place needled him.

Curse him, but the man had a point.

Beth was willful. If he wasn't careful, she wouldn't just be running his household, but his life. George Munro had given his eldest daughter too free a rein, had let her believe she was a man's equal in all things.

He could tell that she wanted to unravel the mysteries of her new husband, to unlock his secrets and make him her slave.

The thought made Niel's lust cool. He had no intention of ever letting that happen.

10

COURAGE, BETH

BETH HAD KNOWN she'd be nervous by the time for the bedding arrived—but she hadn't realized just *how* anxious the impending act would make her.

She'd kept it hidden of course. Few besides Niel himself would have known. He must have noted the dampness of her palms as he led her from the hall, felt the way her pulse galloped under his fingertips.

The afternoon and evening had spun away in an instant. After the feasting and drinking had ended, the trestle tables were pushed back, and the dancing began.

The bride and groom had taken part. It hadn't surprised Beth that Niel was a good dancer. He moved with fluid grace and knew all the dances, from the stately *basse danse*, to the lively circle jigs that had all of them kicking up their heels to the delight of the clapping crowd.

Her sisters had joined in the revelry, even Jean, who rarely danced, for she saw such things as frivolous. Jean had laughed as one of Niel Mackay's warriors swung her around, her frizzy hair flying like a flag behind her.

It had been a wonderful celebration, yet underneath it all, anxiety had slowly tightened in Beth's chest.

Her conversation with Niel during the wedding banquet had revealed that the man wished to control her. His dominance made her want to fight back—and yet, here they were, about to couple for the first time.

Suddenly, her bravery fled.

As they sat side-by-side upon the big bed in the clan-chief's bed-chamber, listening as Father Lucas blessed them, Beth swallowed hard.

Aye, she had a quick wit and confidence, yet she was a virgin. Apart from the kisses she'd received from her suitors, she'd never been touched. And right now, she wasn't feeling that warmly disposed to the man she'd just wed. His overbearing manner earlier hadn't exactly put her in the mood for coupling.

Beth smoothed her still-damp palms upon her skirts. Her pulse now pounded in her ears so loudly, she could barely make out the rumble of Father Lucas's voice.

Moments later, the elderly chaplain shuffled from the bed-chamber, the door thudding closed behind him.

Beth willed her heart to calm itself. She was so nervous now she was starting to feel dizzy. Hands still pressed flat upon her thighs, she straightened her spine and forced herself to look at her husband.

Niel was watching her, his gaze veiled.

She could almost hear his thoughts: *not so bold now, are ye wife?*

Of course, it was easier for her to lock horns with him when they were seated in the great hall, surrounded by kin and retainers. She wasn't so comfortable when the pair of them were alone.

Niel's mouth lifted at the corners then. "Are ye nervous, Beth?"

Beth drew in a deep breath before nodding. She suddenly felt tongue-tied, embarrassed.

The bed they sat on the edge of was huge—a massive canopied affair with curtains to block out the drafts in the bitter winter months. Embers glowed in the hearth, and candles burned around the edges of the room, bathing Niel's features in gold.

It softened his face a little, making him even more handsome.

"I know little of what to expect," she admitted then, cursing the way her voice caught. "My mother never had the chance to speak plainly with me about the subject …

and although I like Laila, I've never felt comfortable asking her."

"I'm afraid I can be of little help," Niel answered with a lopsided smile. "For I have never bedded a virgin before."

His words made heat flush up Beth's neck. That might have been so, but this wouldn't be his first time. She didn't want to think of all the women he'd likely swived over the years. Of course, his time at Bass Rock had been imposed celibacy, but she imagined he'd visited brothels since his escape.

Beth closed her eyes. Hades, this wasn't the time to think about such things.

"Open yer eyes, Beth." Niel's voice rumbled over her. "Look at me."

She did as bid, her gaze meeting his. Niel's eyes were dark in the firelight, although his expression was inscrutable. "I've heard it's a little painful the first time," he said softly, "but I will try to ease ye as much as I can."

Beth quailed inside at his assurance. He was only trying to make her more comfortable, yet her breathing now came in short, panicked gasps.

As if realizing that words weren't going to make the situation easier, Niel reached out and took her hands in his. He then rose to his feet, bringing her with him. And then, without saying anything more, he unfastened the heavy chain about her hips, letting it rattle to the flagstones. Reaching up, he started to unlace the front of her kirtle.

Beth dropped her gaze to where his long fingers moved deftly. Her breasts rose and fell sharply, drawing attention to the deep cleavage between them.

However, when Niel had finished loosening the front of her kirtle, he didn't remove the garment. Instead, he moved behind her and began to unpin her hair. His touch was gentle, although Beth became acutely aware of just how near he was standing to her—she could feel the heat of his body burning into her back like a furnace.

And despite that nerves still clutched at her belly, a warm and tingly sensation crept across her skin, in anticipation of his touch.

Snowdrops and bluebells fluttered to the ground, and the rest of her heavy waves tumbled free over her shoulders. And then, Niel pushed aside her hair and leaned in.

The feel of his lips brushing her neck, before traveling down to the curve of her shoulder, made Beth stifle a gasp. And when he nipped gently at her neck with his teeth, a shiver rippled through her.

What was that? Was it fear—or something else entirely?

He'd barely touched her, yet as Niel busied himself with removing her kirtle, her knees started to tremble. He slid the garment off her shoulders, pushing it down so that the heavy velvet rustled and pooled around her ankles.

She now stood before her husband in nothing but a filmy lèine.

Beth swallowed again before wetting her parched lips. No man had seen her in such a state of undress before. Mother Mary, she wished she didn't feel so anxious. She'd hoped their conversation during supper would have made her feel more at ease in this man's presence, yet it had done the opposite. In truth, the thought of lying with her husband on their wedding night hadn't cowed her in the past. But that was before she'd met Niel Mackay.

Nonetheless, despite her nerves, Beth's body appeared to have a mind of its own. Glancing down, she saw that her nipples strained against the fine linen.

Niel reached around, his hands cupping her breasts, while his mouth returned to her neck. His thumbs stroked her nipples, teasing them into two hard pebbles. Darts of pleasure arrowed out from his touch, and before she could stop herself, Beth gave a soft groan. And when his lips traced a path up to the shell of her ear, the tip of his tongue following its inner curve, her eyes fluttered shut, a deep, shuddering sigh escaping.

"Do ye like that?" he asked, his voice husky.

"Aye," she whispered back. Her body quivered now, as it anticipated what he'd do next.

"Good," he murmured.

A moment later, Niel reached down and pulled up the hem of her lèine, drawing it over her thighs, hips, and belly. Instinctively, Beth raised her arms high, allowing him to pull it up and over her head.

Gooseflesh shivered across her skin as she stood there naked. But the reaction wasn't due to cold, for the air was warm inside the bed-chamber.

Her breathing caught as his fingertips trailed down the curve of her spine to the indentation above her bottom.

"Ye have a lovely body, wife," Niel said, his voice roughening further. "Luscious."

Heat rose to Beth's cheeks. She'd always envied Neave and Eilidh their willowy figures. When standing next to them, she often felt like a sturdy garron beside two delicate palfreys. Yet the appreciation in her husband's voice, the way he'd almost growled his approval, made her glad of her curves.

Warmth pooled low in her belly. At least he was admiring something about her other than her ability to manage his household.

She heard him shift back from her then, followed by the creak of leather and rustle of fabric as he disrobed.

Beth closed her eyes once more, drawing in a deep, steadying breath. If her heart beat any harder, it would leap from her chest.

Courage, Beth. Where was the bold lass who let nothing daunt her? Her bravery had deserted her tonight, it seemed.

A moment later, Niel stepped back to her, and Beth gasped at the feel of his nakedness pressed along the length of hers. His skin was so warm, his body so hard. And despite her tension, she inhaled the smell of him: the clean, spicy scent of his skin.

Her belly fluttered, and the delicate flesh between her thighs started to ache.

His hands explored her once more, sliding up from her thighs, over the soft curve of her belly, to her breasts. He cupped them, feeling their weight in his hands before he shifted his attention to her nipples again, rolling them between forefinger and thumb and teasing them so that they began to ache.

Beth squeezed her eyes shut as his lips, teeth, and tongue continued their exploration of her neck and the sweeping curve of her shoulder. Dizziness swept over her, and without meaning too, she leaned into him.

One of his hands left her breasts, traveling a lazy path down her body, to the soft dark curls between her thighs. He then slid a leg between hers. The lean muscular strength of his thigh and the roughness of hair covering it contrasted against the smoothness of her own skin. A moment later, he nudged her legs apart.

And when his fingers slid into the cleft between her thighs, Beth squeaked, her body going rigid at the invasion.

"All is well, lass," he murmured into her ear. "I won't hurt ye."

Eyes still clamped shut, she leaned against the hard wall of his chest, drawing in a deep breath and then another, before she eventually let her thighs fall open.

She had to trust him in this. He was her husband, after all—and although the intimacy of this situation was almost too much for her, he was treating her gently.

Niel began to stroke her then, and Beth's limbs went molten.

A ragged gasp escaped as pleasure pulsed through her loins. She sagged in his arms and would have surely collapsed if he hadn't been holding her up. His touch addled her wits, made her nervousness flee.

Niel caressed her until she was boneless and trembling. Eventually removing his hand from between her thighs, he stepped back and guided her toward the bed. "Lie down, Beth," he murmured. "On yer back."

Beth's stomach swooped, sweat beading across her skin. The blend of softness and steel in his voice made dizziness sweep over her. She obeyed him, shifting onto the bed and rolling onto her back.

And when her gaze fell upon Niel's nakedness, her breathing caught.

The man was a sight. He was lean—thinner than most warriors of his height—yet his torso, shoulders, arms, and legs were still strong and finely muscled. A mat of dark hair covered his chest, arrowing to a thin line upon his belly and down to the nest of hair at his groin.

Beth's attention slid down his torso, her attention seizing upon his thick shaft that strained against his belly. Its swollen, rounded tip gleamed wetly in the firelight.

Beth's breathing caught. Hades, he was big. She wasn't sure how he was supposed to fit such a large appendage inside her.

Niel moved to the bed, shifting onto his knees as he nudged her legs apart. He spread her thighs wide so that he could gaze properly upon her.

A faint sheen of sweat coated his face and chest, and his high cheekbones bore a flush. His lips had parted slightly as he stared at her, his chest rising and falling quickly now as if he'd been running.

"Are ye ready, lass?" he eventually rasped.

Their gazes met and held. Beth's own breathing came in short gasps now, and her heart hammered a wild tattoo against her breastbone. But her apprehension had subsided—a restless, needy sensation replacing it. "Aye," she whispered.

11

SEPARATE CHAMBERS

NIEL DREW IN a deep breath, in an attempt to steady himself—in an effort to rein in the lust that threatened to turn him into a rutting beast.

Beth had no idea of the leash he was keeping himself on. He'd decided to take this slowly, to undress her gently to ease her nerves and ready her for what was to come. He'd sensed her nervousness, had felt how her body had trembled when he touched her.

Aye, she'd responded to him, yet she was wary.

And she was right to be. Right now, he was so aroused he could barely see straight. The sight of her—spread out before him, her gaze glassy with sensual awakening, her creamy skin flushed—made it difficult to cling to any rational thought.

But he had to, for he didn't want to hurt her. And he didn't want to lose control either. He'd made the nature of their relationship clear during the wedding banquet, and he had to continue to do so. This encounter would set the tone for things to come. He would lead, and she would follow—and that would be the way of things between them.

Clenching his jaw, Niel moved closer to his wife. The urge to lean down and kiss her reared up, but he shoved the desire aside. He'd kissed Beth briefly during the wedding ceremony, and his rod had sprung to attention at the feel of her full, soft lips molded against his.

The act was too intimate. It was best if he avoided it, especially if he wished to maintain the upper hand.

Instead, Niel grasped Beth by the hips and pulled her up so that the tip of his shaft rested in the dampness between her thighs. He'd thought he might need to oil his rod before taking her, to make this first coupling easier for his virgin wife, but she was so wet there was no need for that.

She was anxious about what would happen next, he could see it in her wide hazel eyes, yet she wanted him all the same.

A moan escaped Beth then, and his belly clenched with wild lust in response.

Christ's bones, how was he supposed to maintain control when she made sounds like that?

Slowly, he inched himself into his wife, letting her stretch to take him before he pressed in farther. In response, she gave a whimper, her eyes going wide.

"Am I hurting ye?" he grunted.

"No." She gasped out the reply. "Don't stop."

A growl tore from Niel's throat, and he thrust the rest of the way in, sheathing himself fully.

Beth gasped once more, her lush mouth forming an 'o' of surprise.

Niel stiffened. Curse him, he *had* hurt her.

An instant later though, Beth's face relaxed. And then, to his surprise, she tentatively circled her hips against his. She arched back, a shudder rippling through her as she let out a long, sensual moan.

Sweat trickled down Niel's back, between his shoulder blades.

Being buried inside her tightness, her heat, while Beth moaned and writhed under him, was too much. Aye, he'd planned to take her slowly, with care—but now that she was wrapped around him, he cast his intentions aside.

He leaned forward, held himself over his wife, and started to pound into her. Instinct overrode reason, and he took Beth in hard, deep thrusts.

In response, she wrapped her legs around his hips, drawing him deeper each time he plowed into her.

Niel's eyes fluttered closed. He was lost. His climax gathered inside him, tension and heat coiling at the base of his spine and in his lower belly. Beth shuddered under him once more as the storm broke, washing over him with a force that made his body go taut, his spine snapping straight.

Jaw clenched, Niel swallowed the cry that clawed at his throat. His limbs trembled as he emptied himself deep within his wife.

Afterward, breathing hard, his pulse pounding in his ears, Niel held himself up above Beth. His eyes remained tightly shut while he struggled to compose himself.

Lying beneath her husband, her limbs still quivering in the aftermath of their coupling, Beth tried to make sense of what had just happened.

Heavens, she hadn't expected *that*.

She'd expected pain when Niel had driven into her the first time. However, she'd only felt some fleeting discomfort while she adjusted to his size and to the new sensation of being filled.

And the strength and hardness of him as he'd thrust deep into her, again and again, had caused her to forget everything else. The way he'd taken her—not roughly but passionately—had unraveled her. Pleasure still throbbed between her thighs and deep within her womb in the aftermath.

Her husband had surprised her. Niel's tenderness, and his desire, made Beth relax properly in his presence for the first time.

She would have liked him to kiss her, but their coupling had been too frenzied for that. Fortunately though, they still had the night before them.

Reaching up, she trailed her fingertips over the damp skin and hair on his chest. She could feel the thundering of his heart. Her hands explored the hard muscle, the arch of his ribs, and the hollow of his belly. Aye, he was still too spare; the man was still recovering from his time at Bass Rock.

Beth's breathing slowed then as she thought of what it must have been like for him—to be locked away for so long—without any tenderness or comfort. He'd taken her in such a storm of frenzied need that she wondered if this was the first time he'd lain with a woman since his escape. Yet there was no way to know such things, and she had no experience of previous couplings, or men, to draw upon.

They remained like that for a short while, neither speaking. Niel held himself above her, his eyes closed as his breathing gradually settled, while Beth let her hands explore the lean angles of his body.

And then, he withdrew from her and rolled over onto his back, one arm thrown over his face.

Beth rolled over onto her side, still gazing at him. She'd never thought to find the male body so beautiful, yet she did. Niel's torso bore a few old scars, silvered now with age, yet the imperfections only added to his masculinity.

But as the moments passed, he still hadn't looked her way.

"Niel?" she said, clearing her throat. "Is something amiss?"

Her husband lowered his forearm from his face. To her surprise, both his expression and gaze were shuttered—a far cry from the raw need she'd seen play across his features and darken his cobalt-blue eyes while he'd taken her. "I meant to be gentler than that," he replied, his voice still husky. "Did I hurt ye?"

She shook her head.

A breath gusted out of him. "I'm relieved to hear it."

Not knowing what to say next, Beth tentatively snuggled up to him, placing her head in the hollow of his shoulder. It was a little awkward now, yet she imagined it was like this for many newlyweds after their first coupling.

They lay in silence for a while, and eventually, sleepiness washed over Beth, enveloping her in its warm embrace.

She was just drifting off when Niel's voice intruded. "I think it's time we retired."

"Aye," she murmured, her eyelids drooping. "It has been a long day."

"Go on then," he replied. "Ye can access yer chamber directly from mine."

A heartbeat passed, and then Beth stiffened. The sleepiness sloughed away as she raised her head, her gaze meeting his. "*My* chamber?"

He nodded, gesturing to the far side of the room. Beth turned her head to spy a doorway to the left of the hearth. She hadn't even noted it earlier; she'd been too nervous to pay much attention to her surroundings. "Aye ... it was once my mother's," Niel went on. "The servants have redecorated it for ye ... I think ye will find it comfortable."

Beth looked back at him, her belly contracting. "What's this?"

Their gazes fused. "Don't look so shocked," he murmured. "It's not that unusual ... many couples have separate rooms. My parents did ... and they were happy with the arrangement."

A chill feathered over Beth's skin. *Her* parents hadn't slept apart, and neither did Laila and her father.

"But this is our wedding night," she replied, careful to keep her voice calm. "I'd prefer to remain here with ye."

Niel's mouth thinned, even as a nerve flickered in his cheek. "No, Beth." His tone was gentle, yet with an underlying core of iron. "I'm sorry, but I prefer to sleep alone."

Beth swallowed, pushing herself away from him and rolling off the bed. Heat washed over her. She couldn't believe he was sending her away. The urge to press the issue bubbled up within her, yet she wisely shoved it down. There was no missing the edge to his tone, and despite the intimacy of what they'd just done together, she was still cautious around him.

"Goodnight then," she said, cursing the sudden huskiness in her voice. Mother Mary, she didn't want to start weeping, especially not when Niel was being so self-contained.

Even so, her vision blurred, and an ache rose in her throat.

Not looking his way, she scooped up her fallen clothes and headed toward the door to her bed-chamber.

"Goodnight, Beth," Niel spoke once more. "I'll see ye in my solar tomorrow morning ... we can break our fast together."

Beth ignored him. Instead, she blindly grasped the door handle, as tears scalded her cheeks, and pushed her way into the adjoining chamber.

The door shut, leaving Niel alone in his bed-chamber.

Releasing the breath he'd been holding, he closed his eyes.

She didn't deserve that. With a murmured oath, Niel raised a hand and dragged it down over his face.

Indeed, he was a callous knave to cast his wife from his bed, without a tender word, look, or touch.

It wasn't Beth's fault. His decision had nothing to do with her, but himself. He just needed to be alone. He couldn't relax otherwise.

Niel sucked in a deep breath, and then another, letting his tension subside.

When Beth had stretched out next to him, her cheek nestling against his shoulder, he'd felt as if he were about to crawl out of his own skin.

He couldn't spend the night with her. He didn't want to hold her close and speak intimately as lovers often did after coupling. Instead, he wished for privacy. He needed to be able to breathe once more. It was an irony really—for loneliness had eaten him up inside during his incarceration. The solitude of his gaol cell had nearly broken him.

Opening his eyes, Niel stared up at the shadowed rafters.

So much for his decision to keep a leash on himself tonight.

His bride was fire. Both in and out of bed, she challenged him.

Frowning, Niel decided that it just as well he'd insisted Beth return to her own chamber. The woman didn't like being told what to do—but she'd learn soon enough.

He'd wed her for a purpose. He couldn't let his bride distract him, or weaken him.

He needed to stay in control.

12

THE THIRST FOR BATTLE

"WHAT WAS IT like?"

The question was one Beth had been dreading, even though she'd known one of her sisters would ask.

She wasn't surprised Neave had been the one to do so. The second-born Munro sister was too nosey by half.

Casting Neave an irritated look, Beth sniffed. "None of yer business."

"Oh, don't ye dare keep such things to yerself, Beth!" Neave countered, eyes flashing. She halted and turned to face Beth, placing her hands upon her hips. "Ye are the first of us to wed ... ye *must* tell us what yer wedding night was like."

Beth sucked in a deep breath. All three of them were staring at her now, their gazes wide and imploring. She didn't blame them for their curiosity—for, in the same position, she too would have been dying to know. However, last night's encounter had left her emotionally bruised.

The four sisters walked along the shore of the Kyle of Tongue, their boots crunching upon the shingle. It was mid-morning, and warm sun bathed their faces. Above them reared the bush-clad, rocky pinnacle where Castle Varrich perched, its sandstone curtain wall etched in sharp relief against a clear-blue sky.

The fortress was an impressive sight, yet when she glanced up at it, Beth's belly clenched.

Niel was up there, meeting with his chieftains this morning. She'd broken her fast with him in the clan-chief's solar—an awkward meal that had passed largely in silence. Toward the end, he'd informed her that he would be occupied all day in discussions.

"It's rare we all find ourselves under one roof," he'd said as he poured cream onto his porridge. "I will not waste this opportunity to start planning our next move against the Gunns."

His comment hadn't come as a surprise—for Beth knew that Niel was obsessed about getting even with those he blamed for his incarceration. She'd noted the flinty determination that flared in his eyes. Her husband was a warrior to the core, and not a man lightly crossed.

"He wasn't rough with ye, was he?" Jean asked then, interrupting Beth's thoughts.

"Did it hurt?" Eilidh's large eyes were as big as moons as she regarded her eldest sister.

Beth cleared her throat, realizing that she wasn't going to evade their questions. She might as well meet them head-on.

"No, he wasn't rough," she replied, even as heated images of Niel Mackay pounding into her caused molten excitement to quicken in the cradle of her hips. She'd welcomed his passion, had thrilled at seeing him unravel. "And no ... it didn't hurt." She paused then, searching for the right words. "It was a little uncomfortable at first, but that soon passed."

Her cheeks started to warm then. She and her sisters discussed most things, but never subjects *this* intimate.

"Is he big then?" Neave asked, her elfin face alive with curiosity. "Ye know ... down *there*?"

Beth coughed to cover up her embarrassment. She started to sweat as she recalled Niel's magnificent shaft, and how he'd felt, buried to the hilt inside her.

However, there were some details she'd never reveal. Not even to her sisters.

"I'm not telling ye such things, Neave Munro," she said, a trifle primly. "What happens between husband and wife in the bed-chamber should remain private. So no, I will not tell ye the size of Niel Mackay's rod ... or what he looks like naked."

Her sisters erupted into peals of laughter at that. Jean had gone as red as an ember, Neave was grinning wickedly, and Eilidh covered her mouth with her hands.

And when the sisters had recovered from their mirth, they continued their stroll along the shore. A light breeze rippled across the water, and Beth was glad she'd brought a woolen shawl. Although spring was upon them, the air still had a sharp edge to it, especially this close to the sea.

"There's something not right with ye this morning though," Neave said then, and Beth cursed the fact that she could hide little from her sister. "Have ye and the Mackay quarreled so soon?"

Beth shook her head, even if her throat constricted. No, they hadn't argued—although she almost wished they had.

"Well, then ... what is it?" Jean asked, concern tinging her voice. "It's not like ye to brood."

Sighing, Beth glanced over at Jean. She noted that all three of her sisters were no longer smiling or giggling. Instead, their brows were furrowed in concern.

"It's probably natural to feel a little overwhelmed," she admitted after a pause. "From one day to the next, my life has changed forever." She pulled a face then. "I imagine I will get used to Niel's ways ... in time."

Eilidh inclined her head. "His *ways*?"

"Aye, he likes to have the upper hand. He doesn't like it when I question him." Beth sucked in a breath before pushing herself on. She hadn't been intending to mention this, yet now she couldn't help herself. "And he prefers to sleep alone. I have my own bed-chamber next to his."

Surprise rippled across her sisters' faces, as she'd anticipated it would. They all knew that things were very different at Foulis Castle. Their father wouldn't have wished to sleep apart from his wives.

"Why would he want that?" Eilidh asked, her tone subdued.

"Some couples sleep separately, Eilidh," Neave replied. "There's nothing wrong with it." There was a slight note of chagrin in Neave's voice at her younger sister's innocence, yet Beth marked the shadow in Neave's eyes.

"No, there isn't," Beth agreed, a trifle too quickly. "I was just taken by surprise ... that's all."

"The Mackay was locked away for a long time," Jean spoke up. "It can turn some folk strange." She then favored Beth with an encouraging smile. "But there's nothing to say things won't change ... once ye get to know each other."

A knot formed under Beth's ribcage, even if she attempted a smile. "I hope that will be the case," she murmured. Even so, she appreciated Jean's words. Although she was the third-born sister, there was a seriousness, wisdom, and maturity to Jean that sometimes made Beth feel as if *she* were the younger sister. Their mother had called Jean an 'old soul'. And at times like this, Beth could see why. "Ye are right ... Niel is likely still recovering from his time in prison ... and we have the rest of our lives to learn to trust each other."

"Aye, that's true," Neave chimed in. "Although there's nothing to stop ye from helping things along."

Beth arched an eyebrow. "Excuse me?"

"Let's face it, asking for marital advice from us three is like the blind leading the blind." She cast Jean a quelling look when their sister made a noise of protest. Shifting her attention back to Beth, Neave's mouth curved. "Castle Varrich is full of wedded women at present ... the likes of Keira and Maggie Mackay have happy marriages. Why don't ye ask them the best way to get Niel to thaw to ye?"

"I want more patrols along our borders ... especially to the south and the west." Leaning over the map he'd laid out upon the oaken table that dominated the solar, Niel traced his finger over the mountain ranges and hill-country that separated the Mackays from their neighbors. "The Sutherlands and the Gunns must be watched."

"Aye," Hugh Mackay of Loch Stach rumbled from the far end of the table. "Don't think they've let things be ... I had cattle go missing last month ... and I'd wager it's the Sutherlands up to their old tricks."

"Let's not start pointing fingers too hastily, Hugh," Connor Mackay spoke up. The younger chieftain was frowning, although his gaze lingered upon the map. "Things have been quiet upon my borders of late."

Niel scowled. "What ... the Gunns haven't been raiding yer villages in the winter? I thought it was a tradition."

Connor huffed a laugh before shaking his head. "Ever since Tavish Gunn took his father's place as clan-chief, we've had little trouble." He paused then. "Perhaps the fact that his brother resides at Farr Castle has made him shift his attention elsewhere."

"His *estranged* brother," John Mackay pointed out. "Ye might not have had difficulties with them ... but we have. While we were engaged with our own clansmen ... and with the Sutherlands, Tavish Gunn raided the villages around Badanloch." Niel noted the hard look upon his cousin's face. He didn't bother to conceal his mistrust of their neighbors, and Niel didn't blame him. John had been forced to deal with much unrest during his time as laird of Castle Varrich after Angus Mackay's death.

"John's right," Niel said after a pause, meeting Connor's eye. "Don't think just because Alexander Gunn lives with the Mackays that the Gunn clan-chief views any of ye with tenderness." Secretly, Niel resented Connor just a little for giving Alexander Gunn sanctuary at Farr Castle. "He's been quiet of late because he's been watching and waiting."

"Aye, hoping the Mackays would feud so bitterly amongst ourselves that he'd be able to swoop in and claim Strathnaver for himself," Hugh muttered. He then cast the chieftains of Balnakeil and Dun Ugadale a scowl. Both men, young chieftains who were yet untried in battle, shifted uncomfortably in their seats. They knew what the older man was referring to. His words were a warning. What with their kin's mutiny in the past, and the treacherous Nielson Mackays forming an alliance with the Sutherlands to bring Angus Mackay down, their clan had weathered much bloodshed of late.

"That's all in the past now," Breac Mackay of Balnakeil spoke up then. Tall and swarthy with a stubborn jaw, the chieftain was frowning. "Maybe we should leave it there."

"Aye, it had better be," Hugh replied, his mouth twisting as he sized up the younger man. "But traitor's blood runs in yer veins, lad … and I'll not forget it."

Breac's expression turned stony, and his lips parted as he readied himself to answer. But Niel raised a hand, and the laird of Balnakeil held his tongue.

Niel then favored the men amassed before him with a grim smile. Hugh had been overly aggressive, yet he didn't mind the chieftain issuing that warning. It was one he wanted them all to heed.

"Before we started squabbling amongst ourselves, this clan was once feared," he said, his voice carrying across the solar. "And I intend to make it so once more." He paused then, casting a glance at Robin Mackay. As usual, the laird of Melness was silent. "Can ye spare some warriors, Robin? I intend to send out a patrol west in a few days."

Robin nodded. Melness was the closest broch of his chieftains to Castle Varrich. "I will return home tomorrow and send twenty men to ye," he assured him.

Satisfied, Niel turned his attention back to the table, his gaze taking in the faces of the men who'd sworn their loyalty to him. Pride swelled in his chest. They would help him make the Mackays a force to be reckoned with again.

"Prepare yerselves," he said, his voice hardening. "For this is the year we strike back against the Gunns."

"Will we call them to battle then?" Connor asked. A faint crease had appeared between his dark-blond eyebrows. Niel wondered if his friend disapproved of his aggressiveness. Niel had always struggled to understand Connor, at times. The pair of them had grown up together, hunted and fought side-by-side for years. He knew the chieftain of Farr wasn't a coward. And he also knew that Connor and his brother, Morgan, were loyal to him, and to the clan. However, Connor Mackay had little love for war. Niel wasn't sure if it was seeing his own father cut down in battle against the Gunns, but Connor was a peace-maker at heart.

It was a trait that irked Niel. Curse him, Connor had every reason to despise the Gunns as much as he did. And yet not only had he wed a Gunn, but he'd let that whoreson Alexander Gunn wed his sister.

The latter especially vexed Niel whenever he thought upon it. And if he ruminated upon it too long, his belly ached. He didn't have a sister, but if he had, he'd have seen her dead before being wedded to a Gunn.

Placing both palms upon the table, Niel leaned over, his gaze fusing with Connor's. "Aye," he murmured. "If they don't march upon us first." He paused then, heat washing over him as the thirst for battle ignited in his veins. "But one thing is certain, Connor ... by the end of this year, Gunn blood will stain the earth red."

13

WOMANLY ADVICE

BETH WINCED, dropping her needle and raising her injured finger to her mouth. She then muttered a curse under her breath. She was a woman with many skills—but sewing wasn't one of them. Nonetheless, she persisted.

Across the solar, seated upon a cushion on the wide ledge next to the window, Keira Mackay cast her a rueful smile. "That must be the third time ye have done that, Beth. That lèine will be covered with bloodstains soon."

"Aye," Beth muttered. She then eyed the neat flowers that Keira had embroidered over the coverlet she was working on. "I'm happier in the kitchen kneading dough than with a needle and thread ... I must admit."

"Our Jaimee is a little like ye," Maggie Mackay piped up with a grin. She was winding wool upon a spindle, and like Keira appeared to be enjoying the task. "Jaimee chafes at being cooped up with us at our sewing and weaving. She prefers to be outdoors."

Beth's mouth curved. It was a pity Jaimee hadn't attended her wedding; she would have liked to have met her. Even so, she had warmed to Keira and Maggie from the first. They reminded her of her sisters.

The three of them sat in the women's solar. The window was open, the late-afternoon sun filtering through and pooling like honey over the flagstone floor. Usually, Beth and her sisters spent a quiet hour together in the solar in the afternoons—a brief respite from a busy day—although today Beth had invited Keira and Maggie to join her while her sisters busied themselves elsewhere.

None of the Munro sisters were idle, and now that Beth was the Lady of Varrich, all four of them had taken on duties. Jean had insisted on doing an inventory of the spence this afternoon, while Neave and Eilidh had gone out to tend the rambling terraced vegetable garden beneath the castle's southern curtain wall.

Beth needed to go over the meals the cooks had planned for the coming week. She also wanted to take an inventory of the granary. However, those tasks would have to wait until later.

First, she had to ask Keira and Maggie's advice. She'd deliberately ensured her sisters wouldn't be present, for she didn't wish for them to witness this conversation. It was bad enough that Neave had convinced her to talk to two women she barely knew about her marriage. She didn't want her sisters listening in and flashing her meaningful glances while Beth died of embarrassment.

As it was, she wasn't sure she could go through with it.

How was she supposed to even bring the subject up?

Clearing her throat, Beth lowered her embroidery to her lap. It was best not to try and sew while she did this—or she'd just stab herself again out of nervousness.

"Do ye mind if I ask ye both a question?" she asked, feigning calmness when on the inside she was beginning to cringe. "About marriage."

Both women halted in their tasks, their gazes alighting upon her face.

"Of course not," Keira replied, flashing her a smile. "What do ye wish to know?"

Interest sparked in their gazes. Of course, there was nothing women liked better than to discuss such things.

Beth cleared her throat once more, embarrassment pulsing like a hot coal in her chest. "I ... ah ... well," she began, cursing how gauche she felt in front of these two poised ladies. "It's just that ... Niel and I don't really know each other at all. How long will it be ... before he relaxes in my company?"

Keira Mackay's blue eyes softened, her expression sobering. Of course, Beth had heard the tale of how Keira and Connor had wed. She'd pretended to be someone else, and when the ruse had been exposed, news of it had rippled across the Highlands. Beth had only been around sixteen at the time, but she remembered her parents discussing the scandal—shaking their heads in amazement at how Connor Mackay had forgiven his wife in the end.

Their marriage had endured though. Beth had watched the laird of Farr and his wife over the past days—had seen the way they looked at each other. The couple were clearly deeply in love.

"It depends," Keira replied after a pause. "On ye both."

"Aye," Maggie agreed. She too was watching Beth with a speculative look. "Ye appear an open and warm-hearted lass, Beth ... but Niel is ... more complex."

Beth nodded. "We are wed, yet he still feels like a stranger to me."

"I'm not entirely surprised." Keira's dark-blue eyes had shadowed. "Even before Bass Rock, Niel was never easy to fathom. Connor's known him for years, yet he's often had difficulty reading Niel ... and our new clan-chief has his father's temper." She halted then, her features tensing as if she realized her words appeared harsh. "Of course, Niel's no fool. And although he's arrogant, he's also able to admit when he's mistaken ... as he was about me."

A pause followed, full of things unsaid. Beth frowned, wondering what Keira was referring to. She wished to ask the Lady of Farr about it, yet something in Keira's expression checked her.

"Niel's mercurial ... a trait that got him into trouble in the past," Maggie added softly. "He's bull-headed too: Morgan once told me that when Niel fixes upon something, he finds it difficult to let go." Her lips curved then. "However, Keira's right. He's sharp ... and deep-thinking. Morgan assures me he's trustworthy."

"Niel will have been scarred by his time at Bass Rock." Keira favored Beth with a tight smile. "But he hasn't lost sight of who he is ... not yet, anyway ... and with ye at his side, he won't."

Beth's throat tightened then, a reaction that irritated her. She'd come to Keira and Maggie for advice, yet their empathy was making it difficult for her to remain composed. Straightening her spine, she drew in a deep breath. She didn't know what the matter with her was these days. Before coming to Castle Varrich, she was the strongest of her sisters. The practical one. Beth Munro had been a woman who merely rolled up her sleeves and got things done.

But Beth *Mackay* was at a loss on how to proceed.

"Niel is fixated upon revenge at present," she admitted after a weighty silence. "And although I admire his strength of purpose, he appears to care for little else."

"Aye, Connor has told me as much," Keira replied, her mouth thinning. "He's had too long to stew over the injustices done to him. It's made him obsessive."

Beth let out a slow exhale. "So, what am I to do?" Her gaze flicked from Keira's face to Maggie's. Both women wore veiled expressions now, something which made unease prickle her skin. It hit her then that they pitied her situation.

They were both wed to kind, open-hearted men.

Maybe Neave was wrong. It seemed they couldn't help her, for neither of them had any experience with a man like Niel.

However, after a pause, Maggie met her eye before a smile curved her lips. "All isn't lost, lass. When I met him, Morgan had no plans to take a wife. I think it surprised him how much he enjoyed a woman's companionship." Her features tightened then. "I didn't make things easy for him, I'm afraid. I should have been kinder." Maggie leaned forward, her gaze never leaving Beth's. "Ye need to be patient ... let him have things his way for the moment, and in the meantime, focus on getting to know him ... on letting him see who *ye* are."

"Aye," Keira agreed, smiling now. "Remember that Niel is still adjusting to being free again ... to being surrounded by folk after a long period of isolation. All of it will be new to him ... and being wed is just one more thing for him to get used to."

"He doesn't wish to sleep in the same bed as me," Beth blurted out. "Last night, he sent me to my chamber ... as soon as we'd ..."

Beth's voice trailed off there as she saw the smile fade from Keira's face and observed how Maggie's gaze narrowed.

Misgiving felt like a rock in her belly. She should have revealed that detail before asking for their advice. They might have spoken differently as a result.

"Ye both look so stern," she said after a long pause. "Is that really so bad?"

Maggie smiled, although this time the expression appeared a little strained. "It's not the end of the world ... yet it shows Niel's frame of mind at present."

Keira nodded. "My advice still stands though, Beth. Connor told me once that Niel had a lonely childhood. His mother only ever bore her husband one child—and fortunately for her, it was a son. Angus and Estelle Mackay weren't close ... so perhaps Niel is merely following the only example he's ever been set."

A little of the tension in Beth's shoulders eased at these words. "That makes sense," she murmured. "He told me that his parents always slept apart. It was obvious that he didn't think there was anything odd in it."

Maggie snorted. "Men," she muttered. "They really can be dolts at times." Her lips curved then as she met Beth's eye once more and winked. "Luckily for them, we women are here to put them right."

"How were the meetings today, Niel?" Beth casually broke the silence between husband and wife. They sat alone together in the clan-chief's solar, drinking a small cup of wine before bed.

They'd just shared their last supper with their guests in the great hall. The following morning, their wedding guests would all be returning to their brochs. Beth's father and stepmother would also be leaving. From now on, Castle Varrich would be much quieter.

Niel glanced up from where he'd been gazing into the fire. "They went well."

"And yer chieftains ... are they united now?" The feuding within the Mackay clan, which had resulted in the Battle of Drumnacoub four years later, was still talked about in the Highlands. Beth wondered if the ill feelings remained or if they had truly been stamped out with the death of the Neilson Mackays.

"It seems they are loyal," Niel admitted, swirling his cup of wine. His mouth lifted at the corners in a hard smile that didn't reach his eyes. "Although they know the penalty if they are not."

Beth nodded, even as her pulse fluttered. It surprised her that her husband's ruthless edge excited her—but it did. The discovery was also a little unnerving. Beth had always told herself that she wanted a kind, gentle-natured husband—as some of her former suitors had been—but the reality was none had stoked a fire in her belly like the proud clan-chief seated opposite her.

Beth cleared her throat. "What are yer plans for tomorrow?" she asked, deliberately changing the subject. Keira and Maggie had encouraged her to talk to her husband, to draw him gently out of his shell. It was difficult to do that when they spoke of certain things.

Niel shrugged before he lifted the cup to his lips and drained its dregs. "I'm not sure ... John wishes to go stag hunting, but I might let him go on his own. Our armory is looking too sparse for my liking ... I need to speak to the smith about forging some new blades."

"Well, let's hope that John's hunt is successful, even without yer assistance. The meat stores could do with more fresh venison," Beth replied, her lips curving. "I could make some more of those pies ye enjoy so much."

Niel huffed a laugh. "Are ye trying to fatten me up, lass?"

"Guilty." She smiled back at him, heat shivering through her belly as their gazes met. She liked the low rumble of his laugh, almost as much as his sensual, cocky smile. "So, John will stay on then?"

Niel nodded.

"I thought he was keen to return to Achness?"

"Aye ... but I've convinced him I need his help here," Niel replied. "There's much to be done in the coming months ... when we strike against the Gunns, I want us to be well-prepared."

Beth stifled a sigh. Heavens, the man had managed to bring the subject of conversation back to revenge once more. It was becoming clear that he thought of little else.

Niel set his cup aside then and rose to his feet, towering above her.

Beth's pulse quickened as she too put down her cup, waiting for him to reach down, take her hands, and draw her to her feet. Despite how awkwardly things had concluded between them the eve before, there was no denying she was wildly attracted to her husband. Likewise, she'd noted the way his gaze lingered upon her face during their conversation just now. He too was aware of her.

Yet Niel didn't draw her to her feet. Instead, he gave a long stretch before yawning. "It's been a busy day," he announced. "I shall retire." He moved away from the hearth, not looking at her now. "Goodnight, Beth. Sleep well."

And with that, he walked off, entering his bed-chamber without another word, the door whispering closed behind him.

Beth sat in stunned silence for a few moments. She hadn't replied to him—yet it didn't seem that Niel had even noticed.

Standing up, she turned, her gaze settling upon the door to his bed-chamber. She could enter her own room the same way, although the finality of his last words had made it clear he didn't wish for company tonight.

"Ye won't beget an heir like that," she muttered to the closed door. Even so, beneath her irritation, hurt constricted her chest. How could she get closer to him, if he shut her out like this? She knew he was as drawn to her as she was to him, yet he'd just pretended as if that wasn't the case.

Beth left the solar and walked the few yards down the narrow hallway to the second door, which also gave her access to her bed-chamber—the one that servants tended to use when coming and going so as to not disturb the laird.

Letting herself into her chamber, she saw Greta had been in already. The maid had stoked the fire and turned down the bed in readiness for her. Like Niel's, her bed was large and canopied, although this chamber was around half the size of his. It was a lovely space nonetheless, decorated with colorful cushions and tapestries. It even had a small shuttered window on the exterior wall.

Niel had insisted the chamber was redecorated before her arrival—a thoughtful gesture that she'd appreciated. Nonetheless, at present, she wasn't in the mood to feel particularly grateful toward him.

Muttering an oath, she walked over to the edge of the bed and sank down upon it.

Greta had already retired for the evening, under the apprehension that the clan-chief would help his wife undress before carrying her to bed.

Beth loosed a heavy sigh. "He's just tired," she counseled herself aloud. "Don't think too much upon it."

Sage advice, and yet she found it hard to follow. The truth was, Niel's behavior frustrated her. Digging her fingertips into the soft coverlet she sat upon, Beth tried her best to let the slight go.

Enough of this.

She couldn't let herself be led by her emotions. Instead, she had to be practical. She had to be patient with him—assure him she was the wife he wanted. And then, with time, he would let her in.

But even as she assured herself that her husband's behavior wasn't a rejection and that she would eventually gain his trust, a stone settled into the pit of her belly.

She'd set herself quite a task in trying to win over Niel Mackay—and at present, she wasn't sure if she would ever succeed.

14

A GROWING FRUSTRATION

Two months later ...

ROLLING HIS SHOULDERS, Niel stepped back from John and flipped the wooden practice sword. He then flashed his opponent a grin. "Ready to go again, cousin?"

A few yards away, John shook his head. "I'm done," he panted.

Unlike Niel, who had exercised bare-chested, John Mackay wore a loose lèine, which now clung to his sweaty skin. Niel knew why John didn't strip off whenever they practiced at sword-play together—the long sleeve of the lèine hid his missing right hand and most likely a few nasty scars too. Although John had never admitted as much to him, Niel sensed his cousin was embarrassed about the stump he now bore instead of a right hand. If he was in company, John usually wore a hand carved of wood. However, he took it off at sword practice.

"Come on," Niel jeered. "Just one more round." He too dripped with sweat, his muscles burning from use, his legs heavy with exhaustion. However, he wanted to push himself further. Summer was upon them, and with each passing day, his impatience seethed hotter.

His body was much stronger now, and he'd rallied men from all over Strathnaver to join him. They'd arrive within the next day or two.

The time to march on the Gunns was fast approaching. He'd invited his chieftains back to Castle Varrich in time for the annual summer fair in Tongue—

and he intended to unveil his plans then. Nonetheless, it wouldn't come as a surprise to any of them.

John muttered a curse under his breath and tossed his sword aside, holding up his left hand in surrender. "Enough. Ye win."

Niel snorted. He had, but only barely. John had lost his fighting hand in battle four years earlier, yet he was now just as deadly with his left hand. Niel enjoyed sparring with him, for his cousin pushed him. When they'd begun their practice months earlier, Niel had felt weak and clumsy. But these days, he moved with the same agility and strength he had as a younger warrior.

"Very well," he replied. "Let's go in and get ourselves some cool ale … we've got a little time before I meet with the armorer." Niel was having a new hauberk made, and the armorer in Tongue had assured him it would be ready that afternoon.

Turning, his gaze swept over the sun-soaked bailey. It was the hottest day of the year so far. A rainy May had slid into a warm June. The surrounding stone glowed under the hot sun. Niel could feel it sting his bare shoulders, although he welcomed the sun's kiss. How often had he longed for it when he'd been at Bass Rock? He'd stretched his fingers through the tiny barred window of his cell, in the vain hope of feeling the sun's warmth upon his skin. Yet it had always eluded him.

And as his gaze shifted toward the gates, he spied a familiar figure. Beth had just passed under the stone arch. She now stood before it, watching him. One of her sisters—Neave—stood at her side.

Niel tensed. He hadn't realized they'd had an audience. A moment later, his spine straightened and his shoulders drew back. It had been a good fight, and he'd emerged the victor. As such, there was a part of him that preened at the thought that his wife had been watching him.

Vain cockerel, he chastised himself as Beth moved toward him, Neave following close behind. Why was it that men loved to show off in front of women? He recalled only too well what he'd been like as a young warrior. He'd enjoyed the clan gatherings, where comely lasses cheered the men on as they competed in strength and fighting contests.

"Did ye enjoy that, wife?" he greeted Beth with a grin, unable to prevent himself from gloating over his victory, just a little.

"Aye, husband." The husky note to his wife's voice enveloped him like an embrace. He also didn't miss the way her gaze boldly slid down from his face and over his naked torso before she met his eye once more.

Niel hardly saw Beth during the day at present, for he was kept busy with his duties as laird of Varrich and readying himself and his men for battle—but they had supper together alone every eve. And afterward, he sometimes took her to his bed.

He took care *not* to enjoy her every night. It was a tremendous exercise in will, for the more Niel had of Beth, the more he wanted her. But just like a rich dish, such as roast swan or those delicious custards the cooks made at Yule, Beth wasn't a pleasure he let himself indulge in too often.

Aye, he could have taken her nightly—and indeed his groin throbbed at her brazen stare just now—but he deliberately limited himself.

There had been so much to do of late, so much to plan, and he didn't want any distractions. Nonetheless, he lay with his wife frequently enough to get her with bairn—although as yet, Beth's womb hadn't quickened.

"That was a good fight, John," Neave quipped cheerfully. "Ye nearly had him during the last bout."

"Aye, but he didn't," Niel reminded her.

Even so, John's mouth quirked, his blue eye glinting as his gaze met Neave's. "He knows my fighting style too well these days," he admitted. "Maybe I need to learn a few new tricks."

Niel snorted before turning his attention back to his wife. "I don't usually see ye out here at this hour," he noted.

"Neave and I have just been down to Tongue," Beth replied, her full-lips curving. "We've been helping the villagers ready the market square for tomorrow's fair."

"Aye, there will be archery, hammer throwing, and wrestling contests," Neave said, her voice tight with excitement. "As well as musicians, dancing, and mummery."

"Indeed." Beth's smile widened, her gaze upon Niel. "I was wondering if we might attend together?"

Niel quelled the urge to frown. His wife's request wasn't an outrageous one, yet he hadn't actually intended to go down to Tongue for the fair. Ever since his escape from Bass Rock, he found large groups of people suffocating. Instead of attending the fair, he'd planned to go over fighting tactics and battle plans with John and his chieftains in his solar. Still, he'd glimpsed the hope in Beth's eyes. They'd hardly seen each other of late. To refuse her would have been rude, even for him.

He supposed he could spare a little time in the afternoon, for most of his chieftains weren't due to arrive before then anyway.

A heartbeat passed before Niel smiled back. "Aye, wife ... it should be a pleasant day."

"What am I doing wrong?"

"The bread looks fine to me ... much neater than the braid I've just done."

Beth made an impatient noise in the back of her throat. She then straightened up from where she'd just made a plaited loaf with boiled eggs nestled amongst it.

Neave wasn't exaggerating. *Her* braid was untidy, the eggs placed in a haphazard fashion.

"I wasn't talking about the bread," Beth replied. She then carefully lifted the braid onto a large wooden paddle before transferring it to the roaring oven behind them.

It was mid-afternoon, and the two sisters were making breads to add to the baking that the cooks had labored over during the past days. The servants would bring the breads, cakes, and pastries down to Tongue to distribute among the crowd. It was a yearly tradition for the laird of Castle Varrich to distribute food to the locals during the summer fair.

Beth and Neave were alone in the kitchens this afternoon. In an hour, the cooks would return to begin preparation for supper, but at present, the sisters had the run of this space.

It was usually a time that Beth enjoyed, for the kitchens could be loud and chaotic. Yet this afternoon, she was on edge.

She turned back to the flour-dusted table to see Neave eyeing her. "Ye weren't?" her sister asked with an arched eyebrow.

"No, I was referring to my marriage."

Neave inclined her head. "I thought things were better between ye and the laird?"

Beth's mouth pursed. "Keira and Maggie counseled me to be patient," she said after a moment. "But it's been *two* months, Neave. These days, I rarely see Niel."

A groove formed between Neave's brows. "But he has agreed to join ye tomorrow ... for the fair?"

"Aye, only because I asked. If I hadn't, he would have remained in the keep, poring over his maps and obsessing over his next move against the Gunns." Beth grabbed another lump of dough and began to bash it with her fists.

Moments passed before Neave spoke once more. "Does he not bed ye?"

Beth cleared her throat. "Aye ... twice a week."

Curiosity illuminated Neave's eyes at this comment.

Beth glanced away, suddenly wishing she hadn't answered so openly. She and Niel had indeed settled into a routine. The couple took a cup of wine together in the evenings after supper and twice a week—usually a

Wednesday and a Sunday—her husband would take her by the hand and lead her into his bed-chamber.

Beth's belly swooped then, as she thought about what he did to her on those nights. Her husband was a quick study. He knew just how to touch her, where to kiss in order to make her sigh and tremble. However, whenever she reached for him, he evaded her. Instead, he'd throw her onto her back or sometimes take her on all fours in a wordless storm of passion that left her gasping in its aftermath. But once they were done, he'd wait until they'd both recovered sufficiently before bidding her 'good-night'.

And despite that Niel just had to look her way to set her pulse racing, Beth's frustration grew daily. In all the weeks that had passed since their wedding, he hadn't kissed her again on the mouth. Not once.

"He's likely hoping my womb will quicken soon." Without realizing what she was doing, Beth placed a hand upon her belly, leaving a floury imprint upon the linen apron she wore over her kirtle. "Niel has been late to start a family ... he will want a son within the year."

She stilled then, ice slithering down her spine. She hoped she was fertile. What if she wasn't?

If she failed to give him an heir, Niel would likely grow to resent her.

An hour later, Beth emerged from the keep, basket slung over one arm, and made for the gates. She'd left her sisters to sew and gossip in the women's solar this afternoon, while she collected some culinary herbs. Earlier in the day, when she and Neave had returned from Tongue, she'd spotted a patch of garlic growing near the base of the promontory, and some dandelion and nettles growing farther up. The herbs added an extra level of flavor to dishes, and so Beth wished to fill her basket with them.

The wind caught her hair, whipping it around her face, when she emerged onto the path and made her way down the hill.

And as she did so, her gaze swept over the vista that unfolded before her.

Even after the time she'd spent at Varrich, the majesty of the Mackay lands still robbed her of breath: the wide sweep of the kyle, the gentle fold of the hills, and the sleeping giants that were Ben Hope and Ben Loyal—the mountains that kept watch upon them. Below, she spied the spire of Tongue's kirk, and the smudge of wood smoke rising from the roofs of the cottages in the village.

Despite her worries over what the future held for her and Niel, a smile curved Beth's lips.

She loved living here. She enjoyed being mistress of her own keep, and the servants had accepted her governance without question. It warmed her to see their smiles when she came down to the kitchens in the mornings.

Beth was also pleased to see how well her sisters had settled in at Castle Varrich. Even Jean, after a few initial doubts, had embraced life in their new home. Like Beth, Neave, Jean, and Eilidh appreciated being able to make their mark here. Many of the villagers in Tongue now looked forward to seeing the sisters regularly. Jean often helped the local healer, and she and Eilidh brought down bread for the poor once a week. Meanwhile, Neave kept herself busy in the terraced vegetable garden on the northern side of the keep. Her green-fingered sister planned to grow enough vegetables to be able to give the surplus to any of the villagers in need.

It took Beth awhile to reach the bottom of the promontory, for she kept halting to pick various herbs along the way. By the time she found the patch of garlic, her basket was already half-full.

She'd almost finished her task when the thud of hoofbeats made her glance up.

Her husband approached on horseback from Tongue, John and three of his warriors with him.

"Greetings, wife," he called out. "What are ye up to?"

Niel drew close and pulled up his stallion, his gaze spearing her.

"Picking garlic," she replied, shielding her eyes from the sun as she tilted her chin up. "It makes mutton stew tastier."

He smiled, his eyes crinkling at the corners. "If ye have finished, I can give ye a ride back up the hill?"

Beth had actually planned to wander a little farther afield. However, her basket was already full, and since she rarely spent time with her husband, she didn't want to squander the opportunity now.

"Aye, thank ye," she replied with an answering smile. Tucking the basket under one arm, she took his hand, placed a foot over his, and sprang up to perch before him.

The strength of Niel's arm, wrapping around her waist to steady her, made warmth seep through Beth. Her husband held her rarely, yet when he did, she felt protected. She leaned into him now, savoring the moment. Then they were moving forward, picking their way up the twisting path.

"Were ye checking the preparations for tomorrow?" she asked casually.

"No, I leave such matters in yer capable hands," he replied, his breath feathering against her ear. "I've just been to see the blacksmith's wife. Malcolm Mackee keeled over this morning and is now abed."

Beth's brow furrowed. Mackee was a hulking, red-faced fellow with a booming laugh. She often chatted to the smith on her visits to Tongue. "What's wrong with him?"

"The healer tells me it is some form of apoplexy. She says he's likely never to speak or walk again." He paused then. "Unfortunate timing. It looks as if we will have to send out word for another blacksmith ... and soon. I've got a large order of arrowheads that need delivering by the end of the week."

Beth's jaw clenched. As much as she admired her husband's tenacity, and even his supreme confidence, the latter had just spilled over into callousness. These days, Niel's mind rarely strayed from the campaign he was planning. Even Malcolm Mackee's ill fortune couldn't hold his attention for long.

The urge to chastise him for his heartlessness bubbled up within her. Yet she choked it back. The last thing Niel Mackay would want was a scold for a wife.

Nonetheless, the pleasure at having Niel's arms wrapped around her faded.

15

COMPETING

LAUGHTER AND MUSIC drifted through the village of Tongue, echoing over the rippling waters of the kyle beyond. The loud bray of a Highland pipe drew folk into the large square in the center of the village, where the fair was taking place.

Beth walked, arm-in-arm, with her husband amongst the crowd.

They drew attention, Laird and Lady Mackay. The pair of them had donned clan sashes, looped across their fronts, fastened with amber brooches at the shoulder. Beth wore a sea-blue kirtle, and Niel a matching lèine and dun-colored chamois braies. The blue complemented that of the Mackay clan colors. Beth wondered how onlookers saw them: both dark-haired, the clan-chief tall and lean, his lady small and curvaceous.

Beth walked with her chin high, her shoulders back. For weeks now, she'd longed to be at Niel's side amongst his people, to be seen with the charismatic clan-chief. And now she finally was.

Amongst the crowd, she caught the distinctive red of Munro clan sashes. Beth's chest tightened with pride. Her father had promised Niel that should he ever have need, the Munros would fight at his side—and true to his word, George Munro had sent a company of one hundred warriors to Castle Varrich.

Their clans were truly united now.

However, despite her own buoyant mood, she could sense Niel's tension. The muscles of his arm looped through hers were hard. Glancing up at him, she could see from the set of his jaw that he wasn't comfortable. He had the look on his face that she'd marked a few times over the past weeks: a faraway, distracted expression, as if his mind was elsewhere.

Beth fought the urge to frown. Surely it wasn't so onerous to be out here with her?

Attempting to side-step her concern, she shifted her attention once more to the surrounding fair. It appeared as if folk from all the surrounding villages had poured into Tongue for the festivities. Bunting made of the Mackay plaid fluttered in the warm breeze, and a troupe of dancers was performing upon a raised platform: they danced a lively Highland jig in time with the music.

Her sisters had all gathered before the dais, their faces alive with laughter as they clapped their hands to urge the dancers on. The three of them appeared so carefree—as she had once been before becoming a wife.

The warmth Beth had felt at walking at Niel Mackay's side ebbed, and a chill, lonely sensation filtered over her. She wanted to be carefree like that again.

Husband and wife continued on their way. They passed two bairns, who were hungrily devouring one of the braided loaves that Beth and Neave had prepared the day before. The children were thin with dirt-smudged cheeks. The sight of their pleasure in the food drew Beth out of the mire of her own thoughts.

"It is a fine tradition," she said to Niel, raising her voice to be heard over the surrounding din of voices, laughter, and music. "To give away food to yer people every year at this fair."

Niel glanced her way, smiling, even if his penetrating blue eyes had a slightly hunted look. "Aye, my grandfather began it ... as a way of bringing people to the fair." He paused then, his attention shifting to where the bairns were now squabbling over who got the last boiled egg. "He understood that loyalty is much easier to obtain when a man's belly is full. It's a tradition I intend to continue."

They walked on, passing a ring where a group of warriors were competing at the hammer throw. The men were bellowing insults at each other, trying to put their competitors off before they took their throw.

Niel halted to watch them.

Meanwhile, drawing in a deep breath, Beth gathered her courage. Over the past two moons, she and her husband had fallen into a relationship where they communicated like polite strangers. But today, Beth wished to change that.

"Niel," she said, drawing his attention from the hammer throw. "Ye appear tense today. Is something amiss with ye?"

Niel's gaze narrowed at the question before he shook his head. "I'm well, thank ye."

"Are ye irritated then ... that I asked ye to join me here?"

Niel stilled. "No."

"What then? Ye can deny it all ye want, but I can feel the tension in yer arm." To prove her point, she reached up and placed her hand over the muscles of his bicep. They were as hard as carven wood.

Niel's mouth thinned, and Beth stiffened, bracing herself for his reprimand. She knew the signs by now when her husband was displeased. The day before, she'd held her tongue, for fear of being thought a scold—but surely she was permitted to express concern over his wellbeing?

But Niel didn't respond as she'd expected. "I don't like crowds," he admitted after a pause. "Ever since Bass Rock ... they make me feel as if I'm trapped."

Their gazes held, and something passed between them—a silent understanding. Beth's breathing quickened. Finally, he'd shared something of himself with her, a detail he likely hadn't told anyone else.

"It must feel odd at times." She squeezed his arm gently. "To be amongst folk again."

"It's a weakness," he replied, his tone hardening. "One I must overcome if I'm going to lead men into battle again."

His vehemence surprised Beth. "Ye will," she assured him. "Ye are the most dogged individual I've ever met, Niel Mackay. If any man can vanquish his demons, it is ye."

Niel huffed a laugh before eyeing her once more. "Was that a compliment or an insult, wife?"

"A compliment, of course, clod-head." Beth gave his arm a playful punch. "Bass Rock has killed many men ... but not ye."

They reached the far end of the square then, where an archery contest was underway. Men had set up a bullseye target on the side of a wooden storehouse, while competitors lined up to take their shot.

A smile crept across Beth's face then. "Do ye recall our conversation on our wedding day?" she asked. When Niel gave her a blank look, she made an impatient noise in the back of her throat. "About archery. Ye said ye'd challenge me to a contest one day." She pointed ahead. "Well, here's yer chance."

Niel's mouth curved, and his dark-blue eyes gleamed. "What, *now*?"

"It's as good a time as any?"

He laughed. "Very well, wife. Let's see who has more skill with a longbow."

They took their places in the line, although folk drew back the moment they saw their clan-chief had joined them.

Beth could see from the way her husband was now grinning that he clearly thought he was better than her—and it was likely so. However, she was glad he'd agreed to this. She wanted them to spar a little. She wanted her husband to *notice* her.

The other contestants gave way, and the pair found themselves at the head of the line.

"Are ye competing, laird?" A lad asked, awe in his voice.

"Aye," Niel replied.

"Here, Mackay." The range master—a tall rawboned man with a gleaming bald head—handed Niel a yew longbow and a quiver of ash arrows. "Show us how true yer aim is then."

Still grinning, Niel shook his head. "Soon enough … first, my lady wife would like to give us a demonstration of her skill."

The patronizing edge to his voice vexed Beth a little; nonetheless, she let it go. She would show him that she hadn't been boasting. Her father had taught her how to wield a longbow from an early age—and had once revealed that although men had the stronger arm, women were often more skilled at sighting prey with a bow and arrow. Both she and Neave were keen archers, although Jean and Eilidh had never shown much aptitude or interest.

"Very well." The range master looked her up and down as if trying to imagine this small woman wielding a longbow successfully. "Husband against wife, it is."

A rumble of excitement rippled through the onlookers. Beth allowed herself a wry smile. They'd create quite the spectacle.

"Ye each have six arrows," the range master continued. "The points are as follows: one for the white, two for the black, three for the blue, four for the red … and five for those skilled enough to hit the yellow." The condescending smile the man now wore told Beth he didn't think she possessed such ability. "Go on then, Lady Mackay. Loose yer first arrow."

Beth nodded, ignoring all onlookers, her husband included, as she selected an arrow and checked the tension in her bowstring. She then squared her shoulders, straightened her spine, and turned side-on, drawing the arrow back so it was parallel with her collar bone.

Keep that elbow nice and high, Beth. She could almost hear her father's drawl in her ear. Adjusting her stance, she sighted the target.

The arrow loosed, flying through the air and embedding into the wooden target with a 'thud'—straight into the red ring.

Cheering went up around her, and Beth let out a slow exhale. She was nervous and a little out of practice. The arrow had gone slightly wide.

"Good shot," Niel's voice reached her, and when she glanced his way, she saw that her husband was no longer grinning. Instead, he wore a speculative expression.

Warmth arrowed through Beth's belly. Finally, he was paying her some real attention.

It's just a shame I have to act like one of his men to get him to do so.

Notching a second arrow, Beth focused on the target once more. She needed to concentrate.

The twang of the bowstring releasing cut through the air, and the arrow thudded into the target upon the line between the red and yellow.

More cheering erupted.

Not looking her husband's way, Beth reached for another feather-fletched arrow from her quiver. And this time, her arrow hit the yellow. It wasn't a proper bullseye, for it wasn't dead-center.

Nonetheless, her shot caused a roar of approval from the watching crowd.

Beth did glance Niel's way then—noting that his face was now serious, as was his gaze.

Misgiving tickled at her then. She recalled Laila's advice, a year earlier, about how a wife must not compete with her husband.

"It doesn't do for a man to think ye cleverer and more skilled than him," she'd warned when she'd overheard Beth and Neave congratulating each other after clan games. They'd won first and second place in the archery contest, much to the ire of some of her father's men. "It can make a suitor insecure."

Beth had laughed aside Laila's advice at the time. She'd insisted that a worthy man wouldn't let a woman's skills diminish him. Instead, he'd be proud of her.

However, she wasn't laughing now.

Niel Mackay was a perplexing individual—and despite that they'd been wed since spring, she didn't really know him that well.

Of course, he was a man who preferred men and women to keep to their designated roles. She'd wanted to compete with him today for entertainment, to bring the pair of them closer together. But judging from the shuttered look in his eyes, she wondered if her boldness would merely drive a wedge between them.

Christ's bones, what if I win?

Beth dragged her attention from Niel and withdrew a fourth arrow from her quiver.

A wiser woman would probably throw her aim wide now, allow her husband to save face. But pride surged within Beth. Her father hadn't brought her up to hide her abilities. It occurred to her that he'd likely done her a disservice in championing her so—for not all men liked strong-willed and competent women.

Beth couldn't bring herself to deliberately botch her next shots.

Drawing her bowstring back, she sighted the target.

Perhaps it was nervousness, or self-doubt, but Beth's last three shots weren't as good as her previous ones. All three landed squarely in the red. In the past, she'd been capable of hitting a bullseye. But she didn't today.

Grinding her teeth, Beth lowered her bow. She'd let worry distract her.

"Yer turn now, laird," the range master boomed. "Let's see if ye can best yer lady wife."

She noted that the range master didn't view her with the same condescending air he had earlier as he took back the bow and empty quiver. Nonetheless, Beth was still irritated.

She was capable of much better than the skill she'd displayed.

Steeling herself, she looked her husband's way. Niel had been waiting for her to catch his eye.

"Ye have some ability indeed," he drawled, his mouth quirking into that arrogant half-smile she'd come to know well. "But was that good enough to win?"

Beth choked back the urge to tell him that he'd distracted her—that if she hadn't been so worried about annoying him, she'd have hit a bullseye. Such a comment would have appeared churlish and made her look like a poor loser.

Ye haven't lost yet, she reminded herself. *Let's see if Mackay is as good as he believes.*

He was. The knave hit four bullseyes.

Two of his arrows landed upon the red while four all hit the yellow.

And as he loosed one arrow after the other, Niel's concentration didn't waver. Unlike his wife, he didn't glance away, didn't fret about what others thought of him.

Looking on, Beth thought that in itself was an example of how males and females differed. It was one of the reasons why men ruled the world and women did not.

The watching crowd erupted in cheers when Niel lowered the bow after firing his sixth arrow.

The range master was all smiles as he slapped the clan-chief on the back.

Indeed, four bullseyes at a fifty-yard distance wasn't bad at all.

Niel was smiling when he turned back to Beth, his eyes gleaming with victory. Meeting her gaze, he then winked. "How was that?"

16

NEVER LET YER FOE SCARE YE

HIS WIFE WAS vexed. Aye, she hid it well, yet Niel noted the strain in her smile, the tension in her jaw.

Beth didn't like that he'd bested her at archery.

The realization came as a surprise to Niel. He'd never come across a woman with such a competitive streak as Beth. Frankly, her skill with a bow had also surprised him. George Munro had clearly taken an unorthodox view with rearing his four daughters. Perhaps the man had missed not having sons to instruct, and so had let his eldest daughter fulfill that role.

Beth's aim was true, and her first three shots had worried him.

But then, after she'd glanced his way, her focus hadn't been quite the same.

He'd unnerved her.

Smiling at the onlookers, who still cheered him, Niel stepped away from the archery range, looped his arm through his wife's, and led them back into the crowd.

He leaned close to Beth, inhaling the scent of rosemary from her hair as he murmured. "Never let yer foe scare ye, lass."

As he'd expected, his wife's arm went rigid around his. Her chin kicked up, her hazel eyes locking with his. "Is that what we are ... *foes*?" she replied tightly.

Niel grinned down at her. "When we're competing against each other, we are."

Beth's mouth pursed. "I wasn't scared."

"Aye, ye were ... ye started worrying what I'd do if ye won. It threw ye."

The look on her face told him he'd indeed scored another bullseye.

Moments passed while Beth clearly struggled not to make a tart comment. Niel could see her inner battle, one she eventually mastered. And as he watched her, he realized that he'd enjoyed competing against her.

There had been something alluring in the way his wife handled a longbow. He liked the determined set of her shoulders, the fire in her eyes as she loosed each arrow.

Her manner today reminded him of how she'd locked horns with him during their wedding banquet. Ever since then, she hadn't challenged him again. Instead, Beth's manner had been generally obliging and gently-spoken. Apart from requesting he join her today, she'd asked little of him.

Niel had sensed her demureness was merely a façade, yet he hadn't complained. He'd liked that Beth had allowed him to set the boundaries of their relationship.

But today, her demure front crumbled.

Niel's grin faded. He didn't want her to start demanding things from him.

It was just as well he'd bested her at archery.

"Why don't ye go and join yer sisters for a while?" he suggested casually. "I'm going to test myself at the hammer throw."

Her pretty face tensed, and he saw disappointment darken her eyes.

Irritation tightened Niel's belly—at himself for being observant enough to sense his wife's mood, and at Beth for wishing him to remain glued to her side all afternoon.

The press of the crowd already set his teeth on edge; he didn't need his wife suffocating him as well.

"I'll join ye later," he promised, disengaging his arm and stepping away from her. And then, before she could protest, Niel turned on his heel and strode off.

He felt Beth's gaze upon him as he did so.

Irritation surged once more, and he clenched his hands at his sides.

Enough of this nonsense. He could tell Beth wished to get closer to him, for them to develop a bond, but Niel's skin itched at the thought. He was happy as things were. He didn't want things to change.

Women weakened men. The likes of Connor and Morgan might deny it, yet both men had lost their edge since they'd fallen in love with their wives. Niel couldn't risk that—not with his reckoning against the Gunns so close now.

Weaving through the crowd, Niel headed toward the hammer throw. On the way, he caught the savory aroma of mutton pies. There was a stand nearby, and his belly growled in answer. As such, he made a detour.

He'd almost reached the stand when a heavy-set man stepped into his path.

Niel skidded to a halt to prevent himself colliding with him, his gaze raking over the fellow.

The stranger had a scowling face and heavy brow. He was hulking in size, with massive arm and shoulder muscles.

Niel didn't think he'd met this man before, and yet there was something familiar about him—something he couldn't quite place. His dark hair was cut short against his scalp, a severe style that just made the man's appearance more thuggish. But it was his eyes that caught Niel's attention: purple-grey, like storm clouds. Niel had seen eyes of that hue before, yet he couldn't remember where.

"Afternoon, laird," the man greeted him, his voice a low rumble.

"Afternoon," Niel replied warily. There was something about this man that made his hackles rise—and it wasn't just his intimidating size or scowling face.

"Can I have a quick word?" the stranger asked, stepping closer.

Niel cocked an eyebrow. "Aye?"

The man's gaze locked with his. "I've heard whispers that ye intend to move soon against the Gunns."

"What business is it of yers?"

The man's gaze never wavered. "I wish to aid ye."

Niel's mouth curved into a hard smile. "And what's yer name?"

The stranger's lips thinned, his grey eyes hardening. "Roy Morrison." He moved closer still so that the pair of them were standing chest-to-chest, nearly touching. They were roughly the same height, so they ended up eye-balling each other. The crowd swirled around them. No one seemed to be paying much attention to the pair of them.

The reek of stale sweat filled Niel's nostrils, and he fought the urge to pull a face. Aggression rippled off this stranger in waves. The man was standing too close—and would receive a punch to the guts if he attempted to move any nearer.

"Out with it then," Niel said through gritted teeth.

Morrison's lips curved. "If ye are waiting for the Gunns to make the first move, ye will be disappointed … Tavish Gunn won't attack ye."

The way the man spat out the name of the Gunn clan-chief piqued Niel's attention. There was hatred there: white-hot, venomous loathing. Morrison was no friend of the Gunns. Instead, Niel wagered that he bore them a deep grudge.

Finally, the man was speaking Niel's language. Revenge was something he understood.

"He's above such things now is he?" Niel asked, his lip curling. "That hasn't stopped the Gunns from raiding our border villages."

Morrison's face twisted. "Raids are one thing … an open challenge is another. Gunn wishes to keep the peace. If ye want him to come to ye, I suggest ye provoke him."

Niel inclined his head. "I'm listening."

"Dounreay is where ye should strike."

Niel frowned. Dounreay sat just beyond the Strathnaver-Caithness border, a wild area on the northwest coast.

"How so?"

"It once belonged to the Mackays, did it not?" Morrison said with a thin smile. "Until old Iain Gunn tore it from ye?"

Niel frowned. Indeed, it had.

"It's good land ... excellent grazing for sheep and cattle. Its villages prosper these days. Perhaps it's time ye took Dounreay back."

Niel didn't answer immediately. Instead, he stared back at this stranger, taking his measure. In truth, he hadn't considered the northwest as the right place to strike the Gunns. His plans had been focused more on the mountainous area that formed their eastern border.

However, this man had a point. Dounreay was valuable—and attacking it would enrage Tavish Gunn.

Maybe he would discuss this as an option with his chieftains this eve, once they had all arrived. Even so, Niel was a little disappointed with Morrison's suggestion. From his attitude, he'd expected something more dramatic. Aye, the man had given him a location for a possible attack—but nothing more. "Is that it?" he drawled.

The man stepped away then, mercifully taking the reek of stale sweat with him. However, his gaze burned. "It's just a suggestion, Mackay," he growled. "Do with it what ye will."

"And what's it to ye, Morrison?" Niel demanded. He already sensed that this man sought vengeance, yet he wished for him to admit it.

"Let's just say that it's personal between me and Tavish Gunn ... and that being so, I wish to see him cut down," the man admitted, his reply irritatingly vague. "Make sure that ye face him in battle ... and that he kisses steel."

Niel frowned. "Who *are* ye?"

"Someone whose advice ye should heed," Morrison replied evasively. "Good day, laird."

And with that, the big man turned and shouldered his way through the crowd. Niel watched him go, wondering at the strange encounter and whether he could trust the advice of such an individual.

~ 143 ~

Roy Gunn walked away from the Mackay clan-chief with a smile upon his face.

Seven long years he'd waited to have his reckoning upon his elder brother—and there had been times when he'd almost despaired.

After he'd tried—and failed—to kill Tavish, he'd been banished from the Gunn territory, on pain of death, and in the years following had moved around the Highlands. He'd been forced to adopt a new identity, to learn a skill so he wouldn't starve. Roy Morrison was now a blacksmith, and he'd discovered that he had a real talent for the craft.

Like Alexander.

Roy's mouth thinned. Aye, it was an irony both exiled Gunn brothers had turned to the same trade. Roy had heard that his elder brother was now Farr Castle's blacksmith.

There was no danger of him living like a peasant now—for his skills were in demand wherever he went. He should have started afresh, should have left the past behind him. But he couldn't.

Every night, he lay abed thinking of the various ways he'd like to kill Tavish: all of them methods that involved extracting the most pain possible before he ended him.

Those fantasies drove him on, even as his frustration grew.

To return to Castle Gunn and wield a knife against his brother would be foolish indeed. Roy had no intention of martyring himself in order to gain his revenge.

Instead, he'd ensure it was Niel Mackay that brought Tavish Gunn down.

Still smiling at his cleverness, Roy made his way through the crowd.

The fair was still in full swing, and a woman's voice rose amongst the din. Her singing was lovely, and Roy's stride slowed. His errand done, he'd planned to leave Tongue, yet the song made him linger.

Turning, he let his gaze travel over the clusters of stalls selling hot food, to the podium where a troupe performed a courtly dance—in contrast to the lively jig he'd spied earlier.

The singer stood to their right.

It was a haunting song—one that told of forbidden love between a laird's daughter and one of his men, and the tragedy that befell them both—but it wasn't the song that caught Roy's attention so completely.

It was the woman who sang it.

Roy's breathing slowed as he stared at her. Never had he seen such a lovely creature. She was small in stature and lithe, with chestnut brown hair tumbling down her back and elfin features that made her look like a faery lass.

Entranced, Roy moved closer, his gaze taking in the plum-colored kirtle that hugged her willowy frame. He noted that she had luminous green eyes flecked with brown and rose-bud lips.

And she sang like an angel fallen from the stars.

Warmth spread over Roy, and for a few instants, he forgot his quest for revenge, forgot the hatred that pulsed within him.

For the first time in the thirty-one years of his life, Roy Gunn found himself utterly ensnared by a woman. He'd never considered taking a wife—after years of enjoying the servants at Castle Gunn, he preferred to relieve himself with whores instead these days—but in just a few instants, he re-evaluated his decision.

If he had a woman like this one, he'd never darken the door of a brothel again.

The songbird continued, her luscious mouth curved as if she were inwardly smiling at a secret only she and Roy shared.

Roy's pulse quickened, and he licked his suddenly parched lips.

His reason for visiting Tongue was complete. The Mackay hadn't given his word that he'd take Roy's advice, yet he'd done what he could to convince him. To push it any further would only draw unwelcome attention upon himself. Roy had been planning on traveling south afterward, to find work near Inverness for a spell.

However, the sight of this beauty made him change his mind. Instead, he would linger at this fair awhile and gaze upon her some more, and then he would visit the local forge.

Perhaps it required a smith.

17

NO TURNING BACK

"THIS IS THE best fair I've ever been to," Eilidh exclaimed as she rejoined Beth and Jean. "I didn't expect so many people to attend." She'd just been on stage with the dancers, while Neave had dazzled the crowd with her lovely voice. The onlookers applauded lustily, and Neave favored them with a smile in return.

"More!" a man called out. "Give us another song, lass!"

"Folk have come from all over the territory," Jean replied, raising her voice to be heard over the din. "Look ... the Mackays of Farr have just arrived."

Following her sister's gaze, Beth looked right to see, indeed, a knot of newcomers were making their way through the press. Connor Mackay's golden mane was distinctive, and hard to miss, as was the height of him and his brother. Both men towered over many others in the crowd.

At that moment, Neave began another song. This one was livelier than the last, and the dancers gave a whoop and started to whirl. Eilidh gave a squeal, and Beth glanced back to see her sister pick up her skirts and hurriedly rejoin them upon the dais. However, Jean remained steadfastly at Beth's side. Although Jean had danced during Beth and Niel's wedding celebrations, her sister's serious, shy nature meant that she usually avoided drawing attention to herself.

Smiling, Beth swiveled to focus on the Mackays of Farr once more. Keira, Maggie, and their brood of offspring followed in their menfolk's wake. Spying Beth and her sisters, Maggie waved.

Beth waved back, although her attention didn't remain upon Maggie for long—for she caught sight of her husband making his way toward the brothers. Niel embraced them both, a warm smile illuminating his features.

Beth tensed, her own smile fading. She never saw such warmth on Niel's face when he looked at her.

For a short while earlier, she'd thought she was making a breakthrough. Niel had revealed that his time at Bass Rock had made him leery of crowds, and he'd agreed to compete at archery with her.

But in the aftermath, he'd stepped away from her.

It hadn't helped that she'd been a poor loser. She wasn't usually—but the situation had needled her, vexed her. She'd wanted her husband to notice her, and he had—just not in the light she'd hoped. Beth had berated herself for her reaction afterward, but it was too late now.

Niel had been only too eager to send her away, to rejoin her sisters while he was free to enjoy the fair on his own.

Drawing in a deep breath, Beth curled her hands into fists while frustration beat like a Beltaine drum within her.

Even though she'd gotten him to accompany her to the fair, there was still a gulf between her and Niel. Despite the time they'd spent together today, she wasn't being herself around her husband.

Week after week of this—of pretending to be someone she wasn't, of swallowing comments because she didn't want to come across as too demanding or opinionated, of not telling him when he behaved in ways that disappointed her—was taking its toll. She was tired of sleeping alone every night, of feeling neglected.

Demure and obedient be damned.

She needed to be honest with him—if she wasn't, she would explode.

"Can ye trust such a man?" John Mackay's question carried across the long table. "I'm not sure I would."

"I agree with John," Connor replied. He reached over and refilled his goblet of wine from a ewer at the table's center. "Roy Morrison sounds like a shifty bastard."

This comment caused laughter to ripple down the table.

However, Niel didn't join in the mirth. Instead, he looked down at the map he'd unscrolled before them.

The men sat alone in the great hall. Supper had come and gone, their womenfolk had all retired, and the servants had cleared up. The only witnesses to their conversation were a pair of Niel's wolfhounds that lounged next to one of the hearths.

Niel ran his finger across the territory of Strathnaver to the coast before tracing it north.

"The man had a point though," he mused. "Dounreay is in Caithness now ... but it once belonged to us." He glanced up, his gaze spearing Connor. "And it once belonged to yer grandfather."

Connor held his eye. "Aye ... it did."

"And don't ye wish to reclaim it?"

In that instant, Niel saw heat flare in Connor's gaze, giving his answer. Connor Mackay of Farr didn't need to reply. The tightening of his jaw, the way his dark-green eyes gleamed, told Niel all he required.

Connor wanted that land back.

"There's another issue with this ye might not have thought of," Robin spoke up then, his voice low and gruff as if he was unused to speaking. "The folk of Dounreay have lived amongst the Gunns for a while now ... they might not take kindly to us taking our land back."

Niel waved him off. "They won't have any choice in the matter." His gaze swept down the table to where

Hugh had been observing the exchange. "Ye've been quiet, Hugh … what say ye to this idea?"

Hugh leaned forward, his grizzled eyebrows drawing together as he viewed the map. "It's a bold move," he allowed. "And one sure to jab a stick in the hornet's nest."

"Aye," John agreed with a rueful smile. "Gunn will come at us with a pitchfork if ye claim those lands as yer own."

Niel leaned back in his chair, his fingers drumming on the carven armrests. "Aye, John … that's the point," he replied, his voice lowering.

Inhaling deeply, Niel considered what his chieftains had just said. A few of them around the table had remained silent, but that didn't bother him. He could see from the looks on their faces, the steadiness of their gazes, that they'd follow him.

"The decision is made then," he said finally. "We shall march on Dounreay. With the Munro warriors already here, I have no reason to delay any longer." He paused once more, a hard smile stretching his lips. "Return to yer holdings, gather yer warriors, and join me. Summer is upon us, lads … it's time to go to war. Tavish Gunn will no doubt expect me to attack at some stage—but he won't anticipate us striking Dounreay."

Beth paced the floor of the clan-chief's solar, awaiting her husband's arrival.

She didn't usually spend time in here on her own, for this was Niel's domain.

Nonetheless, Beth wasn't in the mood to join their female guests and her sisters in the women's solar this evening. Instead, she'd told them she was tired and would retire to her bed-chamber. She'd purposely avoided being alone with Keira and Maggie today—for she knew they'd both be eager to know how things were progressing with Niel. Meanwhile, her sisters were in high spirits after spending the day at the fair, and their excited chatter stretched her already taut nerves to breaking point.

Greta had offered to help her ready herself for bed, but Beth had assured the maid she could undress herself for once. Only she hadn't gone to her bed-chamber, but to her husband's solar. And as time inched by, and the hour grew late, Beth's nerves started to get the better of her.

I must speak frankly with him, she reminded herself. *Enough of this mummery.*

Aye, she'd made a start at the fair, before the archery contest, but tonight she was out of patience.

The whoosh of the door opening behind her made Beth whirl around, heart pounding as if she'd been caught up to no good.

Niel entered, thankfully on his own, surprise flickering across his face when he spied her. "Ye are up late, Beth," he greeted her. "I thought ye'd spend the eve catching up with Keira and Maggie."

Beth turned to face him squarely, swallowing to ease the lump in her throat. Mother Mary, this man made her so nervous. In the past, she'd have smoothed her discomfort by making a light comment about her sisters' prattle or the fact she was tired.

But not so now. This evening, she wished to be open with him.

"I didn't want to pass the eve with them," she replied, cursing the huskiness to her voice. "Instead, I'd like to speak with my husband."

Niel inclined his head, closing the solar door behind him. "Is something wrong?"

"Aye." The admission came out in a croak, not with the poise that Beth had intended. But now that she'd begun, she plowed on. "I'm unhappy with how things are between us, Niel."

Such a bald statement brought her husband to an abrupt halt. He'd been moving from the door toward her, yet his penetrating gaze now pinned her to the spot. "Excuse me?"

"I feel as if I'm married to a stranger. I don't mind running yer household, yet ye treat me as if I am of as much consequence as one of yer hounds or horses: to do as bid yet demand nothing." Beth broke off there before heaving in a deep breath. "And I cannot stand it."

Under the light tan that the warm summer had given him, Niel's face paled. "I've never mistreated ye, Beth," he replied, his tone soft, yet his eyes had narrowed. "Few women marry as well as ye have."

Heat washed over Beth. He was insinuating that she was ungrateful.

"I'm aware of my 'good fortune'," she countered, clenching her hands at her sides. "And that a woman who buried the three men she was supposed to wed shouldn't end up receiving a proposal from a clan-chief … but I cannot help what I feel."

Niel's sharp features tightened at this admission. However, his gaze never left her face as he moved forward, closing the gap between them. "And what is it exactly ye want?" he asked, his voice roughening.

"I want a husband who shares some of himself with me," she replied without hesitation. Finally, the question she'd longed to hear. "I wish for tenderness, to spend our nights in the same bed, for ye to *talk* to me." She paused then, her breathing coming in short gasps now, such was the force of the emotions roiling inside her. "Most of the time, it feels as if ye look right through me, Niel. Am I that insignificant to ye?"

Her husband continued to hold her gaze. His expression was difficult to read. At first glance, he looked vexed: there was a deep groove between his eyebrows, and his jaw had tightened. Yet she marked the way a nerve flickered in his throat, and how his eyes shadowed. "Of course ye aren't," he said after a pause. "Ye are my wife, and I have treated ye as such."

"And what is a wife? Someone to keep the servants in check and bear yer bairns? What about companionship, intimacy?"

Niel swallowed, tension rippling through his tall, lean body. "I can't give ye those things."

A heartbeat passed before Beth's belly twisted. "Why not?"

Niel's mouth thinned, and then he turned from her and went to the sideboard, pouring himself some wine. Raising it to his lips, he drained the wine in one gulp. Beth could sense his quickening temper, yet she stood her ground. She'd known this exchange wouldn't be an easy one, but there was no turning back now. She'd taken this path, and she'd follow it—right to the bitter end.

"That's not the way I am," he said finally.

Heat washed over Beth once more, her own anger rising. "That's a poor answer," she snapped. "And not one I'm willing to accept."

Niel slammed the cup down and whirled around, his gaze hard. "I don't answer to ye, Beth."

She held his gaze, even as her pulse fluttered in the hollow of her neck under the force of his wintry anger. "Why not?"

"Because ye are my wife," he growled, approaching her now. His stalking gait made Beth's knees tremble. For the first time ever, she was wary of her husband. "And ye clearly forget yer place."

18

PROVE IT

BETH INHALED SHARPLY, fury beating like angry fists against her ribs. It was the only thing that made her hold fast as her husband loomed over her. This close, the heat of his body enveloped her, as did his scent. Awareness prickled Beth's skin, despite her anger.

Curse her, why was she even attracted to this man?

Bull-headed, arrogant, and as inflexible as a lump of granite—she'd made a mistake in agreeing to wed him.

Beth had a passionate nature. She was also observant and clever and liked to share her thoughts with those closest to her. Aye, she had her sisters with her at Castle Varrich—and that was just as well—but the person she wanted to be closest to was her husband.

Niel had just informed her that he would never let her in.

"Mark me, Beth," he continued, his voice low and hard. "I will ensure ye live in comfort and safety ... that our bairns want for nothing ... but I can't be the man ye dream of." His lip curled then. "I doubt such a paragon of virtue exists."

"They do," she countered, her gaze never leaving his. "My father treated my mother like a queen ... and he does the same with Laila. And I've seen how Connor and Morgan Mackay adore their wives ... ye'd have to be blind not to notice too."

She noted then how a nerve in Niel's cheek jumped. Aye, he had.

"I'm not asking for the moon and stars ... just a little warmth," she continued. "And I think all this talk of wives 'knowing their place' is rot." Beth lifted her chin a little higher then, in a direct challenge. "In truth, I believe ye are scared of me."

Niel's gaze widened. An instant later, he barked a laugh. "Scared ... of *ye*?"

Beth had to admit the notion was ridiculous. Why would this warrior fear the likes of her? However, Beth knew that there were different kinds of fear and that sometimes physical courage was easier than baring one's soul.

"Aye, yer years in prison have left a scar ... I know ye seek solitude more than most, that ye sometimes retreat into yer own thoughts, even in the midst of conversation ... but that isn't the whole story, is it?" She stared him down. "The truth is, ye aren't comfortable sharing yerself with others, women especially ... and I'd wager ye have always been this way."

She broke off then, breathing hard.

Niel went still.

Bullseye.

Beth had loosed a number of verbal arrows at her husband since he'd entered the solar, and most of them had merely bounced off his shields.

But this one had hit home.

"Aye ... that's why ye won't share yer bed with me," she plowed on. "Why ye won't even kiss me. Ye *are* afraid to kiss me, aren't ye?"

His dark brows drew together. "No," he replied roughly.

"Prove it."

Heart pounding, Beth stepped closer to him so that they were merely inches apart. He'd provoked her into this, and yet under her burning temper, she quailed. She hadn't intended to take her husband on so aggressively. Her own boldness shocked her.

So much for a wife knowing her place. A pox on that!

Any moment now, he'd likely raise a hand and strike her.

Her father had never hit Beth and her sisters, or either of his wives, but she'd heard that many men had foul tempers and wouldn't let their women best them in an argument.

With her last accusation, Beth had turned their exchange in her favor. She'd exposed him—yet she'd gone too far. What the devil was she doing provoking him so?

Beth's jaw clenched, and she braced herself for his anger.

But her husband didn't hit her. Nor did he curse or insult her. Instead, Niel hauled her into his arms, his mouth crushing against hers in a bruising kiss.

Beth's gasp of shock cut off as he possessively pulled her body flush with his.

And then, leaning her back over his arm, he ravaged her mouth.

The kiss was wild, brutal—and once Beth recovered from his unexpected move, she responded with equal savagery.

Finally. He was giving her what she'd craved for weeks now.

It seemed that words just made things worse between them. But this kiss tore through it all. Niel was angry with her—but at least she'd penetrated his armor.

Need spiked through Beth with such force that she whimpered against his mouth.

This kiss was honest.

Niel might not like to admit it, but there was a connection between them—there had been from the first instant they'd locked gazes in the bailey the day she'd arrived at Castle Varrich. He'd deliberately shut her out: he knew she affected him yet was determined to resist it.

The passionate onslaught continued, and as it did, Niel's kisses softened. They'd almost been punishing in the beginning, yet now they grew increasingly sensual as he teased her lips with his teeth, his tongue mating with hers in a glide that turned the cradle of Beth's hips molten.

Hades, this man could kiss. Why had he denied them both this?

Her past suitors had favored her with a kiss or two, and she'd enjoyed them. But this embrace was something else. If other men's kisses had warmed her like she'd been seated by a glowing hearth in winter, Niel Mackay's kiss was like being consumed by the flames themselves.

Sweat beaded across her skin, and her heart drummed against her breastbone.

She never wanted him to stop.

And he didn't.

The kiss went on and on, gentle and then hard, fierce and then sensual. Niel gave no quarter, and neither did she. Although, if he hadn't been holding her up, she would have melted onto the floor like tallow.

And then, just when Beth's head started to spin from lack of air and the heat that pulsed between them, Niel walked her back to the oaken table that dominated the solar.

He lifted her up onto it and dragged her skirts up to her hips.

Beth gave a soft groan as his lips grazed the column of her throat, his fingers deftly unlacing the front of her kirtle.

An instant later, he'd pushed the garment down to her waist. The sound of rending fabric followed as Niel ripped open the thin lèine she wore under it.

Beth's gasp of surprise turned to cries of pleasure as he lowered himself before her and started to suckle her breasts.

He did so with the same fierceness that he'd kissed her with, drawing each swollen nipple deep into his mouth and suckling until she groaned and writhed against him, her fingers digging into his scalp, urging him on.

Niel continued his exquisite torture of her breasts awhile, and when he drew back, his eyes gleamed with passion and his lips were swollen. His gaze seared hers an instant, and then he dropped to his knees before her, pushing her thighs wide, and baring her to him.

He moved close, his teeth grazing the soft skin of her inner thigh—and then, to Beth's shock, he kissed her there, in her most intimate spot.

In all the times he'd taken her since their wedding, he'd never done such an act.

Beth's shock lasted only an instant as the sensual dance of his lips and tongue drove all thought from her mind.

Beth gripped the table edge as tremors rippled through her lower abdomen and thighs. The pleasure he was giving her, the intimacy of it, unraveled her completely.

Arching back, her eyes fluttering closed, Beth's cries echoed through the solar.

She wasn't quiet. The noise she was making might bring servants running. And if they burst into this chamber, they'd be welcomed with a quite a scene: the lady of the keep half-naked and writhing on the table, with the clan-chief's head buried between her thighs.

But Beth didn't care. They could have had an audience of hundreds, and she wouldn't have paid them any mind.

She was completely lost.

With a guttural cry, Beth bucked violently then, shattering against Niel's mouth.

Breathing hard, he rose to his feet, and through half-closed lids, she watched as he began to unlace his braies.

Pushing herself up, Beth leaned forward and reached for him. She had to touch his naked skin, had to feel him against her, inside her. Her hands trembled when she lifted his lèine, her fingers tracing the hard planes of his belly.

She lifted the tunic higher, a whimper of frustration escaping her. Sensing her need to see him, Niel stopped unlacing his braies and helped her, shrugging off his lèine.

Beth leaned in, tasting his skin. The firelight gilded her husband's lean body, highlighting the well-defined muscles he'd worked hard to build since his return to

Castle Varrich. He was no longer as lean as a hound; instead, he was strong, fighting fit.

Beth's tongue traced down his breastbone before she nipped one of his nipples gently with her teeth.

Niel's swiftly indrawn breath emboldened her, and she trailed kisses down his chest to his belly.

He'd released his shaft from the prison of his braies. It thrust up proud and eager.

"Oh, Niel," she whispered, aching for him. "Ye are beautiful."

Her small hand wrapped around his girth, reveling in the contrast between the velvet skin and the steel underneath. This was the first time he'd allowed her to touch him like this.

Hunger twisted in her belly, and she wriggled forward, intending to slide off the table onto her knees before him. She wanted to pleasure him as he had her.

However, Niel halted her.

Taking her wrists, he drew them back behind her, placing her hands firmly upon the table. The position caused Beth's breasts to thrust up into his face, and with a growled curse, he released her wrists and cupped her breasts, pushing them together so that he could bury his face in them.

An instant later, he reared back, parted her thighs wide, and thrust deep into her.

A cry tore from Beth's throat. Niel had never taken her at this angle before. He filled her completely, his shaft touching her in places that caused her limbs to tremble, caused her to writhe. Pleasure coiled in her lower belly, and sweat bathed her skin.

Heavens, this felt so good she thought she might faint.

"Aye," she gasped. "Like this, Niel!"

His mouth claimed hers then, in a wild kiss that made her reach for him again. She wanted to trail her fingers over his sweat-slicked body, wanted to drag her nails down his back.

But he took hold of her wrists once more and shifted them back behind her, making it clear where he wanted her. The move was dominant, and the aching pleasure in Beth's womb wound tighter.

He started to move inside her then, and his tongue mimicked the slide of his shaft.

Beth gave herself up to him, her arms trembling as she leaned her weight back on her hands and let him take her as he wished.

Even though she wasn't allowed to touch him, she could feel the tremors in his body every time he thrust deep into her. Niel was on the verge of losing control.

With each glide, each thrust, tension mounted within Beth. And when he spread her wider still, angling himself high inside her, she splintered.

Crying out against his mouth, she went over the edge. Beth's arms gave way, and she would have fallen back against the table if Niel hadn't caught her. He pulled her hard against him, his arms wrapping around her back. And then, tearing his mouth from hers, he buried his face in her neck and thrust deep once more.

She felt his climax barrel into him, felt the heat of him empty inside her, felt the waves of it pulse through him as they clung together, sweat-slicked and panting.

Long moments passed afterward.

For a while, Beth was incapable of speech, incapable of thought. Instead, her world had shrunk to this chamber, this table—to the man who crushed her in his embrace as if he was afraid she'd slip away from him.

This man who until now had held himself back with her.

Eventually, Beth's racing pulse slowed, and as it did, her world expanded. She became aware of the hard polished surface of the table under her backside, of the warm evening air tickling her bare skin.

And, gradually, Niel's hold on her loosened.

He stepped back from her, withdrawing himself from inside her.

The heavy drag of his shaft, the feel of his warm seed upon her thighs, caused heat to flicker to life once more in Beth's lower belly.

She couldn't get enough of him.

Niel straightened up then, and their gazes met.

His chest still rose and fell sharply, a sign he'd not yet recovered from the passion of their joining. His gaze glittered. "Was that proof enough for ye, wife?" he asked hoarsely.

Beth stared up at him. She didn't answer. Frankly, she had no words—not after what had just happened.

But Niel did. "I can't be the man ye want." The words came forth jerkily as if it was an effort for him to speak. His face was all taut angles. "As such, we will not be sharing a bed, and I will not be baring my soul to ye." He paused then, their gazes fusing. "Ye must accept that."

Beth's breathing hitched. A chill washed over her, dousing the languorous warmth of their coupling. She wanted to answer him, yet Niel's words were like a rude slap to the face. Her husband had just made his position clear. She'd believed tonight had been a bridge, a breakthrough, but she was wrong. Niel had used it to prove a point.

He didn't even bother to make excuses this time. He wasn't scared of her. He just didn't want to be close to her.

No plea from her would change his mind.

Niel relaced his braies, scooped up his lèine from the floor, and turned from her.

Beth watched her husband leave the solar and enter his bed-chamber, closing the door firmly behind him. And as he did, she clenched her hands around the table edge, her fingernails biting into the wood.

Icy shock drained away, and fire pulsed in her belly.

Twice now, her husband had wielded physical intimacy like a weapon. On their wedding night, he'd used it to gain her trust before sending her from his bed. And now, he'd exercised it to assert his dominance over her.

Beth glared at the closed door, her jaw clenched.

There won't be a third time, Mackay.

And this eve, unlike their wedding night, there would be no tears.

19

IN CONTROL

NIEL SHUT THE door and leaned against it.

His breathing was coming in short, sharp bursts now, and his pulse throbbed in his ears. His legs felt weak, as if they could barely support him, and his chest ached.

Ye are one nasty bastard, Mackay, his conscience needled him. *How could ye do that to her?*

His wife, who usually had a pert answer and a defiant look, had stared at him with such shock that it had taken everything he had to turn his back on her.

God's blood, the woman wasn't asking for the sky. All she wanted was a husband who shared some of himself with her.

A decent man would give her what she deserved.

But he wasn't decent.

Reaching up, Niel rubbed the ache under his breastbone. His chest hadn't hurt so cruelly in a long while, not since his father's betrayal.

She's seen right through me.

The truth of it was that, even before Bass Rock, Niel had been guarded with women. He'd liked to flirt, and he'd enjoyed a few conquests, but he'd never let any of his lovers in.

He'd never delved into the reasons—for he hadn't cared to—but now he knew there was indeed something wrong with him.

There was a piece of him missing.

Had he ever cared about anything deeply? Aye, despite the tension in his parents' marriage, he'd once worshipped his father, favoring the charismatic clan-chief over his timid mother—but his father had utterly betrayed him, and these days, the only thing that moved him was the desire for revenge.

Whispering a curse, Niel closed his eyes and leaned his head back against the door. Deathly silence reached him from the other side. Beth hadn't left the solar, nor could he hear her weeping.

Go back in there. His conscience stabbed at him once more. *Get down on yer knees before that lass and apologize. Swear that ye will do yer best to let her into yer heart.*

Niel swallowed hard, heat sweeping through him. The constriction in his chest moved up to his throat now, making it hard to breathe. Panic had him in its grip. He started to sweat.

No, he wouldn't be returning to his solar tonight. Nor would he be taking back the words he'd uttered. As hurtful as they'd been, they were the truth.

Niel Mackay was incapable of love.

"Have ye heard? War is upon us."

Keira's voice made Beth glance up from where she was mixing batter for blaeberry cakes in the kitchen. It was that quiet time of day when the cooks and servants all took a well-earned rest, when she had this space to herself. Usually, one of her sisters would join her—Jean especially enjoyed assisting her—but today Beth had chosen to bake alone.

However, Keira's announcement drew Beth from her concentration. The Lady of Farr stood in the doorway, her face pale and strained.

Beth stiffened. "So soon?" She'd thought Niel's campaign was still another month off. He hadn't mentioned anything to her the day before—although, in truth, other matters had occupied them.

"I've just spoken to Connor," Keira continued with a frown. "Niel has decided to strike against the Gunns earlier than planned. Morgan has ridden back to Farr to gather our men. Niel and Connor will join them on their journey north."

"North?"

"Aye, they intend to take back the old Mackay lands at Dounreay ... to provoke the Gunns into battle."

The women's gazes fused. There was no mistaking the edge to Keira's voice.

Keira Mackay had been born Keira *Gunn*, the daughter of a wealthy sheep farmer and wool merchant.

"Do ye fear for yer kin?" Beth asked.

Keira shook her head, waving the comment away with a hand. "The Mackays are my kin now," she assured her. "No, I fear for Connor and Morgan ... and all the Mackays who will follow Niel into battle."

Tearing her gaze from Keira's, Beth added a cup of blaeberries—small blue tart berries some of the servants had collected from a nearby valley—to the batter. She then started to fold them in. Blaeberries reminded her of her father. George Munro had a fondness for these cakes. They would be served at this eve's supper.

"Niel has been impatient to attack the Gunns," Beth admitted. "But I haven't heard him mention Dounreay before now."

"Connor said that Niel spoke to a man at the fair yesterday ... who advised him it was the right place to attack." The flat tone to Keira's voice told Beth what her friend thought of the decision.

Beth frowned at this news. She wondered who could have wielded such influence upon her headstrong husband.

"When exactly are they leaving?" she asked after a pause.

"In four days. Robin Mackay and some of the others who reside nearby have already gone off to rally their warriors and bring them to Varrich ... the others will join them in the north."

Beth stilled. *Four days*. She had no desire to see Niel at present. Resentment still smoldered like a stoked ember within her whenever she thought about the man. Perhaps she could successfully avoid him until his departure. The thought of sitting next to him in the great hall at meals was too much. It was too raw, too humiliating. He'd kissed her, plowed her—merely to teach her a lesson.

He wasn't scared of her.

He wouldn't be influenced by her.

He was in control and always would be.

Like Keira, she didn't like the thought of her husband going into battle. But unlike her friend, there would be no heartfelt farewell, no loving words and tender kisses before he rode out.

The force of her own reaction to the night before surprised her. Right from the first day of their acquaintance, Niel Mackay had wielded a strange power over her. At times, she felt as if she were looking at a stranger, and yet there had been moments over the past weeks when she'd caught a glimpse of the man beneath the shield. From the beginning, she'd been attracted to Niel's strong, determined character. She also appreciated his intelligence, his dry sense of humor, that arrogant quirk of a smile that he sometimes favored her with. And her body sang every time he touched her.

Curse him for that.

Beth scowled then—and, of course, Keira noticed.

"Things haven't improved with Niel, have they?" she asked softly.

Beth shook her head, meeting her eye once more. "It's impossible ... *he's* impossible."

Keira's midnight-blue eyes shadowed. She would want to know why, yet Beth couldn't bring herself to speak of it again. Not at present.

The night before had left her humiliated.

All she could think about were his final words.

I will not be baring my soul to ye.

She'd already weathered her sisters' concern that morning when she joined them in the garden. All it had taken was her to answer Neave curtly over a trifling matter, and her sister had fixed her with a probing look.

"Have ye and Niel argued?" Neave had asked.

Beth had denied it, and apologized for her sharpness—but the expression on Neave's face told her she knew Beth wasn't telling the truth.

She didn't like lying to her sisters, but she couldn't bear to see the sympathy and worry in their eyes. Jean and Eilidh would fuss over her too, and ply her with well-intentioned advice.

Just as Keira would, if she confided in her. No, it was best to keep her lips sealed.

Shifting her attention back to her task, Beth moved away from Keira and transferred the batter to a row of small clay vessels that sat upon an iron tray. She then picked up the tray and slid it into the oven behind her.

Fortunately, the Lady of Farr didn't push her. "Once Connor leaves with Niel, I will travel back to Farr on my own," Keira announced after a pause. "Why don't ye join me ... perhaps some time away from Castle Varrich will do ye good?"

Beth turned to Keira to see she was smiling. Their gazes fused and held for long moments before the tension in Beth's shoulders eased a little. She wasn't one to run away, yet the strain of her relationship with Niel made the idea of taking a break appealing. She'd never seen Farr Castle and had heard it had a breathtaking setting upon cliffs looking out to sea.

"Are ye certain?" she replied, suddenly hesitant that her friend had merely made the offer out of pity. "I don't want to intrude."

Keira snorted. "Nonsense. Maggie and I will welcome the company." Her expression sobered then, her gaze shadowing once more. "We could *all* do with some distraction at present. I for one won't sleep easily until Connor returns home."

20

FAREWELL

"I NEED YE to leave at first light tomorrow, John," Niel informed his cousin as he spooned thickened cream onto the blaeberry cake before him. They were nearing the end of supper, and, as fine as it was, Niel found it difficult to concentrate on anything except his looming campaign. "How many warriors will ye be able to gather at Achness?"

John swallowed a mouthful of cake. "At least a hundred men ... possibly more."

Niel nodded. With all his chieftains—and some of his allies—contributing, their army would be a significant one. John had lingered at Varrich in order to help Niel rally his men, but it was time for him to return to Achness. Once he collected his warriors, his cousin would follow Niel and the bulk of their force north, serving as rearguard.

"All of us are ready." John met Niel's eye then, his jaw firming. "The Gunns won't know what hit them."

Niel flashed him a wolfish smile. "Aye."

John finished off his last bite of cake before letting out a sigh of pleasure. "These are delicious ... have ye taken on a new cook?"

"Not as far as I'm aware," Niel replied, still distracted by thoughts of war. "Although my wife has made some improvements to the kitchen of late."

"Beth baked these," Neave Munro informed him.

Beth's sister sat a little farther down the table, yet she'd caught the men's conversation. Usually, Neave spent mealtimes chattering away like a magpie to Beth,

Jean, and Eilidh. However, there was a gap between the laird and Neave this eve. Beth had sent word that she wasn't feeling well and wouldn't be joining them.

"Aye ... it was our mother's recipe," Jean added.

Niel eyed his sisters-by-marriage, paying proper attention to them for the first time since he'd sat down to his supper. All three lasses were watching him closely this eve, their brows furrowed.

Niel tensed. Beth was close to her sisters. Had she confided in them about what had happened the night before?

Heat washed over him.

Christ's bones, he hoped not. Although Niel told himself he didn't care what others thought of him, he wasn't proud of his behavior.

Suppressing a frown of his own, he picked up his cake and took a bite. The tang of blaeberry exploded in his mouth, complemented by the richness of the cream. Aye, his wife had considerable skill as a baker. Ever since her arrival at Castle Varrich, the quality of his meals had improved vastly. Not only did Beth lend her own skills in the kitchen, but she'd taken it upon herself to teach the cooks new recipes as well. Even Niel's morning bannocks were lighter, crispier.

The delicious cakes aside, Niel didn't appreciate the sisters' bold stares.

When Beth had asked him if her sisters could join her at Varrich, he'd agreed without giving it much thought. The Munro sisters were a busy brood. He'd noted that Eilidh and Neave worked tirelessly in the afternoons in the vegetable garden outside the curtain walls, a terrace of beds of onions, kale, turnips, and an array of other vegetables. Their industry pleased him. That garden had been Niel's mother's joy, but upon his return to Varrich, he'd seen how overgrown it had become.

But despite their hard work, Niel felt outnumbered by females at the table this evening, especially since Connor's wife, Keira, had also joined them for supper. All of his chieftains, save Connor, who'd depart with him in a few days, had already left to gather their warriors.

Over the past months, he'd learned that Munro women all had far too much to say for themselves.

"If I stay on at Varrich much longer, I'll run to fat," John said then, helping himself to yet another cake. "These are too good to resist."

Connor, who'd remained silent for most of the meal, snorted at this. "There's little chance of that ... I swear yer legs are hollow, man."

Niel's lips curved. Indeed, his cousin could eat. Although John had filled out a little over the years, what flesh he had was all muscle. The man was never idle either. If he wasn't training, he was busy helping Niel manage Varrich. John was a natural diplomat, something that came in useful during the weekly councils with Niel's tenants. In the case of disputes or crimes committed upon his lands, the clan-chief acted as a judge and an arbiter. They had another council organized for the following morning—the last before Niel marched to war.

"Well, save some for the rest of us," Neave replied, catching John's eye.

The laird of Achness favored Neave with a boyish grin before winking.

Niel took another bite of cake, and despite himself, glanced at the empty seat beside him.

His wife's absence shouldn't have bothered Niel, yet it did. Nonetheless, he knew why she was avoiding him.

Would she continue to do so until he left?

Irritation wreathed up within Niel at the thought, accompanied by an odd disquiet. Banishing both, he resolved not to let Beth intrude on his thoughts anymore tonight.

Upon the dawn of her husband's departure, Beth awoke early.

Greta would bring her up a platter with a wedge of bannock, butter, and honey, along with a cup of fresh milk to break her fast, but she didn't want to linger in this chamber.

Niel might take it upon himself to bid her farewell.

Nerves danced in her belly as she hurriedly dressed, her fingers fumbling in haste as she laced the front of her kirtle. She'd slip out of the keep and seek refuge in some quiet corner until he'd left.

Fazart, a voice needled her. *Since when did ye let a man cow ye?*

Beth's lips thinned. Since she'd wed a man incapable of feeling. The only thing Niel Mackay cared about was his quest for revenge against the Gunns. Well, he was getting his heart's desire now.

She'd managed to avoid him over the past days—although it wasn't difficult to evade someone who didn't usually seek her out. Ever since that fateful evening in the solar, Beth took all her meals in the women's solar or in her bed-chamber and sent Greta or one of her sisters down with her apologies.

And Niel hadn't come looking for her.

Tying her hair back in a loose braid, Beth set her jaw.

He might fall in battle. She reminded herself then. *Ye might never see him again.*

Her throat tightened. It was hard to imagine her brave husband never returning to Castle Varrich, yet it was foolish not to entertain the thought. She'd seen him fight in the practice yard, with John and the other warriors. He wouldn't be easy to bring down.

And yet, all it took was one well-placed blade to slay the mightiest warrior.

Drawing in a deep breath, Beth resolved to think no more on such things. Instead, she needed to find a hiding place. Hurrying from her bed-chamber, she took the stairwell down to the entrance hall and slipped out of the keep into the glimmering dawn.

A dew lay upon the ground, although the air had a sweetness to it that promised a warm day to come. The first rays of sun were peeking over the top of the keep, lightening the indigo sky, and despite the hour, men and horses filled the bailey. The rise and fall of gruff male voices, the snort of horses, and the jangle of bridles echoed off stone.

Beth's heart leaped, and she pulled the light woolen shawl she'd donned close. She hadn't expected there to be so many folk about yet. But a quick scan of the men below assured her that Niel wasn't present.

However, she did glimpse sight of Munro clansmen amongst the milling warriors. They bore their red and green clan sashes across their chests with pride. Beth's pulse quickened at the thought of any of them losing their lives in the coming conflict.

Bowing her head, lest any of the men spy her, she descended the steps and cut right, making her way to Varrich's chapel.

Her slippers scuffed on the sandstone blocks covering the floor as she stepped inside. Beth let the heavy oaken door whisper closed behind her, shutting out the sounds beyond, before she dragged in a deep breath, inhaling the scent of incense and the fatty odor of tallow from the banks of candles that burned along the walls and either side of the altar.

Although she wasn't an overly pious woman—among her sisters, only Jean was—Beth welcomed the solitude and sanctuary of the chapel. There was no sign of Father Lucas either. She could wait in here until Niel and his men departed—and judging from the industry outdoors, that moment wasn't far off.

Halfway down the aisle, Beth slid onto one of the wooden pews.

Seated there, she found it difficult not to fidget, not to let her mind run away with her. She needed something to occupy herself.

Inhaling deeply once more, she lowered herself to her knees upon a cushion, clasped her hands together—and started to pray. She might have not had Jean's dedication to the Lord, but she knew all the most common prayers off by heart. Their mother had ensured her daughters committed them to memory.

She wasn't sure how long she knelt there, whispering to the Virgin Mary, but it did indeed provide some distraction. The words also loosened the knots in her belly.

Beth had just murmured the last of the prayers she knew, when she heard the creak of the door opening behind her.

Her whispers died upon her lips, and she froze.

Booted feet approached—a man's long, determined stride—and Beth's heart bucked against her ribs.

He's found me.

Keeping her eyes clamped shut, her hands still clasped together in prayer, she willed him to turn around and leave her in peace.

Instead, he approached her pew, halting just behind her.

"Praying for my safe return, wife?" Niel's voice rumbled through the church.

Beth swallowed, inwardly cursing him. She *had* whispered a prayer to the Virgin that her arrogant husband might live through the coming battle, but she didn't feel like admitting such to him. Beth wasn't playing games. She wasn't trying to manipulate or wound him—for how could she hurt a man who didn't care for her?

"Or perhaps hoping that Tavish Gunn will sink his dirk into my belly."

Beth's eyes flew open, and she swiveled around, glaring at him. "Why the devil would I wish such a thing?"

Too late, she saw the slight curve to his mouth, the glint in his eyes. Curse him, Niel Mackay was teasing her. He didn't seem uncomfortable or embarrassed in her presence as she'd thought he might be. It was as if the other night hadn't happened.

Niel shrugged then. "Ye wouldn't be the first woman to wish her husband dead."

Beth flinched. Christ's bones, no wonder she'd been avoiding this man. How could he make light of such things? "I don't wish for that," she replied tightly.

Their gazes fused, and a brittle silence fell between them. Niel's expression sobered, and when he broke the hush, there was an edge to his voice. "Ye are a difficult woman to track down, Beth."

She resisted the urge to frown. "How did ye know I was here?"

"One of my men saw ye head toward the chapel earlier." He paused then, his gaze narrowing. "We haven't seen each other in days. Did ye really expect me to leave without saying 'farewell'?"

Beth squared her shoulders, lifting her chin. "Aye," she replied, aware of how cool and calm her voice was. Good—she'd been far too vulnerable with her husband of late. She needed to gather what little was left of her dignity and shield herself from him.

Niel's gaze shadowed. "And why's that?"

"Ye know why."

She wasn't going to engage in mummery with him. If he wanted to bid her farewell, then let him be done with it.

In truth, Niel's presence was doing strange things to her pulse.

The sight of him standing before her, clad in leather and mail, a dirk at his hip and a claidheamh-mòr strapped to his back, was distracting. This morning, Niel Mackay looked like the warrior he was: fell and proud. His dark hair fell over his shoulders, his sharp-featured face kissed by the glow of the nearby candles. She pitied any man who came within reach of his blade.

Another pause stretched between them, and Beth clenched her hands into fists at her sides. Clearly, her husband hadn't sought her out to apologize. Instead, he appeared to be waiting, as if he expected her to say something.

She wasn't sure what he wanted. Awkwardness twisted within her, and Beth cleared her throat. "I wish ye good fortune on yer quest for vengeance, husband," she said finally. "May it bring ye the relief ye seek."

His cobalt gaze glinted. "Aye, it will." There was no doubt in his voice, only unwavering purpose. He favored her with a nod then. "Take care, Beth ... I'm sure ye shall look after things well in my absence."

She nodded back, even if defiance arrowed through her. She hadn't told him that she wouldn't be remaining at Castle Varrich while he was away. Neave would fulfill the role of chatelaine admirably, while she accompanied Keira to Farr Castle. She wondered if she should let him know, yet something prevented her.

She wasn't sure if he'd deny her.

When Beth didn't say anything else, Niel stepped back, turned, and headed toward the chapel door. He'd almost reached it when Beth called to him. Blood roared in her ears now, her heart pounding. "Niel."

He halted, twisting his head to meet her gaze over his shoulder. "Aye?"

"Try not to get yerself killed."

Her husband flashed her an answering smile. "I'll do my best to stay alive, wife."

21

A FRESH PERSPECTIVE

"JUST LIKE OLD times, eh?" Niel glanced Connor's way and cast him a grin. "Brings back memories of when we used to go into battle together."

Connor pulled a face. "Aye ... back when we had more courage than sense ... when we thought our hides were made of iron and blades would just bounce off us."

Niel laughed. "Don't ye still believe that?"

"No ... not since Harpsdale."

Niel grew serious at this comment. He'd been there upon that fateful day—the battle between the Mackays and the Gunns that had brought King James's wrath down upon them. It was the battle where Connor had lost his father, Rory Mackay. He and Morgan had watched, unable to prevent it, as a Gunn warrior gutted the chieftain of Farr.

Lips thinning, Niel reflected that he too had lost his father. But unlike Connor, whose green eyes still shadowed when he spoke of the man he'd adored, Niel felt nothing but a lingering burn of resentment when he thought upon Angus Mackay.

Niel and Connor rode at the head of a column of warriors. The morning sun warmed their faces as they traveled over the hills that would take them northwest, and eventually to Dounreay. They would pass Farr on the way, where Morgan would be waiting for them with more men.

Even so, an impressive army of warriors on horseback—and men at arms following on foot behind, their pikes bristling against the blue sky—already followed them. The Munro warriors had definitely swelled their ranks. Robin Mackay had also arrived late the evening before, with a force of eighty men. The chieftain rode behind Niel and Connor this morning, in silence.

Glancing over his shoulder, Niel's gaze settled upon the laird of Melness. Despite his loyalty to Niel, and his readiness to go to battle on his behalf, Robin's mood was dark. It was as if a shadow lay over him constantly these days. His face, once open and good-natured, bore lines that made him look older than his years.

Although it had been a year since his wife and brother's betrayal, the laird didn't appear to have put the unpleasant episode behind him. Instead, the bleak look in his eyes revealed that the opposite was true. If anything, the laird of Melness's demeanor had become even more withdrawn of late.

Behind Robin rode Hugh Mackay of Loch Stach. Hugh's holding was bigger than Robin's, and he'd managed to gather over a hundred men.

A grim smile curved Niel's lips as he swept his gaze over the snaking column behind him. With Connor's men, and those that John would bring for reinforcements, they were a mighty force.

Tavish Gunn wouldn't have time to gather much of a defense.

It wouldn't be a fair fight—but then life wasn't fair.

Niel had learned that first-hand.

Turning back to the direction of travel, Niel's thoughts turned then, unbidden, to his wife.

The image of Beth's face, pale and framed by dark curls, her hazel eyes wide, taunted him. The evening before, vexed once again that she hadn't shown her face at supper ever since the incident in the solar, Niel had told himself that he wouldn't go looking for her the following dawn.

But he had.

He'd been unable to prevent himself.

And when he'd entered the chapel and spied her kneeling at one of the pews, her head bowed, a disquieting sensation had flooded over him.

A constriction of his chest.

A tingling across his skin.

An ache in his throat.

Shoving the unwelcome reaction aside, he'd steeled himself to face her. It had taken an iron will to drawl a welcome and to keep his manner casual.

For, when she'd turned to face him, Niel's heart had started to thud against his ribs.

He'd fled from her presence four days previous, and seeing Beth again flustered him.

The realization had come as a shock. Niel Mackay never got flustered. He couldn't remember a time, even when he'd been a gauche lad, that he'd felt tongue-tied in a woman's presence.

But this morning, as he'd stood before his wife, Niel had felt awkward. He hid it well, but every word that came out of his mouth had been forced. It had been a relief to bid her farewell and make for the door.

Try not to get yerself killed.

Her words had been clipped, yet the haunted look in her eyes told him that she cared what happened to him. And that knowledge had caused a kernel of warmth to sprout under his breastbone.

Ye don't deserve yer wife's well-wishes, he reminded himself. *Not after the way ye treated her.*

Niel clenched his jaw, forcing his thoughts away from Beth then. He needed to get a grip on himself. First, he'd sought out his wife when he'd promised himself he wouldn't—and now he couldn't stop thinking about her.

It was a weakness he couldn't allow himself. Instead, he needed to focus on the coming battle—on dealing the Gunns a blow they'd never forget.

And yet, even as he urged his horse into a brisk canter, moving ahead of Connor up a hill carpeted in purple heather, Niel noted the tightness in his throat and chest.

He'd made his position clear; Beth now understood how things would be between them. Nonetheless, the pain he'd witnessed in those luminous hazel eyes disturbed him. He'd won the battle-of-wills between them, yet it was a hollow victory.

He hadn't needed to be such a bastard about it—to hurt her as he had.

Beth urged her garron forward so that it drew alongside the Lady of Farr and her leggy courser. "Ye weren't lying, Keira … yer home is truly bonny."

Keira cut her a glance, a smile flowering across her face. "Aye, the first time I saw it was from the water … and it took my breath away, perched upon the cliffs like an eagle's eyrie."

Beth nodded, her attention straying ahead once more to where a square keep thrust up against a windy sky. Indeed, Farr Castle had a precipitous position, teetering on the edge of sheer cliffs, looking west over the sea. Bare, velvet-green hills surrounded them, stretching away to the east and south like folds of a rumpled blanket. There were few trees here, and what shrubs Beth did spot in the kirkyard, as they rode through a village on the way to the gates, grew on a slant, molded by the harsh winds on this part of the coast.

They'd left Castle Varrich with the dawn, just a day after Niel, Connor, and their warriors had departed, following the same road over the spine of hills that separated Tongue from the lands that Connor Mackay oversaw.

As they'd set out north, Beth had been uneasy.

She wished that she'd told Niel of her plans. Initially, she'd thrilled at defying him, but once he'd departed, she regretted it. Things would never mend between them if she dug her heels in.

An escort of ten men rode with the two women. Maggie had already left Varrich with Morgan a few days earlier, and Keira had left her bairns at home on this trip—and so they had no other traveling companions. Five of Connor Mackay's warriors rode out front, the others bringing up the rear of the small party.

Beth's stocky Highland pony had struggled to keep pace with Keira's courser during the journey, and as they reached their destination, the poor beast's sides were heaving.

Reaching forward, Beth patted the mare's sweat-slicked neck. "I'll make sure ye get an extra handful of oats, Clover," she murmured. The garron had been with her for the past eight years—a gift from her father upon her eighteenth birthday. And although she didn't have the speed of a courser or the elegance of a palfrey, Beth was loath to part with the honey-colored pony.

The journey had eased a little of the knot of tension in Beth's gut. With each furlong that took her farther from Castle Varrich, she started to feel better.

Now that Farr Castle approached, she was glad she'd agreed to this trip. It was what she needed—a change of perspective. And Neave would run things admirably while she was away. A rueful smile lifted the corners of Beth's mouth at the thought. Like her, Neave was born to boss others about.

Following Keira into the bailey, under a wide stone arch, Beth decided that she'd indeed done the right thing in agreeing to come to Farr for a few days. The distance from her new home, and time away from Niel, would hopefully allow her to regain her equilibrium and focus.

Beth was rarely defeated for long.

Swinging down from her mount, Keira waved to the two lanky lads—Rory and Quinn—who rushed out to meet her. Beth had met them both at her wedding, as she had Rose, Connor and Keira's daughter. The lass appeared at the heels of her younger brothers, clutching a puppy to her breast.

Hugging all three of her bairns, in turn, Keira then greeted Maggie. Her sister-by-marriage had just descended the steps from the keep, accompanied by her daughter, Tara, a lass of around eight winters.

Maggie was smiling, although her heart-shaped face was tense, her blue eyes shadowed.

Beth tensed. The look on Maggie's face reminded her that war affected them all. A large portion of their menfolk had gone off to fight, including Maggie's husband.

"How did Morgan fare in rallying the men?" Keira asked Maggie as she approached.

"Well enough," Maggie replied with a grimace, "although it was chaotic. The army left at first light this morning." Her throat bobbed. "The keep seems so quiet without them."

Keira nodded, her own expression shadowing. "Aye," she replied huskily, "and so it will be until they return home."

Taking a sip of bramble wine, Beth sighed. Seated in the hall of Farr Castle, enjoying a supper of rich venison stew and oaten dumplings, she could feel the tension of the past days draining out of her.

As much as she loved Castle Varrich, she was relieved to be away from it for a short while. It was the first time in years Beth had been apart from her sisters, yet even that brought a little solace. Neave, Jean, and Eilidh were her confidants, her best friends, yet their worrying, their fussing over her, just made Beth feel worse of late.

Here at Farr Castle, she didn't need to explain herself. Keira and Maggie didn't know her well enough to pry. They were merely happy to have her as a guest.

Swallowing a mouthful of stew, Beth's gaze strayed across the table to the couple seated there. In truth, she'd kept glancing their way ever since she'd taken her seat in the hall.

They made a striking pair, but that wasn't the only reason her gaze kept returning to them. Apart from the garrison left to protect the stronghold, few men of fighting age had remained at Farr Castle. Indeed, the dark-haired man with storm-grey eyes and hulking muscles looked like he should be cutting a swathe through the enemy with his claidheamh-mòr, rather than taking supper amongst his womenfolk.

However, Alexander Gunn had been bid to stay behind.

It was clear why. Although judging from the tense set of the man's jaw, and the glower that furrowed his brow, the former heir to the Gunn clan-chief chafed at not being able to fight.

Watching him, Beth wondered which side he'd join if given the choice. Aye, he was wed to a Mackay—the lovely woman with red-gold hair who sat beside him—but he'd always be a Gunn.

Had Niel's campaign made Alexander reconsider his loyalties? Did he wish to fight at his brother's side?

"Did ye manage to get all those blades ready in time, Alex?" Cait, a small dark-haired woman who Beth had learned was wedded to Connor's cousin Kennan, asked. "They were working ye hard."

Alexander Gunn glanced up from his stew and dumplings and nodded. "Aye," he murmured, his voice a low rumble. "With Brodie and Stewart's help ... we got there in the end."

Jaimee favored her husband with a smile. "Just as well ye took on two apprentices last winter."

Of course, Beth realized—Alexander Gunn's formidable musculature came from the hours he spent working in Farr Castle's forge. He was the blacksmith.

Once again, Beth wondered what this man, who'd once been set to inherit the title of clan-chief and whose reputation as a ruthless warrior had traveled far and wide across the Highlands, truly thought about the choices he'd made.

Beth's attention shifted to Jaimee. The woman was dressed in a plain, dun-brown kirtle, yet her loveliness outshone every other female at the table. Beth noted she had her brothers' piercing pine-green eyes. Her smile, which held an edge of mischievous humor, reminded her of Morgan, while her proud bearing recalled Connor.

And as supper continued, Beth marked the way Alexander glanced often at his comely wife, the way their gazes would meet and hold.

The heat, the connection, between them was palpable.

An unwelcome jolt of envy jabbed Beth in the guts then.

By blood and bone, what she would give to have Niel look upon her like that.

Everyone in the Highlands knew the tale of Alexander Gunn and Jaimee Mackay, of how she'd tamed the fierce warrior. He'd given up everything to be with her, and despite the permanent groove between his dark brows this evening, it was clear with every look, every light touch, that Gunn adored his wife.

Perhaps he had no regrets after all.

Jaimee laughed then, the merry sound drifting across the table. Glancing across at the couple once more, Beth watched as Alexander leaned down and kissed his wife, oblivious to the fact that they had an audience.

Beth dropped her gaze to her half-finished bowl of stew and tried to ignore the envy that speared her once more. Some women made it look so easy.

Ye know it's not as simple as that, lass, she chastised herself. Once she would have thought that it was Jaimee's charisma and beauty that had made Gunn go witless over her—but these days, she'd lost such idealistic notions.

The truth was that Alexander Gunn felt no shame in wanting his wife, in loving her. He didn't seem to have a problem with Jaimee having a sharp mind and pert tongue. Unfortunately, Niel Mackay preferred meeker women.

An ache rose under Beth's breast bone. Raising a hand, she rubbed at it with her knuckles. Watching

Jaimee and Alexander together made her consider that perhaps her marriage had been doomed from the start.

After all, she couldn't change her husband's tastes.

Drawing in a deep breath, Beth glanced back at the happy couple. Aye, their marriages were vastly different. Even so, a woman like Jaimee would be wise in the ways of men. It wouldn't hurt to get her view on matters.

22

RIGHTEOUS

*Dounreay—Caithness
Gunn territory*

FURY PULSED THROUGH Niel as he slashed at the press of mail and leather-clad warriors that came at him.

He needn't have worried that he'd feel panicked by the wall of bodies around him. Once bloodlust sang in his veins, he forgot all else.

"Fall back!" Through the din of battle, the roar of Hugh Mackay's voice reached him.

Gripping his claidheamh-mòr two-handed, Niel clenched his jaw and drove the long blade into the gut of the man who bore down upon him with an axe. The warrior crumpled, his howls of pain cleaving the air.

"Fall back!" Hugh Mackay shouted once more.

Rage burned hotter still, turning Niel's vision crimson. His mouth tasted bitter, sweat poured off him, and his body ached from the vicious skirmish just south of the village fort of Dounreay.

This wasn't the battle he wanted to be having. It wasn't the folk of Dounreay he wished to clash with—but the Gunns.

The day was drawing out, the roar of Forss Water thundering behind them. After reinforcements had joined the defenders at Dounreay, Niel had been forced to retreat. They now fought on the northern banks of a fast-flowing river that foamed over sharp rocks. They were deep in Gunn territory here, not far from Thurso, the mainland's northernmost port.

Years earlier, Dounreay had been Mackay land—but the locals allied themselves with the Gunns these days.

Niel had planned to lead a raid on the village and broch, an act that would send a clear challenge to Tavish Gunn, but as they fought their way toward the gates of Dounreay, a host of mounted warriors had surged over the hills to the north to join the locals. Despite Niel's hope that they'd traveled north unseen, the locals had known they were coming and had already sent out a call for assistance.

The warriors had hurtled toward them, screaming like banshees at the Mackays' approach, and a violent battle had taken place on the bare hills south of the settlement. Eventually, the Mackays had been forced to withdraw south, only to turn and fight once more when they reached the rapids of Forss Water.

However, the battle was turning against them here, too.

Aye, it tasted like gall in Niel's mouth, yet he had to face the truth.

If they didn't withdraw, they'd suffer a crushing defeat here and wouldn't be able to press on. Niel would be robbed of the reckoning he longed for.

Hugh was right. They had to fall back.

Niel moved away from his attackers, his boots sliding on gore, and bellowed, "Retreat!"

His warriors obeyed, closing in around him like a shield wall of old, and carrying their clan-chief to safety. They surged into the foaming river, linking arms as they struggled to cross. Shouts and cries split the air, rising above the roar of the rapids, as some of the Mackays were swept away.

The water clawed at Niel too, seeking to drag him under. Teeth clenched, he fought it, although his heart pounded painfully when he finally dragged himself up onto the far bank.

Lips twisted into a snarl, he turned to glare at the jeering warriors back on the other side. Arrows peppered the air then, and he was forced to move back, following his retreating army to safety.

But with every step south, Niel reminded himself that this wasn't a defeat.

He was just saving his strength for the fight that mattered. The Gunns had escaped punishment a decade earlier, for their role in the feuding. Niel would never forget the smug look on George Gunn's face that day in the great hall of Inverness Castle, the victory that lit in the bastard's eyes when King James condemned the Mackays instead.

This campaign wasn't just about revenge—it was about righting a grievous wrong.

The Mackay force drew back to Sandside Bay, a crescent-shaped beach of golden sand farther down the coast from Dounreay.

The wounded nursed their cuts and bruises. A handful of the injuries were serious, and when Niel visited these men, he doubted they would last the night. Hide tents went up next to the shore, and the clan-chief set a watch on their perimeter, just in case the folk of Dounreay, and their allies, became bold overnight.

Stalking around the perimeter, his gaze trained on the hills to the north, Niel found it difficult to contain his restlessness. Battle fury still smoldered in his veins. Despite that he knew they'd made a strategic choice in retreating, he longed to head back to that broch, smash down the walls, and take it for his own.

But such a reckless act would come at great cost, for both him and his men.

Striding to where Connor and Morgan were talking together at the eastern edge of the camp, Niel addressed the brothers without preamble. "Has word been sent to John?"

Connor nodded, his blood-splattered face grim. "Aye."

"Any idea when he'll get here?"

"As soon as he can," Morgan replied. Connor's younger brother's face was drawn with fatigue, although frustration burned in his eyes. Like Niel, defeat didn't sit well with Morgan Mackay. "Drum Hollistan is some distance south. He's not likely to reach us until tomorrow."

Niel ground his teeth, dragging a hand through his hair. He needed to calm down. Instructing John to wait had been his idea, after all. He'd told his cousin to protect their rear, just in case the Gunns attempted an attack from behind.

He now wished he'd kept John, and the forces he commanded, closer.

"He'll be here soon enough," Connor muttered with a scowl. "Not that it matters … the fighting has ended for today."

Drawing in a deep breath, Niel nodded. Connor was as vexed as he was at having to withdraw, yet his friend had a calming effect upon him. Connor always had, since when they'd hunted together as lads.

However, Connor then muttered a curse under his breath, casting a baleful look north. "Bastards."

"Aye," Morgan bit out. "They definitely had wind of our arrival. We didn't spot any scouts on the way up here … but *someone* saw us."

"Or someone warned them ahead of time," Connor replied.

The chieftain of Farr's green eyes glinted when his gaze speared Niel's. "That man who advised ye to attack Dounreay … was he really trustworthy?"

Niel snorted. They'd already had this discussion back in Varrich. Did they think him that gullible? "Most likely not," he growled back, "but I know what I saw in his eyes. Hatred." Aye, raw loathing had pulsed off the man in waves, and it hadn't been directed at him. "Whatever his reason, that man has a score to settle with the Gunns, not us."

Connor's lips thinned; he still looked unconvinced.

Niel wasn't worried. He knew in his gut that they hadn't been betrayed. Instead, they'd underestimated how wary and well-defended the men of Dounreay were.

Not a mistake he'd be making twice.

"Of course, whether or not we managed to raid Dounreay, ye will have achieved the end ye wanted,"

Morgan pointed out then, his mouth twisting. "Riders will have gone out to Castle Gunn. All we have to do is sit tight and wait for Tavish Gunn to come to us."

Niel nodded, even as he clenched his jaw. He wanted to strike right now, but he needed to curb his impatience and settle down to wait a day or two. Castle Gunn, located on the eastern coast, was a decent ride away. The wait would give John time to reach them, and for Niel to come up with a strategy to ensure they emerged the victors from the coming battle. "Aye," he replied, flashing Morgan a savage smile. "And he *will*."

Dusk gradually faded into night, and a waxing crescent moon sailed high overhead. The camp settled down, the voices of the men low murmurs against the rumble of the surf.

And beyond the Mackay camp, the world went quiet.

After a brief supper of bread, cheese, and small sweet onions, washed down with ale, Niel prowled the perimeter once more.

Despite his talk with Connor and Morgan earlier, he was still agitated. The silhouettes of his men at watch, helmeted figures outlined against the sky, put his nerves on edge. If he could see them this easily, then so could the enemy.

No doubt, the folk of Dounreay knew exactly where they'd made camp and were probably discussing the wisdom of attacking them.

Niel halted, his gaze spearing the darkness north of the camp.

His skin prickled.

Battle. It set him alight, made him feel alive.

But there was something else that quickened his senses.

Beth.

That night in the solar, when she'd confronted him—it had been a battle of another kind. It might not have drawn blood, yet when they'd locked horns, part of him had reveled in it. And when he'd kissed her, touched her, lost himself deep inside her, nothing else in the world had mattered.

For a few moments, his hunger for vengeance had faded like mist on a summer's morn. In its place, a sense of peace, unlike any he'd ever known, had settled over him.

Would it be such a bad thing—to surrender to it?

Beth was right, he thought grimly. *She sees the truth, even when I hide it from myself.* Indeed, he blamed Bass Rock, the Gunns, and his father's betrayal for making him so angry—but all of it was a shield. His rage prevented him from facing what was truly broken inside him.

Niel clenched his jaw, glaring out into the darkness as if daring the enemy to close in. He didn't want to surrender. Even as a bairn, he'd been self-contained, in control of his emotions. He didn't want to make himself vulnerable, even to his wife.

Not if he wanted to keep his edge.

And a clan-chief needed an edge if he was to lead his people to greatness.

"Ye are dedicated, Niel." A low, gruff voice intruded then. "I didn't think to find ye on the watch tonight."

Tearing his gaze from the night-shrouded hills, Niel glanced left at where a shorter, yet strongly built, figure approached. Robin Mackay had found him. He couldn't see the man's face, yet his voice and shape were distinctive.

"Aye," Niel murmured back, careful to speak softly. Noise carried on a still night such as this. "We must all do our part."

Robin stopped next to him. "I'll take over from ye for a while, if ye wish? I sleep little these days anyway."

Niel continued to look at the chieftain. Even though he could hardly make out the lines of his shadowed face, the edge to the man's voice was impossible to miss.

"Keep me company awhile, Rob," he replied. "Two pairs of eyes are better than one."

Indeed, he recalled that Robin had excellent eyesight. Whenever they'd gone hunting in the past, the warrior had always spied prey in the distance, long before anyone else did. Nonetheless, he doubted the man could see at night.

The laird of Melness turned his gaze north, his profile outlined against the darkness beyond. "They won't bother us tonight," he said after a moment, his voice barely over a whisper. "They'll be too busy scrambling for reinforcements."

"And yet, they nearly bested us today." The admission tasted like ash in Niel's mouth. To be chased off by a local rabble still stung.

"They caught us by surprise ... but they won't do so again," Robin replied before spitting on the ground before him. "Next time, we'll slaughter the lot of them."

Niel continued to observe the laird's profile, his brow furrowing. These days, his friend sounded so bitter. Did he want to end up like that too?

Will ye let yer resentment toward yer father steal yer life away?

"What happened to ye, Rob?" he asked finally.

A heavy pause followed before the laird of Melness replied, "Ye must have heard the tale."

"Aye ... some of it."

"Then ye, more than most folk ... will understand what it feels to be betrayed by those ye love."

Niel took in the chieftain's words. "I do," he admitted warily. He then cleared his throat. "So ye haven't been able to track yer wife and brother down?"

"No." Robin's voice was hard and flat. "I paid men to scour Scotland in search of them ... but they disappeared like smoke. I'd say they went south ... to England or Wales."

"Well, if they value their necks, they'll never return to Mackay lands," Niel replied. He shook his head then. "It's a sorry day when brother betrays brother ... over a woman."

"Aye, and yet it happens." Robin's voice turned raw. "I *loved* her, Niel ... and he stole her from me."

Niel didn't reply. He hadn't met the woman Robin Mackay had wed, having been in Bass Rock at the time—yet he'd heard she'd been a beauty. John had told him that the chieftain had struggled to control his wife, right from the first days of his marriage. He'd wed the wrong woman, to be sure—and it was on the tip of Niel's tongue to tell his friend that his treacherous brother hadn't exactly 'stolen' her. The pair had plotted against him, and then when things hadn't turned out in their favor, had fled together.

Nonetheless, Niel refrained from making such a comment. Robin wouldn't appreciate it, and Niel knew from experience that there were some betrayals a man never healed from.

After all, *he'd* never forgiven his father for handing him over to the king in order to save his own hide.

23

SEEKING COUNSEL

*Farr Castle—Strathnaver
Mackay territory*

"MA ... CAN WE ask the cooks to make bramble pie for supper?" Rose Mackay's excited voice carried along the clifftop. The lass skipped toward them, clutching a basket under one arm. "We can have it with cream!"

Keira smiled. "Well, ye will have to ask Elsa," she replied.

Rose's smile faltered, making it clear that the notion didn't appeal. "She's scary."

"I can make bramble pie with ye and Tara," Beth said, favoring Keira with a grin. "If ye wish?"

"Are ye sure?" Keira's brow furrowed at Beth's suggestion. "I'm not in the habit of making my guests cook for us."

"I haven't been in the kitchen in a few days," Beth replied with a grin. "And I'm starting to miss it." She then glanced Rose's way and winked. "Plus, I know an *excellent* recipe for Bramble pie."

Keira hesitated before releasing a sigh. "Very well ... I warn ye though, Elsa can be a dragon ... venture into her lair at yer peril."

Beth laughed, although the shriek of the gulls overhead drowned out the sound of her mirth. It felt good to laugh. She had been so serious of late. Spending time with Keira and Rose—as well as Maggie and her daughter, Tara, who were trailing a few yards behind them on the path—reminded her of what it had been like between Beth and her sisters back at Foulis Castle. "I've faced down kitchen dragons many a time," she assured Keira. "Worry, not ... I can handle Elsa."

They approached the high walls encircling the castle. They'd just been for a walk up to Swordly, a village located north of Farr, where they'd picked brambles next to a burn. The day was cool, the sun struggling to break through the high cloud, and despite that it was high summer, the wind that gusted in from the sea had a bite to it.

Beth imagined that winters could be bitterly cold here, even more so than at Castle Varrich, for although the seat of the Mackay clan perched high on the edge of a kyle, it wasn't as exposed as this fortress. Even so, Beth had enjoyed her days at Farr. She'd gotten to know Keira and Maggie better too. They'd spent long afternoons chatting together in the women's solar as they sewed, embroidered, or wove, and during those conversations, she'd discovered that both women had overcome much to gain the happiness they'd found.

They'd made Beth feel that perhaps her situation wasn't hopeless either.

The women and children entered the landward bailey, waving to the men on the walls as they did so. The rhythmic clang of iron greeted them then, as did the acrid odor of molten metal being forged.

Beth glanced left, her gaze alighting upon the open door to the forge. Inside, she spied Alexander Gunn's brawny figure, bent over a glowing length of iron as he beat it into submission. His two apprentices worked with him, their bare arms slick with sweat. And a lad of around four played with stones in the dirt at the entrance to the smith's forge: Aodhan, Jaimee and Alexander's son.

The couple and their two bairns lived in the annex behind the forge, one that had been extended over the years to accommodate them.

Beth swallowed, nervousness building within her. She'd been putting off having a proper chat with Jaimee but didn't want to leave Farr without doing so. However, she would only remain here another day or two before heading back to Castle Varrich and was running out of time. Although Keira and Maggie had made her feel better, she still hadn't had a private conversation with Jaimee.

"Can we start on the pie now?" Rose asked excitedly, plucking at Beth's sleeve.

Beth's attention flicked back to the lass before she smiled. "Soon ... I was just going to pay Jaimee a short visit first." She glanced over at Keira. "I'll be right up, if ye want to warn Elsa?"

Keira snorted. "Not particularly."

Grinning, Beth picked up her skirts and headed across the cobbled landward bailey. One of Alexander's apprentices had ventured out with a bucket of water for the slack-tub. He cast her a curious look as she passed by.

Beth cut behind the forge and approached the annex beyond. The dwelling hugged the curtain wall, nestled between the forge and the keep. The door was open, and Beth smiled when she caught the sound of singing: a melodious female voice accompanied by the high-pitched strains of a child's warble.

Beth paused on the threshold and peered inside. "Am I intruding?" she asked.

Jaimee glanced up from where she'd been chopping onions. Her daughter worked at her side, mixing batter in a wooden bowl.

A smile flowered across Jaimee's face upon spying Beth. The woman was nearly ten years older than the clan-chief's wife, yet her skin was still creamy and unlined. Her red-gold hair was twisted into a bun this afternoon, emphasizing her slender neck and the elegant lines of her face. "Of course not, Beth. Come in!" Her smile turned a trifle embarrassed then. "I apologize for our humble dwelling ... ye shall be used to much finer places."

Beth waved her comment away. "Nonsense." Her gaze swept the plain yet tidy interior of the annex, noting the small feminine touches, such as bunches of drying herbs and flowers that hung from the rafters, and the colorful tapestries covering the rough stone walls. Doors led off to what Beth imagined were sleeping spaces to the right and left. "Yer home is welcoming indeed."

She ducked under the lintel and entered the cottage, smiling at Jaimee's daughter. "I'm going to teach Rose and Tara how to make bramble pie later, Anice ... would ye like to join us?"

"Aye!" Such was the lass's excitement that she gave the batter a vigorous stir, causing it to slop over the rim.

"Careful there," Jaimee admonished her. "Save some for later. Ye know how yer Da likes plenty of dumplings with his stew."

Shrugging off her mother's caution, Anice continued to gaze at Beth. "Are Rose and Tara back from picking brambles then?"

"Aye."

Anice turned to her mother. "Can I go to them?"

Jaimee peered into the bowl her daughter had been stirring, her brow furrowing. "Very well, lass. Be sure ye are back for supper, mind."

"I will!" Anice stepped back from the table, wiped off her hands, and made for the door.

"I'll meet ye and the others shortly in the keep's kitchens," Beth assured her.

Anice flashed her a grin in response. "Aye, Lady Mackay. Thank ye!"

A moment later, the lass had disappeared, the patter of her footsteps dying away.

Jaimee gave a rueful smile. "I swear, Anice grows more headstrong by the day." She snorted then. "Hardly surprising with Alex and me as parents." She picked up her chopping board, carried it to an iron pot hanging over the fire, and scraped in the chopped onions with the back of her knife. Returning to the table, Jaimee started to chop up carrots.

"Can I help ye prepare the stew?" Beth asked.

"Och, no." Jaimee appeared horrified at the notion. "I can't have the clan-chief's wife running around after me."

Ignoring her protest, Beth rounded the table, rolled up her sleeves, and dusted the worktop with flour. She then added more flour to the bowl so that the batter thickened to a workable dough. Tipping it out onto the table, she started to mold the soft dough into dumplings. Working alongside Jaimee eased a little of the nervousness that fluttered like errant moths in her belly. She might be the clan-chief's wife, but this woman made her feel dowdy in comparison. "I'm never happier than when I'm cooking," she admitted to Jaimee with a smile. "It's where I find solace."

Jaimee huffed a laugh. "I wish I did."

Beth cut her a sidelong look. "Do ye mind if I ask ye something, Jaimee?"

Jaimee's mouth curved, her pine-green eyes twinkling. "No ... although by yer tone, I'd guess yer question won't be an easy one to answer."

Beth cleared her throat, suddenly embarrassed. She focused on shaping the dumplings and placing them on a tray until she gathered her courage enough to continue. "Have Keira and Maggie ever spoken to ye about the state of my marriage to Niel?" she asked, meeting the woman's eye once more.

Jaimee tensed, her smile fading. Sensing her panic, as if she'd just caught the three of them at gossiping, Beth hastened to allay her fears. "Fret not ... I'm not trying to catch ye out. It's just easier to broach the subject if ye already know some of my story."

Jaimee gave a cautious nod.

Exhaling sharply, Beth considered her next words. "The truth is ... I feel truly out of my depth with Niel. Maybe I was proud ... or just merely foolish ... but I believed he would fall in love with me." She paused then, heat washing over her. Hades, this was embarrassing to admit. "But the more I try to win him over ... or to penetrate his reserve ... the worse things get between us."

Face burning now, Beth kept her gaze riveted upon the last of the dumplings she was forming. What a daft woman she must think her. Jaimee had won over

Alexander Gunn for pity's sake. Surely, she imagined Niel Mackay a much easier prospect.

However, when Jaimee replied there was no chagrin in her voice or scorn. "Niel was always an enigma," she said after a pause, her tone thoughtful.

Beth glanced up to see that Jaimee was watching her, a slight smile upon her lips. "He was an incorrigible flirt when he was younger—brash, and yet elusive, with women."

"I heard he was once interested in ye," Beth replied. She couldn't help it; her belly twisted as she made the comment. Did Niel secretly regret losing his chance with Jaimee?

The woman's mouth quirked. "Aye ... he flirted with me at any given opportunity, despite my lack of encouragement. He also took a liking to Maggie for a spell." She shook her head then. "But Niel had no intention of settling down during those days."

"I believe he's only taken a wife now out of necessity," Beth replied. She couldn't help the hurt that crept into her voice. "He needs an heir to secure his bloodline."

Jaimee's gaze held hers. "Are things that bad?"

"Aye," Beth replied huskily. "Keira and Maggie suggested that I give him time to get used to being wedded to me. I thought if I became the 'perfect' biddable wife, he'd warm to me ... but after a while, I couldn't keep up the pretense. He still insists we sleep apart, and whenever we spend time together, he holds himself back. It's like being wed to a stranger."

"Have ye spoken to him about it?" Jaimee asked.

Beth nodded. "I decided that if demure wasn't going to work ... then I would challenge him instead." She paused and cleared her throat, embarrassment creeping over her once more. She wasn't going to recount what had happened that eve in the solar. "It didn't go well ... and Niel made his position clear: he won't give me the marriage I wish for."

"And what marriage is that?" Jaimee queried softly.

Beth's throat tightened. "Devotion ... the kind ye have with yer husband."

Jaimee favored her with a rueful smile. "Men can be skittish creatures," she said, with a shake of her head. "They need to feel in control of their lives, their fate. Alex gave up everything for me ... but I would never have demanded that of him." She paused then. "The best thing ye can do is focus on the things in yer life that bring ye joy ... and busy yerself in them. If yer husband one day misses ye, and seeks ye out, then ye two may have a chance. But trying to alter how he feels by sheer will is futile." Her gaze softened, sympathy darkening her eyes. "I'm sorry, Beth ... that wasn't likely the advice ye wished for."

Beth attempted a smile before reaching for a cloth to clean her hands. No, it wasn't, but Jaimee had spoken the truth—Beth knew it in her gut. "I asked for yer counsel," she replied with a shake of her head. "And ye have spoken wisely." Wiping off her hands, she blinked rapidly, forcing back the urge to cry.

Mother Mary, she was a fool.

"Beth," Jaimee asked softly, drawing her attention once more. "Can I ask *ye* a question?"

Beth nodded, forcing herself to meet the woman's gaze once more.

Jaimee favored her with a gentle smile, even if her gaze speared her. "Do ye love yer husband?"

24

RECKONING

Sandside Bay—Caithness
Gunn territory

A BRINE-SCENTED WIND raced in off the sea, whipping strands of hair into Niel's eyes. He'd tied his hair back with a thong at the nape of his neck, but the force of the wind this morning had loosened it.

Blinking as his eyes watered, he kept his gaze fixed north—at where a line of warriors approached, sunlight glinting off their blades. Animosity rolled across the sand, breaking over him like the waves that kissed the shore. One look at the feral expressions twisting the faces of the warriors in the front line, and a smile stretched Niel's lips.

His heart started to kick against his ribs.

At last, his foe had come to face him. Tavish Gunn was here.

Scanning the advancing army, Niel searched for the Gunn clan-chief. He was looking for a man who resembled George Gunn, or even Alexander: big and broad-shouldered.

However, the man who stepped forward didn't resemble either of them closely.

Aye, he had the same dark hair as his sire and exiled elder brother, and at this distance, it looked as if he had the distinctive 'Gunn' storm-grey eyes—but this warrior was tall, lithe, and sharp-featured.

Like Niel, Tavish's dark hair was pulled back from his face.

And just like him, the look on the Gunn clan-chief's face spoke of violence.

"Niel 'Bass' Mackay," Gunn shouted, his voice carrying along the strand. "Come forward … show yerself to me." A gap of around a furlong separated the two armies. Behind Tavish, Niel spied Gunn standards of dull green plaid snapping in the wind.

Niel snorted. He'd heard that folk in the Highlands had started referring to him by that name of late. He didn't care. Let them. Bass Rock was part of who he was now—for instead of shattering him, it had tempered him.

That prison had proved he was a difficult man to break.

Tavish Gunn would know it too.

Shouldering his way out of the line, Niel met his enemy's gaze across the sand. "Here I am, Gunn." He then drew his broad-sword from across his back, metal scraping against leather. "Ready to kiss steel?"

Gunn stared him down, his lips twisting as if he'd just spied something distasteful. "Turn around now, Mackay," he called, his voice rough, "and I might not chase ye home. This is Gunn land, and ye are despoiling it."

A chorus of insults from the Gunn lines followed these words. Instants later, answering curses echoed across from the Mackay force.

When the noise had died down, Niel spat on the ground between them. "This is *Mackay* land. Yer grandsire stole it from mine … and I will have it back."

Gunn's laughter rippled down the beach. "Never."

Niel inclined his head. "Then we are done talking."

"Aye, Mackay … we are."

The two clan-chiefs moved back into line, and a heavy silence, pregnant with leashed violence, fell upon the wide, crescent-shaped beach.

Seabirds whirled above them, their cries haunting, and the wind gusted against the warriors, who stood eyeballing each other across the sand.

Niel sucked in a deep breath. Mixed in with the brine scent of the sea, he tasted the metallic tang of fear and the heavy musk of animal aggression. There was nothing like the smell of the air moments before battle—the promise of death made a man keenly aware of his mortality.

Niel's gaze swept down the enemy lines. Tavish Gunn had brought quite a force with him, yet John Mackay had arrived the day before with much-needed reinforcements.

We won't be beaten back this time, he vowed silently.

This was a fight to the death—and every Gunn, every Mackay standing upon this strand, knew it.

For the first time since the Battle of Harpsdale eleven years earlier, the two clans would clash in open combat. The reckoning Niel lived for had now come.

From the instant the two sides collided, the battle was furious.

It was a slaughter.

Gunn and Mackay gave no quarter, even as men fell, their blood soaking into the sand.

Niel hacked his way through the fray, seeking out Tavish Gunn. The Gunn clan-chief fought in the thick of things, his lean form moving with the same precision Niel had witnessed in his elder brother at Harpsdale.

And he was just as deadly as Alexander.

Jaw clenched, Niel cut down warrior after warrior yet got no closer to his quarry. Nearby, he caught sight of Connor Mackay, his blond hair glinting in the sunlight, his face twisted with savagery.

His friend had been reluctant to go to war against the Gunns again, but now that he had, Connor didn't hold back. Men fell under the savage arc of his claidheamh-mòr. Likewise, John Mackay fought like a man possessed, wielding a longsword in his left hand as if he'd been born favoring that hand and not the one he'd lost. Robin Mackay wielded an axe just a few yards from John, his face a cold, brutal mask as he felled a huge Gunn warrior and then finished him off with a dirk-blade to the throat.

They fought like gods as battle rage sang in their blood.

Niel took blows but was barely aware of them. He felt no pain, no fatigue, even as his boots slipped on the oily sheen of blood that now flowed across the sand.

However, as the crimson tide of his fury ebbed and flowed, he became aware that the tide was turning—in their favor.

Slowly, yet inexorably, they were pushing the Gunns back.

And then, all of a sudden, the enemy lines broke. The Mackays howled as they chased their foes down the beach.

Reaching a loop in the bay, where the crumbling walls of Cnoc Stangar, a Pict fort, rose from sand dunes against the wind-streaked sky, some of the Gunns turned to face the Mackays once more.

But it was in vain.

They butchered them there, under those ancient walls. And when the survivors fled, John led a group of men after them as they raced toward Dounreay.

Panting, as exhaustion finally barreled into him, Niel bent double, sucking in deep breaths. The dead lay scattered around him like broken poppets, the iron-taint of blood filling his nostrils.

The sprint down the beach and the final assault had pushed his body too far. Around him, he heard the rasp of his men's breathing, the stifled groans as they struggled with their injuries.

However, they were standing while the enemy was not.

Staring down at the blood-soaked sand, Niel waited for elation to surge through him, for vindication to quicken in his blood. He'd awaited this moment for so long.

And yet he felt little—save bone-deep exhaustion and a dull ache under his left arm.

"We've got one of the Gunn brothers ... alive!" Morgan Mackay's shout made Niel raise his head. A few yards away, Morgan had pinned a warrior to the ground, his knee pressed firmly between the man's shoulder blades.

"Let's have a look at him," Niel called back.

Together Morgan and Connor hauled the warrior to his feet. Catching a glimpse of wild black hair and grey eyes, Niel stilled before realizing that the man before him wasn't the Gunn clan-chief.

Of course, there had been six Gunn brothers, although only four—Tavish, Blair, Evan, and William— were rumored to live at Castle Gunn these days. Niel wondered which of them hung before him.

"Yer name?" he barked.

The man was barely conscious, blood streaming down his temple. However, he still managed to snarl a curse at his captors. A swift punch to the belly from Morgan yielded a name, however.

"William," Gunn grunted.

Niel's mouth twisted into a grin. They'd captured Tavish's youngest brother. He glanced north then, wondering if John had caught up with the surviving Gunns yet.

Would he bring Tavish Gunn's head back to him on a pike?

"What do ye want us to do with him?" Connor asked.

Niel straightened up fully, stifling a gasp as the dull ache under his left armpit flowered into something deeper and nausea washed over him. An instant later, he broke out into a cold sweat. "He's coming back to Castle Varrich," he replied with a grimace, trying to focus. "Where he will live out his days as my prisoner ... let's see how much a Gunn likes having freedom stolen from him."

Connor nodded before his blood-splattered face went rigid. "Niel ... ye are injured."

Glancing down at himself, Niel saw that his friend was right. He didn't even remember the blow, yet blood wet his left side, running down from under his arm. And the crimson staining the ground around his feet didn't belong to his enemies, but to him. Judas, he was bleeding like a stuck pig.

"Just a scratch," he replied, even as his voice slurred and a sickening wave of nausea hit him. His ears then started to ring. "I'll be fine."

Those were his last words before a dark veil dropped over his eyes, and he collapsed.

25

UNPREPARED

*Farr Castle—Strathnaver
Mackay territory*

"THE MEN HAVE returned!" Jaimee burst into the women's solar, where Keira, Maggie, and Beth sat sewing together. It was Beth's last afternoon at Farr. She would depart for Castle Varrich the following morning.

Keira's lips parted, and she cast her sewing aside, rising swiftly to her feet. "So soon?"

"Aye ... they had a victory against the Gunns," Jaimee replied, the words coming in gasps as she recovered from what had clearly been a sprint up the spiral stairwell to reach them. "Tavish Gunn managed to escape, but they captured one of his brothers." Her gaze then snapped to Beth, and the alarm she saw in their depths made an icy shiver of misgiving trace down Beth's spine. "Niel has been badly hurt."

Beth's heart lurched into her throat. The lèine she'd been embroidering the hem of fluttered to the ground, forgotten, as she jumped to her feet. "Where is he?"

"Cullodina ... our healer ... is with him in one of the guest chambers," Jaimee replied. "I'll take ye to them now."

Without another word, the two women fled the solar—with Keira and Maggie close behind.

And as she followed Jaimee, Beth's mind whirled. Niel had always seemed invincible to her. He was so strong, so stoic. She couldn't imagine her husband gravely injured.

However, when she slipped into the chamber, while Jaimee, Keira, and Maggie waited outside, her belly clenched.

Naked to the waist, her husband was sprawled unconscious upon the bed. A small woman with a round face and long, deft fingers worked on Niel, her brow furrowed deeply in concentration.

Beth sucked in a shocked breath. Niel's face was so pale. He looked as if he were already dead. Her ears started to ring, and her knees wobbled under her. Reaching out, she steadied herself against the wall. Suddenly, it hurt to draw breath.

Calm down, she counseled herself. *The healer wouldn't be tending him if he were gone.*

Upon Beth's arrival, Cullodina glanced up.

"I'm his wife," Beth gasped, hurrying to the bed. "Can I help?"

The healer nodded. She was an older woman, with a steady gaze that Beth instinctively trusted. "Aye, lass … if ye have a strong stomach?"

"I do," Beth assured her. She wasn't the type to faint at the sight of blood.

Nonetheless, when she stepped closer and saw the deep gash that ran down from Niel's left armpit to just below his ribs, her gorge rose. She could see muscle and the white glint of bone, and despite her assurances, the roast mutton she'd eaten at noon churned in her belly.

Mother Mary, how is he still alive?

"He's lost a lot of blood," Cullodina informed her, as she bent down once more, examining the wound. *Too much*. The woman didn't need to say it; her tone told Beth the truth. "I'm trying to ascertain if the pike that gored him cut anything vital," Cullodina continued. "I'll then sew him up and apply a poultice of woundwort."

Dizziness swept over Beth. *A pike?*

"What do ye need me to do?" she asked weakly.

Cullodina glanced up once more, the corners of her eyes crinkling as she smiled. "Fetch me that vinegar from the table, lass. I shall wash the wound and see what we're dealing with."

"How is he?"

Keira's soft question roused Beth from where she drowsed, slumped in a chair next to Niel's bed.

Blinking sleep away, she focused on where the Laird and Lady of Farr stood just inside the doorway. She then glanced over at where Niel lay, still insensible, the shallow rise and fall of his naked chest reassuring her.

"Still breathing, at least," she replied, forcing a brave smile.

"Cullodina says it's one of the worst battle wounds she's ever seen," Connor murmured. The chieftain neared the bed, his gaze shadowing as it settled upon Niel's face. "I'm sorry, Beth."

Beth's breathing hitched, heat igniting in the pit of her belly. She knew Connor meant well, yet he was talking as if Niel were already dead. What had the healer actually said to him? Cullodina hadn't given her such ill news before leaving earlier that evening.

Perhaps she was just trying to spare me.

Beth swallowed. Cullodina's calmness, her skill and strength, had been Beth's rock over the afternoon and evening she'd spent helping the healer tend Niel's wound. The women had spoken little, yet Beth had hoped that Cullodina's silence boded well for Niel.

But clearly, it didn't.

Maybe I truly am cursed, she thought then, ice slithering down her spine. *What if any man who links himself with me will have his life cut short?*

Cods, her voice of reason snarled back. *Don't entertain such foolish thoughts!*

"He shall rally," she said firmly, her attention shifting once more to Niel's face. His skin was still waxy and pale. "He's strong."

"Why don't ye retire to yer chamber?" Keira asked after a pause. "I can stay here with Niel awhile."

Beth shook her head. She wasn't moving from this spot.

"But ye should get some rest."

"The chair is comfortable enough." That was a lie; the chair was like an instrument of torture, but Beth was resolute. She wouldn't move from Niel's side. Not tonight.

"I'll bring ye some cushions and a blanket then." Keira's voice was subdued now. "And something to eat."

Beth wasn't hungry. Nonetheless, she stiffly nodded her head. Keira was only being kind and trying to help.

Swallowing the lump that now felt lodged in her throat, Beth looked at Connor once more. His handsome face appeared more severe than she'd ever seen it, deep lines bracketing his mouth and nose.

"So, it was a great victory for the Mackays?" she asked, desperate to change the subject from Niel. If they kept discussing him, she'd crumble. She could feel panic looming, clawing its way up her throat, at the thought he might not survive this.

Connor nodded, his green eyes still troubled. "Aye," he murmured. "Niel got his vengeance. Meanwhile, Tavish Gunn managed to outrun John and his men. He'll now be licking his wounds … and cursing us all to hell."

Beth's mouth thinned. "Jaimee said ye'd taken one of the Gunn brothers captive?"

"Aye, William … the youngest."

"So it's over now?"

Connor's mouth twisted into a smile. However, there was little humor in the expression. "For a while, at least."

Connor and Keira didn't stay long. Bidding Beth goodnight, they left the bed-chamber. Shortly after, servants brought up cushions and a blanket, and a tray of mutton broth, accompanied by a wedge of bannock and a slice of bramble pie—left over from the batch she'd made with Rose, Tara, and Anice.

But Beth couldn't touch the food. Not tonight.

Instead, she wrapped herself in the blanket.

It wasn't a chill night, for they were in the midst of summer and a lump of peat burned in the nearby hearth. Yet the shock of seeing her husband so close to death settled deep into her bones, making her shiver.

Pulling up her chair close to the bed, Beth watched Niel's face, willing his eyes to flutter open, for him to favor her with that cocky smile of his.

But Niel remained asleep.

Do ye love yer husband?

Jaimee's words of a day earlier taunted her. It was a simple enough question, and yet it had floored her. She'd gaped at Jaimee for a few moments before finding her tongue and answering honestly. "I don't know."

Jaimee's face had stilled before she'd inclined her head. "Then the problem of yer marriage doesn't just lie with Niel, does it?"

The woman's comment had shocked her, and if Beth was honest with herself, anger had cramped her belly as she'd stalked back into the keep. She hadn't felt like showing the lasses how to make bramble pie, yet she'd made them a promise—and she'd kept it.

Nonetheless, her exchange with Jaimee had haunted her ever since.

Reaching out, she placed a hand upon Niel's naked chest, feeling its steady, albeit shallow, rise and fall. Her brow furrowed when she noted his skin was warmer than she'd expected and damp. He was developing a fever.

Beth let out a long sigh.

The choking panic and fear that grasped her around the throat when she'd hurried to his side earlier revealed that her feelings ran deeper than she'd realized. She'd been attracted to Niel from the first, and there was much she admired in him.

But attraction, and even admiration, wasn't love.

Beth had never been in love with any of the men she'd been betrothed to. She'd been fond of them all, and had grieved to hear of their deaths, but her attachment to them hadn't gone deeper than warm affection. They hadn't spent enough time together for love to bloom.

She'd thought romantic love would feel similar to what she felt for her kin: a deep, reassuring bond that brought out her protective instincts.

But that wasn't the emotion that Niel stirred up in her.

Her throat constricted painfully then as she dug her fingertips into the crisp dark hair that covered his chest, her gaze never leaving his face. Niel's sharp features softened in sleep, gleamed as sweat rose in a sheen.

This man roused feelings that made her chest ache. He made her want to rail at him *and* wrap herself around him. Beth sucked in a shallow breath. She'd once thought she understood life and her place in the world.

But at present, she knew nothing.

If this was love, she wasn't prepared.

Why hadn't anyone warned her it hurt this much?

26

THE TWISTS OF FATE

NIEL'S FEVER WAS worse by morning.

Despite her best efforts, Beth had fallen asleep during the night. Seated at her husband's side, she stirred now at the sound of the door creaking open. She'd slumped forward, lying against Niel's chest. Blinking, she pushed herself up, to find her cheek wet with his sweat.

Her gaze shifted to his face, her chest constricting when she saw his cheeks were flushed. The day before, he'd been as pale as a corpse, yet the color on his face she saw now didn't bode well either.

Wincing as she attempted to loosen the knots in her neck and back, Beth's gaze flicked to where Cullodina approached, a wicker basket under one arm.

"He's sweating," Beth greeted her, a note of panic in her voice.

The healer nodded. "It's to be expected, lass. I did my best to clean the wound … and I will apply some more woundwort now" —Cullodina patted her basket— "but his body will be in shock after such an injury. We must do our best to make sure the wound doesn't fester."

Beth nodded, her lips thinning. She would do everything she could.

She helped Cullodina while she removed the poultice she'd applied the day before, cleansed the stitched wound with vinegar, and then applied fresh woundwort.

"When will he awaken?" Beth asked the healer as they worked.

"Soon, lass." Cullodina nodded toward the small clay bottle upon the bedside table. "He will be in pain … so

I've brought something to ease it. Just four drops to a cup of boiled water thrice a day … no more, mind." The healer's gaze shifted to Niel's face then, and with a sigh, she reached across, pushing a strand of dark hair off his sweat-slicked brow. "I hope for his sake our clan-chief remains insensible for a while longer."

But Niel didn't. He awoke shortly after noon, his long dark lashes fluttering against his cheeks as he rose from unconsciousness.

Seated at his side, Beth watched as his usually sharp blue eyes blearily stared up at the rafters, unfocused.

A moment later, a low groan escaped him, pain rippling across his face.

And when her husband's gaze shifted to her, it was fever bright, dark with agony.

Rasping a curse, Niel licked parched lips. "Beth … am I home?"

She shook her head. "No … ye are at Farr Castle." She paused then before giving his hand a gentle squeeze. "Do ye recall what happened, Niel?"

Moments passed as his eyelids fluttered shut and a spasm of pain twisted his face. "Aye," he grunted. "The last thing I remember was standing under a ruined fort upon the beach, blood running down my side."

"That was two days ago. Connor brought ye back to Farr … his healer has been tending to ye."

Niel's eyes opened, his attention settling upon her once more. "Ye arrived here quickly, lass," he said, his voice hoarse.

Beth inhaled slowly. "I was already resident at Farr," she admitted. "Visiting Keira and Maggie while ye were away."

Niel nodded. Of course, he was too ill to be vexed by this news.

Their gazes held for a few moments before he spoke once more. "How bad is it?" the words came out in a croak.

Bad.

Beth gazed back at him. Even Cullodina didn't think he'd make it—she'd seen it in the woman's eyes as she'd departed earlier. But Beth wouldn't let the despair that had settled over this keep infect her as well.

"It's a deep wound, yet the healer has stitched ye up," she said, struggling to keep her voice low and sure. "Now ye just need to rest and let yer body mend."

"I feel as if I've been kicked in the ribs by a carthorse."

"Aye, that's to be expected." Beth released his hand and moved to the bedside table. "But I have something to help the pain." She unstoppered the bottle Cullodina had given her. The woody scent of herbs, mixed with something much sharper, drifted out. As bid, she added four drops to a cup of cooled boiled water and moved back to Niel, placing an extra pillow under his head so that he could sip from the cup.

Even that small action taxed him. And when he'd taken a few sips, Niel fell back against the pillow, panting. His face glistened with sweat. The tincture no doubt tasted foul, yet he didn't complain.

He was in so much pain he likely hadn't even noticed.

Silence fell in the bed-chamber, broken only by the rasp of Niel's breathing. Weakly, he then raised a trembling hand, reaching for hers. Moving closer, Beth entwined her fingers with his, squeezing tight.

"Am I dying?" he asked finally, his voice barely above a whisper.

"No," Beth replied, cursing the tremor in her voice. "Ye are going to rally, Niel Mackay ... ye won't let a wee scratch best ye."

He managed a weak smile. "A *wee scratch* ye say?"

"Aye." Beth leaned forward, her pulse hammering in her throat. "Ye didn't weather all those years at Bass Rock to fall now. Ye are strong, Niel. Ye must fight."

It was mid-afternoon when Beth finally left Niel for a spell. He'd fallen into a fitful sleep, and Cullodina had returned to his beside.

Returning to her bed-chamber, Beth found an iron tub filled with steaming water awaiting her.

Her vision misted at the kind gesture. She had planned to wash quickly, change clothes, and return to Niel's side, yet the bath beckoned.

Her body and soul ached.

Stripping off her clothes, she climbed into the tub, sighing as she sank into the hot water. Steam, scented with lavender, drifted up, filling her senses.

With a sigh, Beth rested her neck against the rim of the tub, closed her eyes—and promptly fell asleep.

When she awoke, the water had cooled. Wincing, Beth sat up, rubbing her stiff neck. Then, grabbing a cake of lye soap, she washed before clambering, shivering, out of the tub and going in search of clean clothes.

She hadn't meant to fall asleep in the bath, yet the rest had reinvigorated her. However, when she opened the shutters to her chamber, she saw that the light was fading outdoors.

And as night fell late this time of year, she realized that she'd been asleep for longer than she'd thought.

Goose, drowning yerself in the bath isn't going to help Niel.

Her pulse quickened. She needed to get back to him.

Leaving her bed-chamber, she collided with Maggie.

"There ye are." Maggie took her firmly by the arm, leading her in the direction of the women's solar—and not Niel's sickroom. "Keira's had supper brought up for ye ... come on."

Beth tried unsuccessfully to pry her arm free, yet Maggie had it in a vice-like grip. "I should get back to Niel."

"He can wait ... his cousin is visiting him at present. Ye need to eat something, Beth ... or ye will be no help to him ... or yerself."

They entered the women's solar, to find both Keira and Jaimee there. The former sat at her loom by the window, while the latter fidgeted upon a chair nearby as she wound wool onto a spindle for her sister-by-marriage. Both their faces lit up at the sight of Beth.

"Ye look as if ye got some rest?" Keira greeted her.

Beth grimaced. "Aye ... although I fell asleep in the bath."

"Here." Maggie guided her over to a small table near the hearth and pushed her down into a chair. "Eat."

Before Beth sat a tray of bread, cheese, and vegetable pottage. It was simple fare, but since Beth's appetite still hadn't returned, she couldn't have cared less. Casting Maggie a look of chagrin, Beth picked up a piece of bread. "Very well, Maggie," she muttered. "Ye don't have to loom over me."

Mollified, the woman moved to a chair opposite and picked up her embroidery.

Meanwhile, Beth forced herself to eat her supper.

Silence settled over the women's solar. Even so, Beth sensed the tension that simmered just underneath Keira, Maggie, and Jaimee's calm.

None of them asked how Niel was faring. And she kept catching Jaimee watching her when she thought Beth wasn't looking. The shadow in her usually bright green eyes made Beth uneasy.

No doubt they'd already been updated by Cullodina. A chill washed over Beth. Did they know something she didn't?

"Has the healer given ye any news, Keira?" Beth asked as she finished the last of her vegetable pottage. She tried to keep her voice steady, yet the quaver in it betrayed her.

The Lady of Farr met her gaze across the chamber, her hands stilling in the midst of weaving a shuttle through the weft of her loom. The chill turned to a lump of ice in Beth's belly, and her supper churned.

Keira had such expressive midnight-blue eyes. And they didn't lie. "She thinks it's just a matter of time,"

Keira admitted softly. "She's seen similar injuries before ... usually when a hunter is gored by a boar, and—"

"But the pike didn't damage his innards," Beth cut her off. "Cullodina said so."

"Aye, but he's lost a lot of blood ... and the cut is long and deep." She faltered then. "He might not be strong enough to fight the fever that now rages through his body."

Beth straightened her spine, the chill replaced by the heat of determination. "He *does* have the strength to fight it," she told Keira firmly. "And if he falters in the days to come, I shall lend him my own."

"I'm sorry we let Gunn get away, Niel." John Mackay's voice rumbled across the bed-chamber. "Once the bastard reached the walls of Dounreay, we couldn't touch him."

Propped up on a nest of pillows, Niel managed a tight smile.

If he hadn't felt so weak, so wracked with pain, he might have laughed at the irony of the situation. Tavish Gunn's force had been decimated, and his youngest brother was now a Mackay captive. However, the Gunn clan-chief had escaped with his life, while Niel—the victor—had been gravely injured.

The twists and turns of fate never failed to surprise him.

Swallowing, Niel drew in a deep breath, trying to ignore the deep, sickening pain that burned down his left side. It pulsed in time with his heartbeat. His limbs felt leaden, weakness pressed him down in the bed as if a heavy hand splayed across his chest, and heat rolled over him in waves.

At present, whether or not Tavish Gunn had escaped was the least of his worries.

However, he understood why John was apologizing to him. Frustration smoldered in his cousin's gaze. Even though he'd lost his left eye and now wore a patch over the empty socket, his look hadn't lost its intensity.

Raking a hand through his curly black hair, John muttered an oath under his breath. "This wasn't how it was supposed to end," he muttered.

"No," Niel replied. "But take heart, cousin. We won."

"Aye." John moved closer to the bed, staring down at him. "But at what cost?"

Silence stretched between them, before Niel asked, "How many of our men fell?"

John's gaze shadowed. "Nearly two hundred."

Niel sucked in a deep breath.

Two hundred souls ... gone. His belly clenched. They'd died for him. Aye, he'd had his reckoning. Yet it had come at a price. Victory suddenly tasted as sour as spoiled milk in his mouth.

Another ponderous hush fell in the bed-chamber before Niel gestured to the chair next to the bed. "Stop hovering," he croaked. "Sit down, man. I wish to speak to ye."

Frowning, John did as bid, although tension rippled off his body, and his expression was wary. It was as if he knew what Niel was about to say.

"Things aren't looking rosy for me, cousin," he said after a pause. There was no self-pity in his voice, no fear. Every man had to die, and few warriors ever reached old age. Maybe his time had come. "I need ye to promise that ye will rule in my stead if it comes to that."

John held his gaze, his throat bobbing. Yet he didn't answer. After a moment, he nodded.

Niel grimaced then, as a particularly intense spasm of pain lanced across his chest. Speaking was taxing him. He could feel malaise pulling him down into its clutches. The fever was fogging his mind. He had to say this before it addled his wits completely. "Beth must be taken care of ... promise me ye shall take her as yer wife if I die."

John's right eye flew open wide. "Niel?"

Something twisted deep within Niel as he held his cousin's gaze. John would never know how much it cost him to make the request. And as the words left his lips, his belly clenched in helpless jealousy.

John Mackay was his cousin, and yet they'd become as close as brothers of late. Nevertheless, he couldn't stand the thought of John being able to spend the rest of his life with Beth when he could not.

John would be able to lie with her, lose himself inside her, see her raise her chin in defiance, and listen to the musical warmth of her voice in the evenings as they sat opposite each other in the solar, enjoying a cup of wine before bed. Would he lock horns with her as Niel had?

Likely not. John's character didn't have the jagged edges that Niel's possessed. He hadn't yet taken a wife, although of late, Niel sensed his reluctance had more to do with the fact that he was maimed, and carried a deep embarrassment about it, rather than an inability to let himself love and be loved.

No, that was Niel's problem, not his cousin's.

"I wouldn't ask this of anyone else," Niel whispered. "Only ye, John."

John's blue eye glittered. "Christ's bones, Niel," he muttered. "Don't ye give up just yet."

"I'm not ... I just want things to be settled." Niel continued to spear his cousin with his gaze. "Will ye wed her?"

Moments passed before John nodded. The gesture was jerky, as if it was taking every ounce of will for him to agree. "If she'll have me," he replied roughly.

"Good." Niel sank back into his nest of pillows. Lord, he was exhausted. It hurt to breathe, to think, to concentrate. But, even so, a tight knot of misery had tied itself under his breastbone.

Beth.

Where was she? He wanted his hand in hers, to hear her voice. Ever since he'd awoken, all his visitors—Connor and John among them—viewed him with fear in their eyes. But his wife didn't. When Niel stared up into

Beth's warm gaze, he could almost believe he'd live through this.

She was his strength, his anchor. He needed her at his side.

27

TRAITOR

BETH SHIFTED POSITION upon the chair and stretched out her back. It was early morning. Her body ached, her backside was numb, and her eyes burned with fatigue. Yet she didn't go to her bed.

Next to Beth, her husband groaned and thrashed, a nerve in his face flickering as he fought the fever that pulled him under, like a Kelpie, dragging him to the depths of a deep dark loch.

"Don't let it best ye," she whispered, reaching for a strip of cloth on the bedside table. Dunking it in a bowl of cool water, she wrung it out before mopping Niel's fevered brow. "Show us yer indomitable spirit, Niel. *Fight*."

He couldn't hear her, for her husband had slipped into this state earlier the evening before. But Beth continued to talk to him. She spoke to him frankly, as she never had when he was awake. She told him how much she admired him—how, despite everything, the sight of him brought her senses alive, and that she was sorry for pushing him so hard.

She promised Niel that when he awoke, they'd start over. Instead of demanding he give her things he wasn't capable of, she'd focus on finding fulfillment in her life by other means. She was indeed blessed, for she was a clan-chief's wife and had her beloved sisters living with her. And she had plenty of interests to keep her busy.

She'd give him his freedom and not look to him for all the answers. They'd be happy together then.

Beth talked to him until her throat was dry and sore, clasping his limp hand in hers. And as she spoke, the determination that burned in the pit of her belly burned hotter still.

Niel *would* live. He had to.

Alexander Gunn ventured out into the landward bailey, his gaze narrowing as it swept to the keep. It was just after dawn, and the sun crept over the castle, warming the cool stone. Connor was making his way down the stairs, heading toward him.

Connor's expression was grave as he approached.

"Is he dead then?" Alex asked. It was a blunt question, yet he wasn't a man given to bandying words.

The chieftain of Farr shook his head. "Not yet. Niel's tough." Connor gave a humorless smile. "And his wife has a will of iron. Beth has barely left his side."

Alex's gaze widened. It had been nearly seven days since they'd returned from the north, bringing their injured clan-chief with them. It had been a tumultuous time, for despite the Mackay victory, they'd still suffered heavy losses. Joy blended with sorrow within the walls of Farr Castle.

There had been a number of burials in the days following the battle, and now they awaited one more.

A shadow had fallen over Farr, as the inhabitants all waited for the hammer to fall.

Surely, Niel Mackay couldn't last much longer. And yet he did. Jaimee had reported to Alex that the man had thrashed about in a fever for days now, rising into consciousness briefly now and again before delirium took him once more. His wound hadn't festered, yet Cullodina had informed them that the clan-chief likely bore injuries inside that she hadn't been able to see.

"Jaimee tells me Beth has a stubborn streak that would rival hers," Connor said with a rueful smile.

Alex huffed a laugh. "Aye, well, the Mackay will have met his match then."

The two men's gazes met and held, an unspoken message passing between them. After a decade living at Farr Castle, Alex had become part of Connor's family. It had taken awhile for the chieftain to trust him completely—a process that Alex hadn't tried to hurry.

He didn't need Connor Mackay to see him as a brother. His wife and bairns were all that Alex required to be happy. His work as the keep's blacksmith was tiring, although now that he'd taken on two apprentices, he was no longer dead on his feet at the end of the day.

Aye, Alex was content in his life here at Farr—more than content if he was honest—and yet over the past week, he'd been on edge, troubled.

Seeing the look on Connor's face, Alex realized that the chieftain knew why.

"Ye want to see yer brother, don't ye?" Connor asked after a pause.

Alex drew in a slow breath.

It was a strange thing, the hold that blood ties had upon a man. He hadn't seen any of his brothers in years and rarely spared a thought for them.

But knowing that his youngest sibling, Will, was here, locked up in one of the cave cages beneath the fortress, niggled at him like a sore tooth.

Connor was right, Alex wished to see him.

He nodded, and Connor flashed him a rueful smile. "Go on then ... I told the guards to expect ye this morn."

Alex's mouth lifted at the corners, and he cast a glance back over his shoulder at where his apprentices waited for him in the entrance to the forge. "Get started, lads," he called to them. "I'll be with ye shortly."

He then turned back to the chieftain, meeting his eye once more. "Thank ye, Connor."

Making his way down the steep, narrow stairs outside the curtain walls a short while later, Alex reflected at life's ironies.

He hadn't been down here in ten years, not since he'd once been a prisoner in one of these cages. The cave cages were nooks carved out of the cliff-face. There were around a dozen of them, and Alex found his brother in the lowest cell—the same one *he'd* occupied all those years earlier.

The fine hair on the back of Alex's neck prickled as he approached. It was a reminder of how fragile, how blurred, the line was between friend and foe.

The morning sun sparkled upon the sea and warmed Alex's face. A sharp sea-breeze tugged at his hair and clothing, and the fishy stench of shag droppings made his nose sting and his eyes water. However, Alex paid that no mind—instead, his gaze was upon the man seated upon a wooden pallet at the back of the cave cage.

Will had drawn his long legs up under his chin. A wound to his temple had formed a large scab, although his face was clean, revealing that Connor had allowed his injuries to be tended. He wore stained braies and lèine, with a leather vest over the top. And although he was trying not to show it, his brother trembled with cold. His lean face was pale.

Alex's mouth thinned. He'd never forgotten just how cold it got in the cave cages overnight. Fortunately for Will, it was high summer, but even so, the chill from the rocks seemed to drill into a man's bones overnight.

A pair of hard purple-grey eyes—so similar to his own—glared back at him.

Halting before the entrance to the cage, separated by sturdy iron bars, Alex let his gaze roam over his brother.

Although he'd always been lean, Will appeared to have filled out a little with the years. There was more muscle to him these days; he'd lost his youthful lankiness.

Moments stretched out, and then Alex spoke. "Hello, Will."

Will's mouth twisted. "I was wondering when ye'd pay me a visit."

Hostility dripped from his brother's voice, yet Alex merely shrugged. "And now I have."

"Traitor." The accusation cracked through the air between them.

Alex's mouth twitched, and he let out a soft laugh. "I didn't go into battle with the Mackays, Will."

"No, but ye have made yer home here, amongst them."

"Aye."

Will's glare speared him, yet Alex didn't wither under it. Instead, a kernel of warmth bloomed deep in his chest.

By blood and bone, he'd missed the Gunn animosity. He and his five brothers had always sparred—although Alex had tolerated Tavish and Will more than Evan and Blair. And the third-born son, Roy, had been impossible to warm to.

"How are things at Castle Gunn?" he asked casually after a brief pause.

Will's dark brows crashed together. "Why do ye care?"

"I don't particularly ... I'm just curious."

Hades, if looks could kill, he'd have been writhing on the ground right now. Will's hands had clenched into fists.

"Tavish rules the clan well," Will ground out in reply. *Better than ye would have done.* The words were unspoken yet clear by his tone. "He and Robina have four bairns now, all lads."

"And the other brothers?" Alex wasn't exactly sure why he was asking, only that the need to know about his kin pricked at him now. Aye, the Mackays treated him well, but on one level, he'd always be an outsider here.

Will knew it too, for he sneered. "Blair and Evan both have families of their own too."

"And Roy? What's that bastard up to these days?"

Will barked a harsh laugh. "Who knows? Tavish cast him out a few years ago ... after Roy tried to kill him."

Alex cocked an eyebrow, even if he wasn't surprised. Roy had always chafed at not being the first-born son. "And ye, Will," he asked finally. "Do ye have a wife and a brood of yer own yet?"

His brother's lean face tensed, his eyes narrowing. "I'm wed." And although he didn't elaborate, Alex caught the edge to his voice. He'd always been able to read his brothers well, an ability that hadn't dimmed with time, it seemed.

If Alex was to hazard a guess, he'd say his brother was regretting his choice of wife.

Silence fell then as the brothers eyeballed each other.

"So, are ye here to gloat?" Will asked eventually. His tone wasn't any warmer than earlier, yet a weariness had crept in. Things weren't looking rosy for the youngest of the Gunn brothers.

"No," Alex replied honestly. "I just wanted to see ye … before they take ye to Castle Varrich."

Will leaned forward then, his gaze spearing Alex. "Is Niel Mackay dead yet? Last time I saw him, the whoreson was bleeding out over the ground."

"He lives still," Alex replied, his tone emotionless. "Although, perhaps not for much longer." He paused then, inclining his head. The Mackay had lost a number of years to Bass Rock. Most likely, he wanted one of the Gunns to taste what it was to have one's freedom, one's future, ripped away. He'd enjoy making Will suffer. "For yer sake, ye'd better start praying his end is near."

28

COME BACK TO ME

SHE NEVER GAVE up hope. Even as her husband's strong body wasted before her eyes, even as his eyes sank into their sockets and the vitality leached from him.

However, Beth *did* start to dread leaving Niel's bedchamber.

She couldn't bear the shadowed gazes, the pity. The folk of Farr believed their clan-chief doomed. None of them voiced their thoughts, yet it was evident in every averted stare, every forced smile. Word had been sent to Varrich of his deteriorating state. But all anyone could do was wait and see.

Keira and Maggie asked Beth to join them in the evenings in the women's solar, yet she declined. Her world became her husband's chamber. She had her clothing brought in and a pallet made up for her before the fire. She bathed there, took all her meals there.

And never strayed far from Niel's side.

Eventually, even Cullodina's serenity started to show cracks. Upon the eighth evening after the battle, the healer packed up her things into her basket, a rare frown marring her brow.

When she met Beth's eye, her gaze was grave. "Prepare yerself, lass," she murmured, her tone uncharacteristically flat. "He cannot go on like this much longer. If yer husband's fever doesn't break by dawn, he will lose this fight."

Beth didn't answer Cullodina. She merely stared back at her, a coil tightening deep within her chest. The healer had been her North Star throughout this ordeal. Yet the resignation she saw in her eyes made a chill skate down Beth's spine.

But after Cullodina left, Beth settled down upon her chair at Niel's side and reached out, taking his limp hand in hers.

"Ye have reached a crossroads now, Niel," she murmured, squeezing his hand firmly. "And ye must choose which path to take." She drew in a shaky breath. "Come back to me, mo ghràdh. Come back."

Mo ghràdh—*my love.*

The words had slipped easily from her tongue, and as they did, something eased within her. Aye, it was true. There was no longer any doubt. She could now answer Jaimee. She did love him, and knowing it brought her peace, as if a missing piece of her had just slid into place.

Love wasn't perfect. It wasn't rosy sunsets and a chorus of angels singing—but it was real. Niel didn't feel as she did, but her love might give him the strength he needed to win this battle.

Love didn't mend everything—if it had, her mother would still be alive—but all the same, she knew how powerful it was. Its energy crackled inside the chamber and made the fine hair on the back of Beth's arms prickle.

She had to believe in it.

The rest of the eve passed silently. A servant brought Beth in a light supper, and she consumed it—out of necessity rather than enjoyment though. Niel received no visitors afterward, and Beth was grateful for it.

She wasn't sure she could face anyone this evening.

Cullodina would likely have told Connor that Niel's condition had reached a crisis.

All of them were waiting to see what the morning would bring.

Sipping from a cup of wine, Beth settled into her chair at Niel's side and watched over him. Later, instead of retiring to her pallet in front of the fire, she climbed onto the bed next to him. She stretched out against his right, uninjured, side. It wasn't comfortable, perched there upon the edge of the mattress, and the heat of his fevered body seared her like a furnace, yet Beth didn't care.

She needed to be close to him tonight.

Laying her cheek against his chest, she stretched out her hand and placed it over his heart.

"Come back to me, mo ghràdh," she whispered to him once more, even as the bitter irony of the situation hit her. How she'd longed to share her husband's bed at night. And now she was—just not how she'd hoped.

Her throat ached. Tears stung her eyelids, leaking out onto her cheeks and wetting Niel's chest.

Beth let them flow.

She'd done all she could and wished she could have done more. The rest was up to Niel.

She didn't think she'd be able to sleep, not when she was so worried about her husband, but lying next to him, intense drowsiness came over her, and before she knew it, exhaustion swept her away.

Beth awoke slowly, the fog of sleep drawing back to release her. Stretching, she snuggled into a warm male body, sighing.

She'd slept better than in a long while. What a relief it was to feel properly rested.

Eyes opening, she saw that light filtered in through the gaps in the wooden shutters. The fire in the hearth had long since died, yet it wasn't cold in the bed-chamber.

A low male groan drew her attention then, and Beth glanced back to the man lying beside her.

Niel Mackay lived still.

Beth's breathing caught as it occurred to her that, although his body was warm, it no longer burned with fever. Reaching out, she felt his brow. It was dry.

Slipping out of bed, she padded over to the window, unlatched the shutters, and threw them open. Warm air, sweet with the scent of summer, filtered in. Beth turned then and went back to bed, stretching out once more next to Niel, and propping herself up on an elbow to watch his sleeping face.

Were her eyes deceiving her, or did he look a little better this morning?

The lack of fever was a good sign indeed, and now that she had light to see him by, she noted that the high spots of color on his cheekbones had gone.

And as she gazed upon him, Niel's eyes fluttered upon.

He looked up at her, his eyes bleary for a few moments before he focused on her.

"Beth?" he rasped softly.

"Aye," she whispered, her vision blurring. She couldn't help it. Tears started to trickle down her cheeks.

"Why are ye weeping?" His voice was weak, yet she didn't miss the note of concern.

"Relief," she hiccoughed, scrubbing at her cheeks. "Ye teetered on the brink last night, Niel ... but I asked ye to come back to me ... and ye have."

He gazed up at her, and then his throat bobbed. Was Beth imagining it, or were his eyes gleaming with unshed tears too?

Moments stretched out before Beth pushed herself upright, sniffing as her nose started to run. She needed to regain control, for she was on the brink of unraveling completely. It was hard to breathe.

"How are ye feeling?" she asked, her voice hoarse.

"Better," he croaked. "It no longer feels as if I'm wading through a peat bog."

"Ye must be thirsty?"

Niel managed a feeble smile before nodding.

Beth clambered off the bed and poured a cup of water from a ewer on the bedside table. Seated next to him, she helped him drink a few sips. "I'll have some mutton broth brought up this morning," she said. "Ye need to regain yer strength."

He huffed. "Aye ... I don't think I can even sit up." Their gazes met and held. "But I'm alive, lass ... thanks to ye."

The pressure in Beth's chest increased, and she swallowed hard. "I'm not the one to thank," she murmured. "Cullodina's healing skills should be praised instead."

Niel nodded. His gaze never left Beth's, while his hand slid across the coverlet, capturing hers. Niel's fingers entwined through her own, and Beth's heart started to gallop.

"I don't remember much of the past days," he admitted, his voice turning huskier still. He gestured to the cup she still held, and Beth leaned forward, allowing him to take another sip or two before he continued. "It was as if I'd journeyed far from here, and only glimpses of it remain with me." He paused there before his lips curved. "But I recall *ye*, wife."

Beth swallowed once more. "Ye are a fighter, Niel Mackay, I'll give ye that," she replied, trying to lighten the mood. She was dangerously close to collapsing upon his chest in a sobbing mess. Admitting her love the night before had given her strength, yet now she felt brittle, as if one more word would cause her to shatter. And she was afraid of what might happen if she did, of what she might say.

Things were too raw this morning. Niel had just emerged from rubbing shoulders with the grim reaper.

"Aye," he agreed softly. "But I married one too."

"Of course, we all knew ye'd rally." John clasped forearms with Niel, a grin splitting his face. "Ye were never going to let the Gunns best ye."

Niel snorted before casting a glance at where Beth sat a few yards away. She was embroidering a garment, although the face she now pulled told him that John's heartiness was feigned.

They'd all thought he was done for.

In truth, so had Niel. During the few moments in which he'd awoken since the battle, he'd been sure the end was approaching.

Propped up on a hillock of pillows now, he actually felt on the mend. After a bowl of mutton broth and a few mouthfuls of bannock, the weakness and tremors that had plagued his body upon waking had faded. And then he'd managed a noon meal of boiled egg, fresh bread, and butter.

He wore a loose lèine over his torso, yet when Cullodina had changed his dressings earlier, Niel had seen how thin he was—thinner even than when he'd escaped from Bass Rock. His belly was concave, and he could count his ribs.

It would take a few more meals before he regained some flesh, and even longer before he'd be well enough to build muscle again. The healer had told him sternly that he would need another six weeks at least before he considered lifting anything heavier than a tankard of ale—and many more before he'd be able to swing a blade.

Her advice hadn't bothered him. Niel didn't intend to wield a sword for a while.

For the first time in a long while, he wasn't plagued by restlessness. He couldn't blame his quest for revenge for that either—he'd always been impatient, always looking for a fight. That was why his father had been able to lay the blame upon him before the king. After the Battle of Harpsdale, Niel had indeed insisted on leading raids against the Gunns, despite King James's repeated warnings to cease.

But today, as he met his cousin's bright gaze once more, Niel wished for nothing more than what he had right now.

They'd all come to see him: Connor, Morgan, and their wives, as well as Hugh and Robin. Their eyes shone with relief, and Niel was humbled. He'd laughed with them, enjoying Connor and Morgan's gentle teasing. He was still weak, yet his body had won the battle it had been waging. The shadow that had once darkened this bed-chamber had lifted, and the summer breeze that drifted in through the open window tickled his face.

Niel drank it all in, with the senses of a man who understood how close he'd come to losing everything.

He'd lost much already in that battle. Nearly two hundred warriors, men who'd followed him unquestioningly, were now fodder for the worms.

"Tavish Gunn will be disappointed to hear ye have survived," John teased, in an attempt to lighten the somber mood. "He's already sent word ... demanding that we release his brother."

Usually, even hearing the name 'Gunn' quickened his temper. But not today.

He was too busy thinking about all the women who'd been left widows, all the bairns who'd grow up fatherless. Because of him.

"Niel?" John was watching him, waiting for instruction.

Clearing his throat, Niel attempted to shove his guilt aside. "Ye can send a missive back to Gunn on my behalf," he replied with a frown, "telling him that his brother won't be going home."

Aye, there were some things he wouldn't relent on— *couldn't* relent on. William Gunn would remain his prisoner at Castle Varrich. It was a reminder to his enemies that the Mackays were to be minded in future. There would be no more thieving of sheep and cattle, and no more opportunistic border raids.

Feeling queasy, Niel shifted his attention away from his cousin, to where Beth sat sewing in silence.

She'd been looking down, concentrating on her stitches, yet feeling the weight of his stare, she glanced up.

Their gazes held, and an ache rose at the base of Niel's throat. He swallowed hard.

I don't deserve this woman.

He'd spurned her attempts to get close to him and humiliated her the last time he'd taken her. She should have hated him for that. But instead, she'd remained at his side. Beth had believed he'd survive, even when everyone else gave up hope.

Heat rose to Niel's face, and his skin started to tingle. Shame wasn't a sensation he'd felt often over the years, yet it flooded over him now.

He owed this woman an apology, and if he had the balls, he'd do it right now—with everyone looking on.

Niel cleared his throat. "Beth."

She cast aside her sewing and moved across to him. John stepped back, allowing her to perch on the edge of the bed. Taking his hand, Beth gave it a gentle squeeze. "What is it?" she asked softly.

"I" —he began, struggling to speak at all, let alone say the right words— "Back in Varrich ... I ..."

His voice trailed off. Suddenly, it felt as if a hand had clamped across his throat and was squeezing tightly.

Fazart! He had the courage to face his foes in battle—yet not to give a heartfelt request for forgiveness.

He tried again. "I wish to ... I need to ..." Again, the power of speech deserted him.

Jaw clenching, Niel dropped his attention to the coverlet, shame pulsing like an ember in his chest. Everyone present had witnessed how useless he was. The room had gone deathly silent. Aye, it seemed he was brave in most areas of life—except where it truly mattered.

"Niel." Beth's whisper made him raise his head so she could meet his eye once more. And when their gazes did connect, their surroundings fell away. Niel's breath caught when he saw that his wife's eyes gleamed with unshed tears—and tenderness. "Ye don't need to say anything," she murmured, her fingers tightening around his once more. "I understand."

29

MAKING FOR HOME

NIEL WASN'T WELL enough to leave Farr for another fortnight.

They eventually departed upon a windy dawn. The sun peeked over the bare hills to the east while a group gathered in the landward bailey to see the clan-chief off.

Niel managed to mount his stallion without assistance, although Beth noted that he'd gone pale and lines of strain bracketed his mouth and nose once he perched atop his mount. She'd been concerned about him riding Stoirm—a fiery bay who usually lived up to his name 'Storm'—although the courser appeared as meek as a lamb this morning.

"Are ye certain ye are well enough to journey home today?" she asked, frowning. "We can stay longer if need be."

Niel shook his head, a little of his old impatience flashing in his blue eyes. "I'm well enough," he replied testily. "Cullodina has given me her blessing."

"Aye, she has," Connor said, viewing his clan-chief with a wry smile. "But remember what she said about not lifting a sword for a long while."

Niel snorted. "Aye ... fear not. I know I'm in no state for that."

Beth let out the breath she hadn't even realized she'd been holding. It was a relief to hear such an admission, for she knew how stubborn Niel could be. He truly was a paradox. She'd never met anyone as strong—and yet it had pained her to see how he'd struggled two weeks earlier. He'd wanted to apologize, to lay himself bare before her, and yet had been unable to.

Watching the battle he'd waged with himself, and lost, she'd finally understood the man she'd wed.

Niel's decision to keep her at arm's length hadn't been designed to hurt her, or even selfishness on his part.

The man was incapable of expressing how he felt.

Beth's throat thickened as she recalled the agony in his eyes. Then and there, she'd resolved to let the poor man be. It was cruel to demand love from someone who struggled so deeply with their emotions.

"It should be a warm day, despite the wind," Morgan piped up. He stood behind Connor, his arm looped around his wife's shoulders. "Have a safe journey back to Varrich."

Niel flashed him a smile. "Thank ye, Morgan." His gaze shifted then to Connor and Keira, who stood at his side. "And thanks to both of ye for ensuring I've been well cared for … I shall never forget this."

Connor smiled back, and the two men shared a long look, a silent understanding passing between them.

Beth met Keira's eye, her mouth curving as she nodded to her friend. Her gaze then shifted to Maggie before she spied a tall, willowy woman with red-gold hair standing to the rear of the crowd.

Jaimee had come to see them off.

Noticeably, Alexander Gunn was absent. However, William Gunn sat upon a cart a few yards away, wrists and ankles bound. The youngest Gunn brother's lean face was inscrutable, although his grey eyes burned as he viewed Niel Mackay.

No doubt he was infuriated that the clan-chief had survived.

Favoring Jaimee with a warm smile, Beth glanced once more at her husband. With each passing day, Niel appeared stronger. He was still painfully thin, but once they returned to Varrich, she would ensure he received meals that would help him regain muscle and flesh.

The Mackays of Varrich clattered out of the landward bailey, traveling under a wide stone arch and onto the road that led through the village, before cutting southeast. It was a day's journey back to the Kyle of Tongue, over scrubby hills.

Warmth filtered through Beth as she thought of her sisters. Despite that Keira and the other women here at Farr had been friendly and hospitable, she'd started to sorely miss Neave, Jean, and Eilidh. The bond she had with them was strong; they understood her in a way that few people ever had. She looked forward to hearing the lilt of Neave's voice, to smiling at Jean's dry wit, and to basking in the warmth of Eilidh's beautiful smile.

Since her marriage, she'd neglected them all a little, as she'd been so focused on gaining her husband's attention.

That would change now.

She saw the world with different eyes.

It warmed her to see Niel's swift recovery, day by day. Despite that he hadn't tried to speak intimately with her again, their rapport had been friendly, easier than it had been in the past. Of late, he often sought her eye and initiated conversations whenever they spent time together.

Beth enjoyed their chats, especially her husband's keen observations on life. Nonetheless, she steeled herself for their return to Varrich. Once Niel recovered his strength and resumed his duties as clan-chief, things would likely be different between them.

As such, she needed to focus on her own life. When she wasn't busy running the household, she'd spend time with her sisters, cooking, and take long walks to gather mushrooms, berries, and culinary herbs. And she'd appreciate what Niel was capable of giving her, instead of lamenting his flaws.

Beth had a good life at Castle Varrich, and, despite everything they'd weathered, she was proud to be wedded to Niel Mackay. She would no longer try to force her husband to love her. For now, it was enough that she loved him—even if she hadn't yet told him. The man wasn't ready for such a declaration, and perhaps he never would be. Today, it was enough for her to see his health was improving.

Her stocky garron couldn't keep pace with the courser that Niel rode, even at a walk—and so she let him draw ahead, alongside John. The two men chatted together, and then Niel gave a soft laugh.

The wind carried the sound toward her. It was pleasant to her ears and made Beth smile. It occurred to her then that Niel hadn't laughed since the Battle of Ruaig-Shansaid—the Sandside Chase—as folk were now calling it. It had indeed been a slaughter, and the loss of so many Mackay warriors, despite their victory, weighed heavily upon him.

Once they'd known Niel would live, the other Mackay chieftains who'd lingered at Farr had returned to their brochs. As such, only Niel, John, their warriors, and their captive traveled with her today. The rattling of the cart near the rear of the company was a constant reminder of the prisoner they brought with them.

Beth's expression sobered as she wondered if Niel would ever let William Gunn go, or whether the warrior would spend the rest of his days locked away in the dungeon. There were caves at the base of the promontory upon which Castle Varrich stood, where locals had once lived. These days, they housed criminals.

Knowing how stubborn Niel was, she couldn't see her husband relenting anytime soon. And, if she was honest, she couldn't blame him. The feuding between the Gunns and the Mackays had been fueled by both sides. But the Mackays had been punished for it, while George Gunn and his sons had all escaped penalty.

Ahead, Niel gingerly turned in the saddle, his face tensing as his healing injury pained him. His gaze speared hers. "What are ye doing riding so far behind, Beth?" he asked. "Come ... ride at my side."

Beth snorted, even as a kernel of warmth flowered in her chest at his words. "I fear Clover is too slow to keep up with Stoirm."

"Then I shall slow him down," he replied.

Niel reined in the stallion, allowing Beth to draw level, while John dropped back behind them.

"It'll take us until midnight to reach Varrich at this pace," she said, glancing right to see her husband was watching her.

"Let it," he answered with a smile. "We aren't in a rush."

Beth cocked her head. His manner was so different of late. The man she'd married had bristled with nervous energy, had been unable to sit still for any length of time. But this morning, Niel acted as if it could have taken them days to return home and it wouldn't have bothered him. He wore his long dark hair tied back at his neck today, a look that emphasized the leanness of his face. Yet his dark-blue eyes were penetrating as they focused upon her, and Beth's breathing accelerated.

They hadn't lain together since he'd awoken from his fever—for his injuries still pained him considerably—and she wondered when he'd reach for her.

Her belly fluttered. It seemed like a lifetime ago now since they'd last coupled, even though it had been little over a month. The wildness of that encounter, the anger that had exploded between them, made her a little nervous about being intimate with her husband again.

They still didn't share the same bed. Every eve, since Niel had begun his recovery, she retired to her own chamber. Back at Varrich, it was likely they'd continue to sleep apart, and the thought sent a jolt of sadness through her—one that she swiftly pushed aside.

Enough of this, Beth, she chastised herself. *Ye know how things are.*

And as disappointing as it was, that was the truth.

"How is yer side?" she asked casually, bracing herself for a frown from her husband. He didn't like her fussing over him. However, she'd noted that he didn't mind if Keira or Cullodina did so.

"A little sore ... but that's to be expected," he replied in a tone that warned her not to fret over him. After a brief pause, Niel continued, "I must admit I'm a poor patient. I've fought in many battles over the years ... but have escaped with little more than a few minor scrapes and cuts." His mouth twisted then. "Fate was saving me for Ruaig-Shansaid, it seems."

"Aye ... and ye nearly met yer maker there," Beth reminded him.

He huffed a soft laugh. "I'm fortunate indeed that my wife has taken such good care of me."

Embarrassed, Beth cleared her throat. "As I said ... that was Cullodina's doing."

He shook his head. "The healer told me of how ye helped her clean, stitch, and dress the wound. She said ye were tireless in yer vigilance over me." His gaze never left hers. "Even when everyone despaired, ye didn't."

Feeling heat rise to her cheeks, Beth glanced away. She couldn't believe Cullodina had told Niel that. "Aye, well, I didn't care to be made a widow so soon."

His gaze twinkled. "I'm glad to hear it."

They rode side-by-side in companionable silence for a spell, crossing heather-clad hills, the wind tugging at their hair and clothing, before Beth spied a huge bird of prey gliding high above. It had brown body plumage, massive broad wings with fingered ends, and a white wedge-shaped tail.

"Look!" she exclaimed, pointing to the predator. "A sea eagle!"

Niel craned his neck. "Aye," he replied, his tone awed. "Iolar sùil na grèine." He'd used the old name for the bird, meaning 'eagle of the sun's eye'. "The fishermen will be happy today."

Beth smiled. Indeed, according to Highland folklore, the appearance of a sea eagle would cause fish to rise to the surface of the sea. Some fishermen even smeared eagle fat upon their bait to increase their catch.

"I haven't seen one since leaving Foulis," Beth said, her gaze tracking the majestic bird across the windswept sky. "There was a female sea eagle that used to circle the castle sometimes."

"I haven't asked ye much about what yer life was like before ye wed me, have I?"

Beth glanced back at Niel to see that he was watching her once more, his expression serious. His eyes had shadowed.

"No, ye haven't," she admitted. It was one of the many things that had disappointed her since coming to live at Castle Varrich. Her husband appeared to have little curiosity about her or her past.

"I was a dolt ... and I wish to make amends for that," he said softly. "I'd like to hear about where ye grew up."

Beth inclined her head. "Really?"

"Aye ... go on. I've never visited Foulis. Describe it to me."

Of course he hadn't. The seat of the Munro clan lay far to the south, and her father had only tended to host local clan gatherings over the years.

"It sits near Cromarty Firth, surrounded by green meadows and an oak wood," she began. "The castle perches high upon a mound with a stone motte and a great tower." Warmth seeped through her at the memory of the Tower of Strath Skiath, as the castle was also known. "Locals call it 'the eagle's nest', for it has a view for many furlongs distant ... as a bairn, I used to climb up to the battlements and imagine I could see all of Scotland from the tower top."

"And what were ye like as a child?"

"Much the same as now." Her gaze held his. "Stubborn and bossy ... the curse of being the eldest sister, I'm afraid."

"There's more to ye than that, Beth."

She raised an eyebrow, inviting him to continue.

Niel cleared his throat, clearly embarrassed. "Ye are courageous ... and warm-hearted," he admitted after a pause, his voice lowering. "I should have told ye that awhile back."

Now it was Beth's turn to be self-conscious. Heat rose to her cheeks. His unexpected candidness had caught her off-guard. She could see from the faint sheen of sweat on his forehead that those words hadn't come easily. She wondered if he'd been working up to this moment.

"We shall pay yer father a visit at Samhuinn, if ye wish?" Niel continued, his gaze never leaving hers. "I should like to see Foulis for myself ... and ye and yer sisters will want to be reunited with kin again."

A wide smile flowered across Beth's face. Joy rippled through her at the thought of seeing her father and Laila once more. "Aye, I'd love that," she replied.

30

WHERE'S MY WIFE?

DESPITE THAT CULLODINA had pronounced him well enough to travel, the journey back to Castle Varrich took its toll upon Niel.

As they approached the castle, its sandstone walls glowing in the setting sun, he sagged in the saddle. They'd taken plenty of breaks en route, but as the day wore on, he'd felt gradually more tired. His back now ached, and his left side throbbed in time with his heartbeat.

It was a bonny evening, and the sculpted edges of Ben Hope and Ben Loyal soared high, etched against a pale blue sky. The wind had dropped to a soft breeze, and the waters of the kyle sparkled.

And despite that the pain had started to make him feel a little nauseated and light-headed, Niel couldn't fail to admire the beauty of his home.

Cottars working the fields, their faces tanned brown from the sun, waved to them as they rode into Tongue, while villagers came out of their cottages to cheer and call to their clan-chief when he rode through their midst.

Niel waved back to them, smiling at the relief on their faces. Word of his victory against the Gunns, the warriors they'd lost, and their clan-chief's subsequent recovery from his life-threatening injury had reached them, it seemed. And when he saw tears glittering in some of their eyes, Niel's breathing grew shallow.

A few of them would have lost kin during that battle, yet they still welcomed him home. These were his people. And he'd prove to them that he was worthy of their love, their respect.

Niel's gaze shifted to the village kirk, and the graveyard behind it—and he thought of his father.

Had Angus-Dow Mackay felt this way about the folk he ruled? It was a great responsibility for one man to shoulder and at the same time an incredible honor. These people looked to him to keep their clan strong and safe—but doing so wasn't as straightforward as he'd once believed.

Leaving the village behind, they made their way toward the winding road that would take them up the promontory to the castle. Along the way, the warriors in charge of the prisoner broke off from the group, heading toward the dungeon at the base of the hill. Niel glanced over his shoulder, his gaze tracking William Gunn. His captive stared back at him, his eyes flint-hard.

Niel's mouth lifted at the corners in a humorless smile. Those Gunns were tough bastards, he'd give them that.

Turning back, Niel urged Stoirm up the incline. And as he rode, Niel caught Beth giving him worried looks. She'd clearly noted that he wasn't feeling well, but given his prickly responses whenever she inquired after his health, had decided to keep her comments to herself.

Niel was grateful.

He didn't suffer weakness of any kind in himself gracefully. The pain made him ill-tempered. All he wished for now was some wine to take the edge off the dull throb down his left side and a bed to stretch out on. A wave of nausea washed over him as he rode through the stone arch, under the portcullis, and into Castle Varrich's wide bailey.

Of course, a crowd had gathered to receive them, and the three Munro sisters were out front.

Cheering erupted, the noise reverberating off stone. Even the chaplain, old Father Lucas, had hobbled out to see him.

The sisters stared at him, gazes wide with worry and curiosity. Niel imagined he didn't look his best, and when he slid down from Stoirm's back, his knees wobbled under him.

A moment later, Beth was at his side. "Yer face is grey, Niel," she murmured, pushing her shoulder under his armpit to help prop him up.

He grimaced. "Aye ... I think this journey might have been too much after all." Maybe they should have stayed on in Farr for another day or two, as Beth had suggested.

"Come, Niel." His cousin appeared before him. He then lent Niel his shoulder before flashing Beth a smile. "All is well ... I shall make sure he gets upstairs."

Beth favored John with a reluctant nod before she released Niel, stepping back from him. "Ye'll want to swap to the right," she advised John. "Ye are standing on his injured side."

"Stop talking about me as if I'm infirm ... or deaf," Niel grumbled.

In truth, however, he was nearly out of fight. He wasn't even sure he could make it up the stairs to his quarters.

Watching her husband go, leaning heavily against his cousin, Beth frowned. She hadn't been exaggerating. Niel's face had paled alarmingly when he'd dismounted his stallion.

She hoped the journey's exertions hadn't set him back.

"Beth!" Neave collided with her, enfolding her in a tight hug. "I missed ye!"

"We *all* missed ye." Eilidh was right behind her, cheeks flushed in excitement.

"Shall I go down to the village and fetch the healer?" Jean, ever the practical one, asked.

Swallowing a lump in her throat, and blinking back tears, Beth nodded. "I think that's best ... thank ye, Jean."

Her sister flashed her a smile. She then picked up her skirts, turning on her heel, and hurried toward the gates.

Beth watched her go before realizing that both Neave and Eilidh were scrutinizing her, their eyes bright.

"What happened?" Eilidh asked, her voice lowering as she stepped closer.

"We heard about the battle ... the losses ... and the Mackay's injury," Neave said, her gaze darting around the bailey, which was now filled with men and horses. "And the prisoner. Where is he?"

"They took him directly to the caves beneath the castle," Beth replied, distracted. Her attention was now riveted upon the oaken door to the keep, where Niel and John had just disappeared.

As much as she wanted to catch up with her sisters, and assuage their curiosity about what had transpired in the time spent apart, she couldn't focus.

Instead, she needed to be at her husband's side.

"He will rest for a while now." Tess, the healer from Tongue village—a tall woman of around thirty winters with a shock of curly black hair—cut Beth a glance before her full mouth stretched into a smile. "I've given him a sleeping draft." She then returned her attention to her patient and placed a hand over Niel's brow. "There's no sign of fever, which is promising."

Beth's shoulders sagged with relief. "And his wound ... it hasn't reopened, has it?"

Tess shook her head. She fixed Beth with a level gaze, her green eyes compassionate. "It's healing well ... but the curing of the skin is much faster than the flesh underneath. He mustn't rush things."

"I'll see he doesn't," Beth assured her.

"Good." The healer moved to a nearby table and started packing her things away into the basket she'd brought with her. "Once he awakes, he will feel much better ... but rest and plenty of rib-sticking food are what the clan-chief needs now."

"I'll make sure he receives it ... thank ye, Tess."

The healer flashed her another wide smile. The woman was striking rather than beautiful, with a large mouth that dominated her face and heavy-lidded emerald eyes. But when she smiled, she was radiant. She wasn't as experienced as Cullodina, yet Beth instinctively trusted her, as she had Farr's healer.

Once Tess left, Beth turned back to where her husband lay sleeping.

Niel's face was drawn and tired, even in sleep, and his dark hair fanned across the pillow. The urge to stretch out next to him assailed her then. She was tired after a day in the saddle and wished for nothing more than to curl up against the warmth of Niel's body.

Instead, she reached out and stroked his forehead.

Niel had been through much of late. Now he was safely home, she'd leave him to rest and recover, while she got on with her chores.

Beth withdrew her hand and stepped back from the bed. Aye, she still had plenty to do: the head cook had asked to speak to her, and Neave wanted to go over a few issues that had cropped up within the keep in her absence.

Turning, she left her husband's chamber.

"Where's my wife?"

The servant glanced up from placing a large suet, beef, and kidney pudding in front of the clan-chief. "She's busy in the kitchens, laird ... this fine meal was made by her hands."

Niel glanced down at the steaming pudding. Indeed, it smelled toothsome and would likely taste even better. He'd been back at Castle Varrich a week, and every noon meal had been better than the last. It seemed that Beth spent most of her day down in the kitchens coming up with new recipes designed to put flesh on his bones.

And it was working. It no longer hurt him to sit on a chair without a cushion under his backside.

Nonetheless, Niel was starting to feel like a goose being fattened up for Yuletide. He was also tiring of taking his meals in his solar alone. Beth continued to break her fast with him in the mornings, yet for the remainder of the day, he rarely saw her. Not until the evening when she'd join him for an hour before they retired.

The servant left the solar, the door whispering shut behind her, leaving the clan-chief alone once more.

With a huff of frustration, Niel dug his spoon into the pudding and took a mouthful.

Lord, it was even more delicious than he'd expected. His wife had great talent.

But then he already knew that. Beth wasn't just a gifted cook, but capable in many areas. She ran his household with ease, and the servants all liked and respected her. The Munro sisters had been welcomed at Varrich, and just yesterday, John had told him that his mother's old vegetable plot had never looked more verdant—thanks to Neave and Eilidh's skill.

Beth's also an able archer, Niel reminded himself as he took another mouthful of pudding. His mouth curved at the memory of the contest they'd had. Her boldness in even suggesting they compete had shocked him. And yet she hadn't been exaggerating her ability. If he hadn't distracted her, she might have beaten him.

Although it wasn't Beth's capabilities that drew him to her—but her warmth, her big heart, and her bravery.

Niel's mood shadowed then, as he recalled the events that had transpired after the fair, in this solar. And as he dwelt on how he'd behaved, and the things he'd said, his fine meal turned to ashes in his mouth.

He still hadn't apologized.

Swallowing his last mouthful with difficulty, Niel pushed the tray away and reached for his goblet of sloe wine.

Ye truly are an arse, Mackay … an arse and a coward.

Was it any wonder that his wife kept her distance from him these days? Even though he'd seen understanding in her eyes in Farr when he'd choked on the words he'd wished to say, she now knew what a coward he was.

Since their arrival at Varrich, he'd noted her gradual withdrawal. Beth was as pleasant and chatty as ever whenever he saw her, but she no longer sought him out. He no longer caught her watching him, her hazel eyes luminous.

And he felt her loss. He also deserved it.

Rising from the table, still cradling his goblet of wine, Niel moved across to the window seat. He settled himself there like a cat, in the center of a pool of honeyed sunlight.

His solar window looked out across the Kyle of Tongue. It was a clear day, and if he peered east, he could just catch the blue swathe of the sea.

The sun's warmth burned into him, and he closed his eyes, leaning against the cushion at his back. The movement was careful so that the scar under his left arm didn't pain him. Of course, he noted it when he twisted his torso or dressed himself, but these days, the injury brought weakness and discomfort rather than pain.

Inhaling deeply, Niel breathed in the warm air, laced with the scents of heather and flowering gorse.

Before his injury, he'd never sat like this, idle in the middle of the day. Restlessness had always beaten inside him like a Beltaine drum. But not so today.

As he sat there, Niel was aware of his deep and steady breathing, of the whisper of a sultry breeze against his face, and how his body welcomed the heat of the sun.

He was alive.

Aye, he'd survived his time at Bass Rock, but one couldn't call that 'living'. It had been mere existence and a terrible one at that. Since his escape, he'd sought to outrun some of his demons while he'd chosen to face others head-on.

But none of it had brought him peace.

Only Beth did that—and he'd rejected her for it.

It occurred to Niel then that he had no idea how to actually live. He felt like a child, exploring a world that was new to him, and observing each discovery with wonder. In the past days, he'd found himself noticing details around him that he'd formerly taken for granted.

He marked what a sunny smile the servant who brought his meals up to him had, how the sandstone keep and curtain walls glowed as if gilded in the afternoon sun, and how Ben Loyal and Ben Hope appeared chiseled by a master's hand in the evening light.

Food tasted better these days, as did wine.

Yet it wasn't his victory against the Gunns that had altered his perspective or his recovery from a wound that had nearly bested him.

It was his wife. And like the craven bastard he was, he had no idea how to bridge the gulf between them.

31

NOT ALL UNIONS ARE LOVE MATCHES

MAKING HER WAY between rows of cabbages and kale, Beth marveled at how well the vegetables her sisters had planted out were growing. She bent down and helped herself to a large cabbage before placing it in her basket. This terraced vegetable garden, protected by the high curtain wall, faced south. White butterflies fluttered amongst the brassicas, and bees buzzed around the flowers that grew amid the vegetables.

Up ahead, she spied Neave. Her sister knelt before an onion bed, weeding. It was a warm afternoon, so she wore a veil to protect her fair skin from the sun. She also wore gloves, yet her fingers worked with nimble precision, pulling out dandelions, buttercup, and other weeds that sought to threaten the onions.

"Where's Eilidh?" Beth asked as she drew near. Usually, the pair worked together in the afternoons.

"She's gone down to Tongue with Jean … to deliver alms to the poor," Neave replied. Sitting back on her heels, she pushed back her veil with a gloved hand. Her attention then settled upon Beth's basket. "That's the third cabbage in a week … I'll need to plant out some more seedlings, or we'll run out."

Beth flashed her a contrite smile. "Niel enjoys my cabbage bake … so I thought I'd make it again for supper."

Neave rolled her eyes. "Of course he does … with all that cheese and cream in it." Her mouth curved then.

"Yer cooking is doing the man good though ... he no longer looks like a scarecrow."

Beth laughed. "Aye ... I'm pleased to see all these heavy dishes are having an effect." In the fortnight since their return to Varrich, she'd noted the change in her husband. Niel's face had filled out, and although he still couldn't do any physical work, he was now able to resume his duties as clan-chief. This morning, he'd settled a dispute between two farmers. And since the noon meal, he'd been ensconced in his solar, going over the accounts with John—a task that was overdue.

She noted then that Neave was favoring her with a penetrating look she knew well. One that demanded answers.

Pretending not to notice, Beth flashed her sister a smile and stepped back. "Well ... I'd better get back to the kitchens. I shall—"

"How go things with Niel?"

Silently cursing her sister, Beth kept her smile fixed to her lips. "Well."

Neave arched an eyebrow.

Beth started to move away once more.

"Ye aren't leaving without giving me a straight answer, Beth." Rising to her feet, Neave fixed her with a fierce stare. "Every time I get close to asking ye about yer marriage, ye rush off. Enough. Talk to me ... like ye used to."

Exhaling sharply, Beth clutched the basket against her. She'd done well to avoid this topic over the past fortnight, especially since all three of her sisters had a habit of sticking their noses into her business—as she always had with theirs. She'd even taken to hiding in her bed-chamber in the late afternoon, rather than join them in the women's solar, as was their habit.

Neave's eyes appeared more green than hazel as she continued to stare at her, a sure sign her sister was vexed. She looked ready to stamp her foot in frustration yet refrained herself.

"There's nothing much to say on that subject," Beth said after a pause. "I'd tell ye if anything had changed."

Neave's gaze narrowed. "So ye don't talk to each other?"

"Aye ... when we see each other in the morning and after supper in the evenings."

"And he still doesn't pay ye any attention?"

Beth stiffened. She really didn't want to have this discussion. While she'd confided in her sisters, Keira, and Maggie about her relationship with Niel in the early weeks of her marriage, she was leery to do so now. After everything they'd weathered, it seemed disloyal, somehow. The truth was that Niel *did* focus on her these days, although an odd tension had risen between them of late—one that had turned their exchanges awkward. "Aye, he does," she reluctantly admitted. "Although, I've been too busy to spend much time with him."

Neave scowled. "Are ye avoiding him?"

"I am." A sigh gusted out of Beth, irritation spearing her. "But it's for the best. I'll not throw myself at my husband again. We're just settling back at Varrich, and I'd prefer to let things be." She paused there, noting that her sister was now scowling at her. "Not all unions are love matches, sister." Her breathing caught as she made the admission. "What our parents had ... was special."

A brittle silence stretched out between them. Usually, Neave's mood was light and teasing. However, this afternoon there was a gravity about her. She was clearly concerned about Beth.

"Ye love him, don't ye?"

The directness of her sister's question made Beth still. "Aye," she whispered.

"And have ye told him?"

Beth's heart started to pound, her palms turning clammy. "It's best I don't ... I might panic the man. He's damaged, Neave. Niel finds it impossible to express his feelings. It would be wise to let things lie for a while."

Or forever. She didn't add that a man like Niel might never be able to accept her love, or return it properly.

Neave folded her arms across her breasts, her bow-shaped mouth pursing in a rare show of anger. "Satan's cods." The curse made Beth wince, yet there was no stopping her sister. "I've always looked up to ye, Beth ... ye are strong, capable, and braver than anyone I know." Neave did stamp her foot then. "But sometimes, ye can be an utter goose."

Beth stiffened. "Excuse me?"

"Nothing worthy in this world is obtained with ease ... ye of all people should know that."

"It's not—"

"I know Niel's behavior hurt ye in the past," Neave went on, cutting her off once more. "But how will ye know how he truly feels, if ye don't talk to him?"

Heat washed over Beth, as frustration slid into ire. "I tried that once before, remember," she pointed out, "and it ended with my humiliation. I'll not put myself through it again. Ye need to stop sticking yer beak in where it's not wanted, Neave. Ye always think ye can mend everything, but sometimes ye just can't. Let it be."

"But—"

"Enough!" Beth snapped. "I don't wish to discuss this further." She knew Neave meant well, yet her sister didn't understand. Turning on her heel and clutching her basket to her side, Beth stalked from the garden.

Neave Munro watched her sister leave,

Her heart hammered against her ribs. She couldn't believe it. Beth had just fled from an argument. Her sister never did that. Beth was one of those people who never backed down.

Her gaze remained riveted upon Beth until she disappeared from sight, and then Neave muttered an unladylike curse under her breath—the second coarse utterance that had left her lips that afternoon.

She wasn't given to swearing like a sailor, yet Beth's bull-headedness frustrated her.

"This won't do." Ripping off her leather gardening gloves, Neave tossed them into a nearby basket and brushed the grass and dirt off her skirts.

If something wasn't done, Niel and Beth would remain locked in this silent battle. Pride, fear, and stubbornness prevented them both from having the conversation that would tear down the walls between them.

There was nothing for it—*she* would have to intervene.

"Will they be sending tax collectors this year?" John Mackay sat back on his chair and pinched the skin between his eyebrows—a sign that he'd had enough of poring over ledgers with his laird.

Niel glanced up, from where he'd just been entering the last chit into the huge leather-bound ledger open before him. Although he'd put this task off, it had provided a welcome distraction from thoughts of his wife—and his inability to put things right between them. "I don't see why not," he replied. "Archibald Douglas will still want our levies to fill the crown's coffers."

Niel glanced back down at the neat column he'd just transcribed. From the looks of things, his father had managed to keep his finances in order, despite his failing health and trouble within the clan. And John had done a fine job afterward. And despite that his memories of the king weren't pleasant, Niel had to admit that James hadn't demanded overly high taxes from his clan-chiefs. He'd indeed been a man of the people—too bad for him he'd had murderous enemies.

After James's murder, Archibald Douglas had been appointed Lieutenant General of Scotland.

When Niel looked up once more, he saw his cousin was frowning. "I can't say I'm happy that one of the 'Black Douglases' is ruling Scotland."

Niel snorted. "Why? They're no worse than most clans."

Despite that the man who'd earned the title of the 'Black Douglas', James, had been dead many years, his descendants still carried his name. James Douglas had fought with the Bruce, and whispers of his presence at a battle was said to strike fear into the hearts of the English.

"Even so ... how long will he be Regent?"

"Until the king's son comes of age." Niel's mouth lifted at the corners. "And that'll be awhile ... since the prince is still a bairn."

John muttered an oath under his breath. Viewing him, Niel wondered at his cousin's irritated mood this afternoon. Aye, he wasn't fond of toiling over the books, but it was unlike him to court an ill-temper. That was usually Niel's role. John's character was different to Niel's. He wasn't a man to hold onto grudges or brood over incidents.

"Does something vex ye, cousin?" Niel asked, glad to be focusing on someone else's troubles for the moment. He'd seen his wife even less than usual over the past days. It was clear now that she was deliberately avoiding him; the situation was slowly making him miserable. These days, he had a permanent ache under his breastbone. "Ye don't seem yerself today."

John raked a hand through his hair once more, making it even messier than usual. "I don't know really," he admitted with a wry smile. "I find myself at a strange point in life. I've spent so many years defending this clan, I can't imagine what I'll do with myself now."

Niel smiled. "There will be plenty to keep ye busy at Achness."

"Speaking of which ... I must return there shortly."

Niel nodded. He understood, although he would miss his cousin's presence at Varrich. "I should like to reward ye, John," he said after a pause. "For yer loyalty over the years." John's blue eye widened at this, his lips parting, yet Niel continued, "In thanks, I shall bestow ye the lands of Lochnaver."

The two men stared at each other before John's throat bobbed. "That's a generous reward indeed, cousin."

Niel's mouth curved once more. "And no less than ye deserve."

A knock at the door intruded then.

"Enter," Niel called.

He was surprised when the door opened and Neave Munro breezed into the solar. As always, the woman walked with a jaunty stride. However, she wore a sterner expression than Niel was used to seeing upon her pixie face.

"What is it, Neave?" he greeted her.

"I would like a word, laird," she replied with a respectful nod. She then glanced at John. "Alone … if possible."

John inclined his head, curiosity rippling across his face.

"Go on then." Niel's interest was also now piqued, although his gut tensed. Was something amiss with Beth? He shifted his attention to his cousin. "We'll go over the details about Lochnaver later, John."

The warrior nodded before unfolding his tall frame and making for the door. On the way out, he flashed Neave a probing look, although she merely inclined her head in response.

Once they were alone in the solar, Niel gestured to the empty seat that his cousin had just vacated. "Out with it then, lass."

Neave moved to the chair and settled down upon it with her customary elegance. She then fixed Niel with a bold look. "I shall not bandy words, laird," she began, her voice low yet sure. "I've come to speak to ye about Beth."

The unease in Niel's belly tightened, and he leaned forward. "Is something the matter?"

"Aye," his sister-by-marriage replied. "Are ye aware that my sister is desperately in love with ye?"

32

WORTHY

NIEL STARED AT the woman before him as if she'd just struck him across the face. "What?" he asked stupidly.

Neave drew herself up, issuing an impatient noise in the back of her throat. "Yer wife loves ye, Mackay."

Niel sat back, aware that his heart now thudded against his ribs. "And how do ye know this?" His voice was barely above a whisper.

"She admitted it to me."

Moments passed before Niel cleared his throat. These Munro sisters were a force of nature. Beth wasn't the only one with much to say for herself. Neave was even more outspoken, it seemed. "And why have ye brought this news to me?"

"Because ye are both unhappy … unnecessarily so."

Niel arched an eyebrow and was satisfied to see a blush rise upon Neave's cheeks. She wasn't as confident as she appeared, and wasn't that comfortable in his presence either.

"I'd say that's something for Beth and me to resolve," he said softly. "Don't ye agree?"

"I believe ye are both too stubborn to do so," she countered, still holding his eye. "Beth loves ye but is determined to go on with her life and pretend yer aloofness doesn't matter to her." Neave broke off there, drawing a deep breath before continuing. "But I know my sister well … and she *does* care … more than she'd ever admit." She swallowed then, her gaze piercing him. "Do ye love her?"

Niel stared back at his sister-by-marriage, poleaxed once more by her audacity. Had she asked him such a bold question months earlier, he'd have thrown her out of his solar before telling his wife that he was sending her mouthy sister back to Foulis.

However, Niel wasn't the same man he'd been upon his return from Bass Rock.

He'd gotten his reckoning and lost far too many good men in doing so. But his victory hadn't elated him as he'd hoped. In the past weeks, he'd started to doubt himself. Aye, the folk of Tongue had cheered at his return, but he wondered if resentment lay beneath their smiles. Did they see a man who'd led two hundred men to their deaths as their protector—or did they curse him for his hubris?

Niel's close brush with death had completely altered his outlook on the world.

For the first time, he cared what other people thought of him. For the first time, he actually *saw* them. It was taking every bit of courage for Neave Munro to face him down—and he found himself admiring her pluck.

Nonetheless, he'd failed to realize that Beth loved him.

"Do ye?" Neave prompted, refusing to back down.

A sigh gusted out of Niel. He leaned back in his chair, raking both hands through his hair. "Aye."

"Well then … why the devil haven't ye told her?"

Niel frowned. "Careful, lass," he growled. "Remember to whom ye are speaking."

Neave sucked in another breath, the blush on her cheeks deepening. Nonetheless, she didn't avert her stare. "I apologize," she murmured. "I'm not usually so blunt in my speech." She clasped her hands together upon her lap. "But I hate to see unnecessary suffering. If ye really do love Beth, isn't it time ye were honest with her? For both yer sakes?"

After Neave Munro left the solar, Niel remained at his desk for a long while.

Despite his still appearance, a storm raged within him.

Why the devil haven't ye told her?

Neave's question taunted him repeatedly until, with a growled curse, he lurched from his desk and crossed to the sideboard, pouring himself a large goblet of wine. He didn't usually drink in the afternoon, but today he'd deviate from his usual habits.

Neave obviously didn't realize that he was a yellow-bellied fazart. She thought pride prevented him from apologizing; she didn't know how terrified he was of what he felt for his wife. The mere thought of facing the truth about his feelings, about himself, made his heart race, made cold sweat bathe his skin.

But he was putting off the inevitable.

Crossing to the window, Niel slugged back the wine in two gulps before slamming the empty goblet down upon the sill. He then dragged a hand down his face.

A pox on him, it was time he stared fear in the eye.

Beth held up the lèine she'd been embroidering, admiring her surprisingly neat needlework in the light of the candle that burned upon the mantelpiece above her. She wasn't the most adept at embroidery among her sisters, yet she was pleased with this project. It had taken her awhile—most of the summer—but she'd finally completed it.

"Ye have done a fine job with that," Niel spoke up.

Lowering the lèine, Beth favored him with a tight smile. "That's just as well, husband ... for it's for ye."

She didn't usually bring her embroidery into the clan-chief's solar in the evening, for the light was poor, and she risked straining her eyes. However, after her words with Neave, she'd been on edge. Her sewing gave her something to focus on—other than the man who sat silently opposite her.

"Then I am fortunate indeed," he murmured. "Can I have a look?"

Beth nodded, handing it to him. Their fingers brushed as she did so, and a jolt of heat rippled up her arm.

Swallowing to mask her reaction, Beth drew back, watching as her husband examined the garment. He traced the intricate needlework around the collar with his fingertips. And when he glanced up, flashing her a smile, Beth caught her breath.

God's bones, she loved his smile.

"N.M. ... ye have sewn my initials."

Despite her nervousness, Beth smiled back. "Aye. Ye like it then?"

Niel nodded, and then to her surprise, he rose to his feet and pulled off the plain grey linen lèine he was wearing. He did so cautiously, and when Beth saw the livid scar that ran from just under his left armpit to his hip, she saw why.

She hadn't seen the injury in weeks—as Tess, the healer from Tongue, had taken care of it—and it was healing well. Even so, it would leave a lasting scar, a token of the battle that had nearly claimed his life.

The sight of his naked torso was distracting. He was still lean, yet Niel was definitely regaining his strength. His stomach was no longer hollowed, and his ribs no longer protruded. Instead, the virility of him, the way the dark hair on his chest arrowed down to the waistband of his braies, caused her breathing to quicken.

Carefully, Niel pulled on his new lèine. "It fits perfectly," he said, admiring the embroidered cuffs. "I shall wear it with pride."

He settled back into his seat opposite her, his penetrating gaze pinning Beth to the spot. "Ye have been good to me, Beth," he said huskily, "even if I've hardly been worthy."

Swallowing, Beth managed a weak smile. She didn't know what to say. Her wits had deserted her this evening. Her encounter with Neave had unsettled her. It had brought everything she'd been trying to ignore to the surface once more. Aye, she longed to tell her husband she loved him, but she was also determined to lead her own life.

When she didn't respond, Niel leaned forward, resting his elbows upon his thighs. His eyes were dark in the firelight, a luminous cobalt blue that drew her in. Her husband wore a vulnerable expression, and a nerve ticked under one eye. "I'm truly sorry." The words came out of him in a rush. "And I wanted to tell ye so weeks ago."

Beth sucked in a deep, steadying breath. She didn't know what to say.

A muscle feathered in Niel's jaw. "I've remained silent because to ask yer forgiveness would mean giving ye an explanation of *why* I'm the way I am."

Beth gave a slow nod. She'd sensed as much that day at Farr Castle. And now, she could see that same war waging within him. Her chest constricted. Lord, it must be hard being Niel Mackay—keeping so much locked inside.

Niel's throat bobbed. "The truth is … I'm scared." When she didn't answer, he pressed on, his voice roughening further. "Terrified, in fact. Ye were right about that … about a great many things." He sat back in his chair, raking a hand through his hair. His expression was haunted now, his eyes wild.

Beth didn't interrupt him, didn't move.

"I've always wanted to be in control," he admitted then, his mouth twisting. "I get that from my father, I suppose. Angus Mackay liked to be at the top of the heap … I don't think I ever saw him show consideration for my mother, or ask her opinion. Not once. I could use their relationship as an excuse, but in reality, I know how a man should treat a woman … Connor and Morgan demonstrated that to me." He paused then, inhaling sharply, before continuing. "I can't blame Bass Rock for my behavior either. Aye, it made me crowd-shy and easily distracted, and I seek solitude far more than I used to … but that's no excuse for sending ye from my bed on our wedding night. That was callous."

Beth swallowed. "And the night of the fair?"

A rueful smile twisted Niel's lips, although his gaze guttered. "I was losing control of the situation … and I didn't like it. I took ye the way I did, and then turned my back on ye, to prove to myself that I didn't need ye." He shook his head then. "But it was futile … all hurting ye did was make me hate myself. I do need ye, Beth. I l*ove* ye."

Silence fell, and they stared at each other for a long, tense moment.

Beth drew in quick, shallow breaths. His words had utterly floored her.

But before she had a chance to respond, Niel continued, "Yer sister paid me a visit this afternoon," he said softly. "She revealed the truth of things."

Beth's breathing caught, ice slithering down her spine. "Is that why ye have confessed yer feelings to me?" she croaked. The chill of shock had faded, replaced with a burning mortification. How could Neave do this to her? She thought her sister cared for her. She'd never thought her capable of inflicting such humiliation. God's teeth, she'd throttle Neave the next time she saw her. "Because ye know already how I feel for ye?"

The words were harsh, yet she felt betrayed—by both her sister *and* her husband. She hated the thought of them discussing her. Niel wasn't the only prideful one, it seemed.

"No, Neave merely gave me the kick in the arse I sorely needed." His gaze shadowed then. "Is loving me so terrible?"

Beth's eyes stung as she blinked back tears. "Of course not," she whispered.

A fragile hush settled between them. And then Niel rose to his feet and crossed to her. Taking hold of Beth's hands, he drew her gently to her feet.

"Look at me, mo chridhe," he murmured. "Please."

Drawing in a fortifying breath, she did as bid.

Their gazes fused. "I thought defeating the Gunns would be enough," Niel said, his voice catching. "But after Ruaig-Shansaid, a great emptiness filled me. Victory on the field of battle means nothing. Ye are what matters."

Beth's vision blurred then, as tears escaped.

Niel reached out, his fingers brushing over her wet cheek. "I didn't want to make ye weep," he said huskily.

A noise, halfway between a laugh and a sob, escaped Beth. "Well, ye have," she gasped. "I love ye ... ye great dolt."

Joy flowered across Niel's face. His dark-blue eyes glittered with tears. A moment later, he drew her into the cage of his arms, holding her close. Pressed against his chest, her ear to his thudding heart, Beth closed her eyes, letting the tears flow. She was soaking his new lèine, but she didn't care. Wordlessly, she wrapped her arms around his torso. How she'd dreamed of Niel holding her like this—only to shove her yearning away, to deny it.

They fitted together perfectly, and for a few moments, they didn't move. Some moments in life had to be savored, and she didn't want this one to end.

But end it finally did, when Niel drew back and cupped her chin with his hand, raising her face so that their gazes met once more. And then, wordlessly, he leaned down, capturing her mouth with his.

The kiss was gentle, sensual, his lips brushing hers a few times before his tongue swept her mouth open.

With a groan, he gathered her against him, kissing her deeply as he cupped the back of her head with his hands.

Beth moaned in response, opening herself to him, her tongue tangling with his. Meanwhile, she reached out, her palms sliding over the wall of his chest. Need pulsed in the cradle of her hips, and she ached with wanting. This kiss was so different to the ones he'd given her on that fateful night earlier in the summer. That embrace, although sensual, had been wild and angry.

This kiss held all the emotion her husband had kept in check.

And when he drew back, Niel Mackay's cheeks were wet.

"Come, my heart," he said softly, catching her hand in his and leading her toward the door to his bed-chamber. "I'd pick ye up and carry ye to my bed ... *our* bed ... but I'm afraid my battle wound might prevent me." He cast her a crooked smile, one that made her chest ache with love. "Will ye forgive me my lack of gallantness?"

33

UNFINISHED BUSINESS

INSIDE THE BED-CHAMBER, in flickering candlelight, they undressed each other. They did so slowly, exploring each other's bodies along the way.

Beth gasped as he trailed kisses down her spine after removing her ankle-length lèine. He then moved around to her front, and she let out a soft, mewing cry when he hooked one of her legs over his shoulder and kissed the delicate flesh between her thighs.

Later, Niel groaned as she pushed down his braies and lowered herself before him, her lips tracing the length of his engorged shaft. Cupping his bollocks, she took his rod in her mouth, tasting him. And as she pleasured him, Niel's fingers tangled in her hair, loosening it from its heavy braid.

His breathing grew heavy, and then rapid, and eventually, he gently pulled Beth up from the floor, causing her to cease her ministrations. "I want to spill inside ye," he growled, drawing her with him as he lay back on the bed. "And I want to watch yer face ... while I'm buried deep within ye."

Her husband's words made wild excitement twist low in Beth's belly. How she wanted that too. Hades, how she'd missed him.

Niel remained upon his back, his gaze riveted upon her while she straddled him. And then, with exquisite slowness, she lowered herself upon his shaft.

Beth's low groan echoed through the chamber, her back arching as he filled her. They'd never coupled in this position before, and the new sensations it aroused made tremors ripple through her lower belly. It made sense for them to do it this way, for he didn't risk hurting himself. However, at the same time, it signaled a loss of control on his part. Niel was surrendering to her, letting her lead for the first time.

Reaching up, he pulled her forward so that he could feast upon her breasts, suckling each one lustily. Meanwhile, Beth undulated her hips, gasping at the pleasure that small movement elicited. She then started to rock against him, bringing him deeper still every time she settled back down.

Groaning his name, she circled her hips, pushing her breasts wantonly against his mouth.

"Aye," he groaned. "That's right, lass. Show me."

His words inflamed her. Despite their troubles, her six months of marriage had taught Beth that she was a sensual woman, and that she delighted in carnal pleasure with this man.

Crying his name, she increased her speed, riding him hard. Meanwhile, Niel's gaze was now riveted upon her face as he gripped her hips, slamming her down hard upon his rod while he thrust up to meet her.

Sweat beaded across Beth's body. She could feel herself losing control. She was vaguely aware of her cries and groans, of writhing against him, her full breasts bobbing to the rhythm of their passion—yet the pleasure that now gathered in her womb made her throw off the last of her inhibitions.

She climbed to the peak, shattering around him with a scream that rattled the walls. A moment later, Niel's own cries joined hers, his fingers biting into her hips while he arched up off the bed, the heat of his seed erupting within her.

Coming back down to earth afterward, Beth hung over him, panting as if she'd just sprinted up the steep path from Tongue village to the castle. Trembling in the aftermath of their passion, she eventually raised her chin, meeting her husband's eye.

Their gazes held and fused, the moment drawing out. Niel's proud face was flushed, and his skin gleamed with sweat. His lips, swollen from their passion, curved into a smile full of sensual promise. With a fluttering excitement deep in her belly, Beth realized that the evening was just beginning.

Indeed, Niel and Beth barely slept that night.

In between bouts of lovemaking, they curled up together on the bed, the silken air of a summer's eve caressing their naked skin. And as they lay there, they talked.

Niel told her of his childhood and adolescence, not of his daring deeds—which he'd boasted of earlier in their relationship—but of the loneliness of growing up the only child of a loveless marriage.

"I thought that was how it was," he admitted as he stroked her back, reveling in the softness of his wife's naked body against his. "My father went to a brothel to satisfy his 'appetites' ... my mother's role was to produce bairns and run his household." Niel paused there, remembering his mother's careworn face, her sad eyes. He wished he'd paid her more attention. But, as he'd taken his father's lead in all things, he'd ignored her most of the time. He regretted that. "But I know better now."

"It was very different in my family," Beth replied, her breath whispering against his naked chest. "My parents were the best of friends ... and Da has a similar relationship with my stepmother, Laila. When I arrived at Varrich, I imagined ye and I would develop the same bond." She halted there, her body tensing against his as if the admission embarrassed her. "It was a foolish notion ... I had a lot of ideas about love that I don't anymore."

Niel wrapped his arms around his wife, holding her close. "Such as?"

"That I can't force others to feel how I want them to," she murmured. "Love has to come to ye willingly ... or not at all."

Her words made Niel's throat thicken. "Aye," he murmured, "but all the same, ye had a stubborn mule for a husband." Dipping his chin, he kissed her upon the crown of her head, inhaling the scent of lavender. "I swear that's all behind us now, my heart."

Neave was discussing the morning's chores with Greta when Beth entered the women's solar. A few feet away, still seated at the small table by the window, Jean and Eilidh were bickering over who would eat the last wedge of bannock.

"Ye've already had three slices," Eilidh pointed out.

"Well that's yer *fourth*," Jean countered, a stubborn expression settling over her features.

Ignoring her two younger sisters, Neave glanced toward the doorway, where Beth had now halted. Their gazes met, and as their stare drew out, a rare flush crept up Neave's neck and colored her cheeks.

"We can go over this later, Greta," Neave said quietly. "Please take the washing down to the laundry first."

Her attention flicking between the sisters, the maid nodded. She clearly picked up on the tension between Beth and Neave, although despite her obvious curiosity, she didn't question them. Instead, she left the solar to do Neave's bidding.

And after she left, Beth continued to eyeball her younger sister. "Why did ye do it, Neave?" she asked finally.

At the sharp tone of her voice, both Jean and Eilidh stopped arguing. They hadn't even noticed their elder sister enter the chamber, but they marked her now.

Beth kept her attention upon Neave, taking another step toward her.

And for once, her sister looked unsure of herself. Clearing her throat, Neave clasped her hands together. "I didn't want to see ye suffer anymore," she replied before clearing her throat. "It was obvious neither of ye would make the first move toward reconciliation … so I just gave ye a wee nudge."

Heat spiked through Beth's belly. Aye, last night had changed everything between her and Niel, and she'd felt as if she were walking three feet off the ground this morning. They'd spent hours making love and talking, eventually falling into an exhausted sleep. And when she'd awoken in his arms, happiness, unlike any Beth had ever known, had suffused her.

However, that didn't change what Neave had done.

"A wee nudge," she growled. "Ye *interfered*."

"Interfered?" Jean piped up. "What did ye do, Neave?"

Her sister swallowed yet didn't answer. A little of Beth's anger subsided then. At least Neave hadn't discussed this with Jean and Eilidh. That would have been too much.

"I was only trying to help," she whispered.

"Aye, but ye should have known better."

Neave's eyes glittered then, and Beth realized she was on the verge of tears. "Did I make things worse between ye?"

Beth heaved in a deep breath, even as her throat constricted. Curse it, why couldn't she stay angry for long at Neave. "No … we are now reconciled."

Neave's eyes widened. Tears did escape then, wetting her cheeks. "I'm so sorry, Beth," she gulped. "Do ye hate me now?"

A strained silence settled between them. Beth was aware of Jean and Eilidh staring at her, yet her attention remained upon Neave's heart-shaped face. Her cheeks now flamed, and her slender frame shook. She'd rarely seen her so distraught. "No," she ground out. "I could never hate ye … I just want to slap ye."

"Go on then." Neave moved forward so that they stood just two feet apart. "I deserve it."

Beth clenched her jaw. Aye, it was tempting. Yet she hadn't resorted to violence against any of her sisters since they were bairns, and she didn't want to start now.

Neave's interference had vexed her, yet fortunately, it had pushed Niel into bridging the gulf between them.

"I suppose I should thank ye," Beth muttered then. "Ye were bold when I was meek. I should have spoken to him."

Neave sniffed before knuckling away her tears. "It's easier for me, Beth ... my heart wasn't involved."

Beth blinked furiously as her vision blurred. Christ's bones, she wanted to stay angry at Neave, yet it was impossible. Her sister should have let things be, but her motives had been pure. She really had been trying to help.

"I'm glad ye have found happiness." Neave reached out and took Beth's hand, squeezing tight. "After Ma died, ye cared for us all. Ye have always given so much without asking for anything in return. Ye deserve to be appreciated for all that ye are."

Those words tipped Beth over the edge. She stared back at her sister, even if tears now blinded her. And then, with a sob, she hauled Neave into her arms, enfolding her in a crushing hug.

Niel walked through the kirkyard, his boots whispering upon the dew-laden grass. It was still early, and the morning air had a crisp bite—a warning that summer was drawing to a close and autumn was almost upon them.

And what a summer it had been.

The most tumultuous season of Niel's life.

Even more so than that fateful spring day a decade earlier when King James had condemned him to incarceration at Bass Rock.

Niel Bass Mackay. He imagined he'd carry that name with him till his dying day, and in truth, it didn't bother him. That lonely island prison was now a part of the tapestry that was his life.

He wondered then about the fate of Amelia Lauder, his kinswoman who'd helped him escape Bass Rock. Niel's brow furrowed. Amelia's act had been selfless and brave. He hoped she and her lover had managed their own escape, but there was no way to know.

Mulling this, Niel made his way across the kirkyard. There was no one about at this hour. Only the gravestones in the kirkyard bore witness as Niel crossed to the far corner, close to where a yew tree grew.

The ancients had believed yew trees sacred and had planted them in places of worship. Yet that wasn't the only reason this mighty yew grew here. As grisly as it was, yew trees were said to thrive on corpses, and having such a tree nearby was useful in times of war—for yew made excellent bows.

This morning, the yew cast a shadow over two familiar gravestones.

Niel slowed his pace as he drew near. After breaking his fast with Beth in his solar, he'd let his wife go off and find her sister Neave. She wished to have 'words' with her, and Niel hoped she wouldn't tear too many strips off the lass.

Aye, Neave had spoken out of turn, but she'd given him the kick in the arse he needed.

He'd forever be grateful to her for that.

Stopping before the graves, Niel's gaze alighted upon the stones. The last time he'd stood here, he'd seethed with hate, with the need to have his reckoning upon the Gunns. In his mind, he'd believed that it would make up for all the years he'd lost—remedy the wrongs that had been done against him.

But his time with Beth had shown him what really mattered.

"It's enough now," he whispered to the silent graves. He reached out, running his fingers along the rough stone of his mother's headstone. "Sleep well, Ma."

Niel then turned his attention to the newer stone beside that of Estelle Mackay's. "Angus-Dow Mackay,

Seventh Lord of Strathnaver," he read aloud, his voice echoing in the stillness. "Born, the Year of Our Lord 1380. Died in 1433."

He stood there, staring at the gravestone and waiting for fury to surge through him, for loathing to churn in his gut.

But nothing happened.

After a while, Niel's mouth lifted at the corners. "Ye did what ye had to, didn't ye?" he murmured. "Ye cunning old bastard." John had told him that Angus had lived to regret his actions, something he'd revealed to his nephew when his health started to fail. Yet the ailing clan-chief had been unable to undo what he'd done.

"Bratach Bhan Chlann Aoidh, father," he whispered then, stepping back from the graves. It was their clan's war cry. "I will continue to carry yer banner with pride … with a strong hand, although I'm done with vengeance."

And as he said those words, a weight lifted off his chest. Suddenly, he breathed easier.

Forgiveness, who would have thought it could bring a man such peace?

Turning, Niel retraced his steps through the kirkyard, back to the gate. Along the way, he spied a rosebush, growing up against the kirk. Its flowers were delicate and pale pink. Niel made a detour to the bush and plucked one of the roses, one that was just opening its petals. Its heady, yet delicate, perfume washed over him.

Niel left the kirkyard then, heading back to the path that would lead him home. However, he hadn't traveled far up the slope when he spied a familiar figure up ahead. A small woman with dark walnut-brown hair was picking her way down the path toward him.

The emerald-green kirtle Beth wore was his favorite. It hugged her curves and emphasized the creaminess of her skin. She wore her hair loose this morning, and it fell in heavy waves over her shoulders.

His wife's full lips curved into a smile at the sight of him, and then she halted, waiting for him.

Approaching, Niel held out the rose he'd picked. "A gift for my bonny wife," he murmured.

Her eyes twinkled, and she took the flower before inhaling its scent. "It's lovely, Niel," she murmured. "Thank ye."

Stepping into the circle of his arms, she kissed him.

It was a gentle, yet sensual, embrace, and Niel's pulse quickened, his groin tightening in response. He had a day of tasks planned, yet all of it could wait. He and Beth would return to his quarters, where they would spend the rest of the day, uninterrupted. He hadn't had his fill of his wife and doubted he ever would. However, he wished to lavish his full attention upon her, to show her just how much he loved her.

Drawing back, Beth looked up, her warm hazel eyes meeting his. "Where have ye been?"

"To the kirkyard," he replied. "I had some 'unfinished business'."

Beth inclined her head, smiling once more. "The dead can't talk back, husband," she chided him gently.

"No." Niel looped his arm through his wife's and steered her back up the path. He then favored her with a wry smile. "But they can listen."

EPILOGUE

BEFORE THE BONFIRE

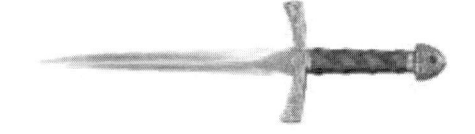

Four months later ...

BETH SMILED AS she walked amongst the revelers. A few yards distant, the bonfire flames licked the night sky, the scent of wood smoke mingling with the dank smell of ice and snow. An enormous oaken log burned upon the fire, as was tradition.

It was a freezing night to be outdoors, yet this eve marked the beginning of the 'Long Night', and Beth wouldn't have missed it for anything.

Nonetheless, winter's chill made her breathing steam before her. Wrapped in a fur mantle, her body was warm enough, although the chill bit at her exposed face and fingers. She was grateful too for the fur-lined boots that encased her feet.

Snow covered the ground, crunching underfoot. Above, the sky was clear—a blanket of glittering stars and a silver moon winking down at them.

"Would ye like some mulled wine, Lady Mackay?" A ruddy-cheeked lass of around sixteen winters appeared before her. She lugged a cart bearing a steaming cauldron behind her.

"Aye, thank ye."

Taking the wooden cup the lass offered, and breathing in the heady scent of clove and cinnamon, blended with rich bramble wine, Beth wrapped her numb fingers around its warmth.

She took a sip and screwed up her nose. Mulled wine was usually one of her favorite things about this season—

however, she appeared to have lost her taste for it tonight. Beth hoped she wouldn't feel that way about the Yuletide sweets she and the cooks had prepared for tomorrow's noon feast: apple cakes, rich custards, and puddings made with dried plums, honey, and clove. Mouthwatering treats indeed.

Working elbow-to-elbow with the cooks over the last few days had brought her a lot of pleasure. The servants at Castle Varrich had accepted her authority without question right from her arrival here—and the once dour mood within the keep had thawed considerably over the months.

Beth now saw Varrich as her home. True to his word, Niel had taken her and her sisters back to Foulis Castle for a trip at Samhuinn. It had been a wonderful visit. Her father and stepmother were delighted to host them, and Niel and George Munro had gone stag hunting together, while Beth and her sisters caught up with Laila. Her stepmother's belly had been swollen with bairn at Samhuinn—and she was due to give birth any day now.

But, as welcoming as the folk at Foulis were, Beth had found herself missing Castle Varrich, and when they returned north, she'd felt a sense of peace and belonging settle over her.

Stopping a few yards back from the fire, Beth let her gaze travel over the surrounding crowd. A woman's voice, fair and lilting, rose high into the air.

Neave was singing *Taladh Chriosda*—Christ's Child Lullaby—an atmospheric melody that caused the fine hairs on the back of Beth's neck to prickle. A man's voice joined her sister's then, and Beth peered through the crowd to see that John Mackay stood next to Neave. He looked like a pirate with his wild raven-hued hair, which fell in unruly curls over his forehead, and his black eyepatch. Niel's cousin had made the trip from Achness in order to spend Yuletide with them.

The song continued, and Beth noted how well Neave and John's voices melded together. Indeed, quite a few folk were gathered around them now, their faces rapt as they listened.

Beth marked then that a man across the fire was staring at her sister. He was a burly fellow with short-cropped dark hair—and he was gazing upon Neave with a poleaxed expression. Beth recognized the man: he was Tongue's new blacksmith, Roy Morrison. Unfortunately, Malcolm McKee hadn't recovered from his fit of apoplexy. He'd died a month after taking ill, but fortunately Roy had been available to replace him.

Misgiving feathered over Beth then. She wasn't sure she wanted Roy Morrison staring at her sister so ardently. Niel had told her that their new smith was actually the same individual who'd suggested they attack Dounreay. It appeared Morrison bore a deep grudge against the Gunns.

Beth frowned. Niel had confided that he didn't overly trust the man—and she didn't either.

"I had no idea John could sing," an amused male voice drawled in Beth's ear. An instant later, strong arms encircled her waist. "He's kept that quiet."

Beth leaned in to her husband's body, careful not to spill her barely touched wine. The warmth of his body made her forget her concerns about the blacksmith. "Maybe he's shy."

Niel snorted in reply. "Who, John?"

"Aye ... just because he's bold on the battlefield doesn't mean he doesn't lack confidence elsewhere."

Niel considered her words, and when he answered, his tone was subdued. "John would never admit as much, but his maiming changed him. I asked him today when he's going to take a bride, and he bit my head off."

"Perhaps he hasn't yet found the right woman."

"Aye, that's likely it." Niel drew her closer then, his lips brushing her cheek. "He and yer sister make a bonny couple, don't ye think?"

They did: John—tall, lean, and dark-haired—and Neave with her elfin beauty, chestnut mane, and twinkling hazel-green eyes.

"Perhaps," Beth replied, "if they saw each other that way." She paused then, her gaze returning to the singers. "As far as I'm aware, John and Neave are nothing more than friends." Over the last year, she'd noted how well the pair got on. Initially, she'd hoped their friendship might develop into something deeper, for John was a good man, yet their relationship, although often irreverent and good-humored, remained platonic.

"Yer sister enjoyed playing match-maker earlier in the year," Niel pointed out. "Maybe ye should return the favor."

Beth huffed a laugh. "I think not, husband ... unlike my sister, I know when to keep my nose out of other people's affairs."

They fell silent then, both of them listening as the lullaby continued. Niel tightened his hold on her, the warmth of his body wrapping around hers. She relaxed against him, wellbeing flowing over her.

"I missed ye today," Niel said eventually.

"There was much baking to be done," she replied with a sigh. "I wanted to make enough cakes for the villagers as well."

"Ye are loved here, ye know?" Niel murmured. "The folk of Varrich and Tongue have never eaten so well."

Beth laughed before stepping out of Niel's embrace and turning to face him. "I'm glad they appreciate my talents," she said, meeting his eye. Firelight suited her husband. It highlighted the sun-streaks in his peat-dark hair and turned his eyes an inky blue. He watched her under hooded lids, his lips curved into a teasing smile.

Watching him, Beth's breathing quickened. She then passed him her cup of mulled wine. "Here ... ye can have this. I won't drink it."

Niel arched a dark brow. "Ye usually enjoy wine, mo ghràdh."

Beth's mouth curved. "Aye ... but the healer told me that when a woman is expecting, she often loses a taste for strong drink ... and it seems I have."

Niel's lips parted, his eyes snapping wide.

Her smile widened. "I didn't spend *all* day baking, Niel. My menses ceased two months ago, and I've started to feel queasy in the morns ... when I'm not seized by the urge to eat everything in sight." She took hold of his free hand and pressed it against her belly. "Tess confirmed what I already suspected to be true."

She paused then, staring deep into his eyes before she spoke once more. "Ye will soon be a father, Niel."

The End

FROM THE AUTHOR

I hope you enjoyed the first installment in the COURAGEOUS HIGHLAND HEARTS series.

Whew, this one was a real gut-punch to write. Niel and Beth's story was emotional, on so many levels, and complex too. I fell in love with them both (as I always do with my characters) and wrote those final chapters with joy in my heart—for although I know that romances always have happy endings, there were times during the writing of this book when I wondered how my hero and heroine were ever going to make it through.

But they did, and they both learned so much about themselves and life itself along the way.

I'm also a sucker for a breathtakingly arrogant, complex, and 'flawed' hero ... and I've been wanting to give Niel Mackay his happy ending for a long while!

Get ready for John and Neave's story, up next. It's going to be a lot of fun!

Jayne x

HISTORICAL NOTES

As with all my novels, I've based HIGHLANDER DEFIED around real historical figures and events.

The feud that underpins the main conflict in this series between the Mackays and the Gunns was a real one. In my previous series, STOLEN HIGHLAND HEARTS, Niel Mackay was imprisoned during the parliament in Inverness (a real council in which King James I dealt out punishment to the warring Highland clans). This took place in 1427, in the aftermath of the Battle of Harpsdale (an actual battle between the Mackays and the Gunns).

Niel Mackay (also known as Niel 'Bass' Mackay after his time at Bass Rock) was a real historical figure, who was imprisoned in the infamous island prison for ten years. In the historical records, his name is spelled both 'Niel' and 'Neil'—I've opted for the former spelling in my novel.

Niel Mackay did marry the daughter of George Munro (the Munro clan-chief and 10th Baron of Foulis), although I couldn't find reference to her name. They had three children: Angus, John, and Elizabeth.

All the historical events mentioned in this novel are true, and I've tried to stick to the timeline mentioned.

The Battle of Drumnacoub (in which John Mackay was maimed) took place in 1433. This conflict was between the Mackays, whereby Neil Neilson Mackay and Morgan Neilson Mackay challenged Angus Mackay's rule (with assistance from the Sutherlands). The battle went in the Mackay's favor, although Angus Mackay was too infirm to be able to fight. In the aftermath, when he was combing the battlefield presumably looking for dead relatives, he was killed by an assassin wielding a bow and arrow.

King James I was assassinated in February 1437 at Blackfriars in Perth during a failed coup. He left behind a six-year-old son and his queen, who tried, unsuccessfully, to set herself up as Regent in the aftermath. As the king's son was too young to rule, the king's first cousin Archibald Douglas (the 5th Earl of Douglas) headed the government as Lieutenant-General of the realm.

In the aftermath of the king's assassination, Niel Mackay escaped Bass Rock (with the help of a kinswoman, who was married to Robert Lauder, the governor of the prison). There aren't any details available as to 'how' he escaped, or what happened to the woman who helped him—so I came up with my own tale in which the governor's wife and her lover assist Niel while trying not to implicate themselves!

The battle at Sandside Bay also took place during the first half of 1437. Niel Mackay led the conflict, most likely fueled by revenge against the Gunns for the Battle of Harpsdale and his imprisonment. The Sandside Chase (Ruaig-Shansaid) took place in Caithness, about 6 miles (9.7 km) west of Thurso. The Clan Mackay launched a raid from Strathnaver towards Thurso until they encountered resistance from the locals at Dounreay. The Mackays then pulled back to Sandside, where they were joined by reinforcements and slaughtered the defenders on the coast north of Reay in the shadow of an ancient fort. There are some historical mentions of Niel Mackay being injured—but the details of the injury he nearly dies from in this story come entirely from my imagination.

Although the characters of Connor Mackay of Farr, Hugh Mackay of Loch Stach, and Robin Mackay of Melness are all fictitious, John Mackay of Aberach is a real historical figure. In reality, he was actually Niel's half-brother, but in my story, I altered his relationship to make him his cousin.

Castle Varrich was the seat of the Mackays. Built out of sandstone, the castle perches upon a high point of rock, overlooking both the Kyle of Tongue and the village of Tongue. The castle's precise origins and age are unknown, although some historians believe it is over a thousand years old, and the medieval castle may have been built atop a Norse fort. The original castle had two floors, plus an attic. The ruin is located around one hour's walk away from the village of Tongue. It has views of the mountains Ben Hope and Ben Loyal.

The Mackays of Farr did reside at Farr Castle (also known as Borve Castle). These days, only the ruined shell of Farr Castle remains. With a stunning position overlooking the sea, the castle was used in ancient times as an outpost for raiding other clans. It is said that a Norseman called Torquil may have built the castle.

I hope you have enjoyed my notes. I really enjoyed researching the history and landscape of this wild and beautiful corner of Scotland.

ACKNOWLEDGMENTS

A huge thank you to Mary Alderson, who provided the name for Eilidh, the youngest Munro sister!

Infinite thanks to my wonderful Tim, who works tirelessly to make these books shine.

And thank you, dear readers—your love of my stories means the world to me!

COURAGEOUS HIGHLAND HEARTS CHARACTER GLOSSARY

The Mackay clan

The Mackays of Varrich
Beth Mackay (neè Munro—Niel's wife)
Niel Mackay (Mackay clan-chief)

The Mackays of Farr
Connor Mackay (Mackay chieftain—laird of Farr Castle), married to Keira (they have three children: Rose, Rory, and Quinn)
Morgan Mackay (Connor's brother), married to Maggie (they have one daughter, Tara)
Jaimee Mackay (Connor's sister), married to Alexander Gunn (they have two children, Anice and Aodhan)
Kennan Mackay (Connor Mackay's cousin), married to Cait (they have two sons, Blake and Logan)

The Mackays of Loch Stach
Hugh Mackay (Mackay chieftain—laird of Loch Stach)
Janneth Mackay (Hugh Mackay's daughter)

The Mackays of Aberach
John Mackay (Mackay chieftain—laird of Achness—Mackay clan-chief's cousin)

The Mackays of Melness
Robin Mackay (Mackay chieftain—laird of Melness broch)

The Mackays of Balnakeil
Breac Mackay (Mackay chieftain—laird of Balnakeil broch)

The Mackays of Dun Ugadale
Iver Mackay (Mackay chieftain—laird of Dun Ugadale)

The Gunn clan
Tavish Gunn (clan-chief)
Roy, Blair, Evan, and William Gunn (Tavish's younger brothers)

The Munro clan
George Munro (Munro clan-chief)
Laila Munro (the clan-chief's wife)
Neave Munro (the clan-chief's daughter)
Jean Munro (the clan-chief's daughter)
Eilidh (pronounced *Ay-Lee*) Munro (the clan-chief's daughter)

Other characters
Greta (maid to the Munro sisters)
Father Lucas (chaplain at Castle Varrich)
Cullodina (healer at Farr)
Tess (healer at Varrich)

ABOUT THE AUTHOR

Award-winning author Jayne Castel writes epic Historical and Fantasy Romance. Her vibrant characters, richly researched historical settings, and action-packed adventure romance transport readers to forgotten times and imaginary worlds.

Jayne is the author of a number of best-selling series. In love with all things Scottish, she writes romances set in both Dark Ages and Medieval Scotland.

When she's not writing, Jayne is reading (and re-reading) her favorite authors, cooking Italian feasts, and going on long walks with her husband. She lives in New Zealand's beautiful South Island.

Connect with Jayne online:
www.jaynecastel.com
www.facebook.com/JayneCastelRomance
https://www.instagram.com/jaynecastelauthor/
Email: contact@jaynecastel.com

Printed in Great Britain
by Amazon